TO KILL A GOD

HOLLOWCLIFF DETECTIVES BOOK 4

C.S. WILDE

CHAPTER 1

THE STENCH of stale beer and sweat invaded Mera's nostrils as she strode toward the bar. Her sharp sense of smell could be a gift or a curse. In moments like this, it was definitely a curse.

A hockey match played on the screen behind the counter— the Downtown Warlocks versus the Growling Pack. A handful of people sat at round wooden tables scattered throughout the place, cheering for their team and drinking, but Mera wasn't there for them. She'd come for the man sitting at the bar, who hunched over his shoulders.

The wooden floor creaked as she approached. When she sat on the red, padded stool next to him, the seat's ripped leather grazed her jeans, scratching her thighs.

"You chose a nice little place to wallow," she offered.

The man took a long gulp of his drink, but didn't acknowledge her presence.

With a sigh, she ordered a beer. The bartender—a tall, furry creature that resembled an overgrown ferret—promptly delivered it with a sharp-teethed grin, the kind that was meant to be friendly but instead looked frightening. He had to be a Puka, though Mera wasn't a specialist when it came to the different types of faeries.

In any case, seeing a fae native working in Clifftown brought a giddy, warm joy to her core. More and more, the people of Tagrad ventured outside their comfort zone, building the dream of a united country.

The nation, and Hollowcliff, still had a long way to go, a fact that became clear when Mera realized all tables in the establishment kept a healthy distance from the man hunched at the bar, but that might not be related to prejudice at all. Maybe it was just survival instinct. Maybe a bit of both.

"My money is on the Downtown Warlocks," she said before taking a long gulp of her beer.

The man chuckled, his sandy-blond hair curtaining his eyes. He focused on the glass of whiskey he was holding, then drained it in one go. "I don't need a babysitter, Mer."

"I wouldn't be here if that was true."

He gave her a weary chuckle. "Checkmate."

"Emma is worried about you. She told me you haven't been feeding."

It was obvious, really. Julian's skin stuck to his bones, and the deep circles under his eyes had a dark purple hue. Thin, blue veins had begun spreading under his pale skin, and ruby-red streaks took over his hazel irises.

"I have been feeding!" He slammed his glass on the counter. "I ate a portion of fries ten minutes ago."

"They don't nurture you anymore, and you're well aware of that." As if to prove her point, his stomach grumbled, and Mera's eyebrow rose. "They'll go straight through your system. You should stay close to a bathroom, Jules. I'm not kidding."

"I know," he scoffed. "Am I pathetic for actually wanting to go to the bathroom? For needing a little normalcy?"

Eyeing the amber liquid in her glass, she shook her head slowly. "Not at all."

It was her fault. If she had protected Julian, if she'd done her job as his partner, he wouldn't be in that situation.

"Look, I can't pretend to know what you're going through, but if Emma hadn't turned you into a vamp, you would have died."

"She should have let me. I prefer death over turning into a fucking bloodsucker."

"You shouldn't call yourself that."

"It's what I am." Julian turned to her with an exasperated look. "I literally have to suck blood to live!"

Her chest tightened with the disgust tainting his voice. "I know, but there's an entire borough of you. You're not alone." She took a sip of her beer. "Also, there are tons of support groups out there. Surely they can help you adapt, but first, you have to accept who you are now."

His gaze bored into hers for an uncomfortable moment; a moment in which Mera wondered if he'd caught her in her hypocrisy.

"Accept who you are…"

Big talk for a siren pretending to be human.

"I'm in control." With a wave of his fingers, he motioned for the bartender, who promptly approached and refilled his drink.

She stared pointedly at his willowy hand. "You're danger-ously close to bloodlust, Jules. If you lose control, I'll be forced to stop you. Please don't make me do that."

He chewed the inside of his cheek, as if he were weighing his options. "Would you stop me if you had to? Would you put a silver bullet in my forehead?"

"Never. Which means you would either kill or hurt me in the process, and probably everyone else in this pub. Would you prefer that?"

His eyes wandered around the space, a certain pain in his gaze. Turning around, he took one long gulp of his whiskey, then hissed through his teeth. "Guess I don't have a choice, do I?"

"Nope." She laid her hand on his shoulder. "The new captain said your post will be waiting for you when you're ready to get back in the force. You can do this, Jules. I know you can."

"I'll try, but I can't make any promises." A heavy breath left his lips, even if he couldn't breathe anymore. Force of habit, she supposed. "It won't be the same without Ruth, though."

Shoving the memory of her mom somewhere deep inside, Mera took another gulp of her beer. After clearing her throat, she nodded to the screen. "Let's finish the game, and then I'll drop you at Emma's. How about that?"

With a small smile, Julian nodded.

They watched the game for maybe fifteen minutes, until the bell above the door jingled, and a man clad in a black suit walked into the pub. The floor creaked as he hurried toward them.

The tall and bulky man, a government agent most likely, wore sunglasses even though it was nighttime. Mera caught a whiff of wet dog hair as he approached.

Werewolf.

Julian's lips curled to show pointy fangs, and the red in his eyes intensified. "Friend of yours, Mer?"

Her brow furrowed. "I have no idea."

"Detective Maurea," the man greeted. "I'll take Mr. Smith to Emma Morrigan's address. Councilor Adams has requested an immediate audience with you."

Julian gawked at Mera. "Are you kidding me? Councilor Adams, as in Peter Adams? The representative of the human borough in the Tagradian Council? *That* Councilor Adams?"

She nodded.

"Since when do you have friends in skyscraper-high places?"

She studied her own feet, her voice nothing but a whisper. "He was a friend of Ruth's."

"Ah." A veil of sadness fell upon his face. "I see."

Mera took one last gulp of her beer and got to her feet, dreading what was to come. There could only be one reason why the councilor wanted to see her so urgently.

Shit.

TO CALL the councilor's office "huge" was an understatement. The place had long walls, a floor built entirely of pearly marble, and a high ceiling that made the space seem way too vast. Walking in there always felt like entering an unending, well illuminated cave.

Mera's boots thumped against the floor as she strode to the dark, mahogany desk at the end. The office's entire left wall was made of anti-reflection glass, which displayed a stunning view of night-time Clifftown.

Councilor Adams watched her approach through kind, hazel eyes filled with worry. As always, he wore a pleated suit. He'd trimmed his blond-going-white hair and beard after the last time she'd seen him—at Ruth's funeral.

The councilor had been in and out of Mera's life, a presence that, in hindsight, had always been there, even if barely seen or noticed.

He used to visit when she was younger, but when she graduated from the police academy, his visits became scarcer. She never took it to heart, since he'd been elected councilor for the human borough that same year. Also, Mera had Ruth, and her mom was enough. She always had been.

Settling on the leather chair that faced his desk, she glanced at him. He watched her sit, his hands steepling on his chin.

"Have you and Detective Dhay lost your minds?" he asked in a placid tone that was anything but.

"Councilor, I can assure you—"

"You want to go to the Isles of Fog, yes?"

"Yeah, but—"

"The natives from the isles haven't been introduced to the modern world, nor do they want to. Also, they happen to be savages." He leaned back on his chair, his manner poised and controlled. "The isles don't have a protection zone, but you're well aware of that. Any siren could waltz in, and rip you and Detective Dhay apart just like they did Ru—" His voice cracked and he went quiet.

After a moment, he let out a weary sigh. "Anyone from the mainland is forbidden to set foot in there. Period. Not to mention the costs, of course. A nightbringer would have to deviate considerably from its route to get there."

"I understand, but I have to go to the isles. Contacting Atlantea is the only way to find a lead on Azinor."

Despite Bast's protests, she'd told the councilor about the prick. After all, how could Tagrad defend itself from an enemy they didn't know? She omitted most parts, of course, especially the fact that the self-named "Poseidon" was her biological father.

Councilor Adams raised one bushy, nearly white eyebrow. "He's Atlantea's problem, not ours. Especially now that he seems to have given up on bringing chaos to land."

"Their problem will become ours. You can bet on that."

Azinor might target Atlantea since his attempt to destroy Tagrad had failed, but eventually, his focus would return to land. Psychos like him didn't give up easily, which was why she needed to get to the isles. Once there, she could waterbreak to Atlantea... but the councilor didn't need to know that.

The prospect of seeing Professor Currenter, Uncle Barrimond, and Belinda again brought fear and joy to her heart, but her feelings didn't matter. Mera had to warn them about Azinor. If they hated her for leaving after she'd killed the queen, then so be it.

Councilor Adams' fingers rhythmically tapped the mahogany surface, close to the form she'd submitted a week ago.

Bureaucracy be damned.

All Mera needed was his approval on that form, but it didn't seem like she would get it.

"So, you want to go to the isles to contact Atlantea," he stated pointedly. "You want to warn them about Poseidon. Maybe even work together with them to stop him."

"That would be a nice plus. Two birds with one stone, as people say."

"I see. And why do you think they won't use the macabre against you on sight?"

"They won't."

"Because you're one of them…"

A loud gasp escaped Mera, and the floor seemed to crumble under her feet. "Of course not! I'm human."

"I was hoping you'd tell me sooner. I wanted the initiative to come from you, but I suppose Ruth taught you a little too well about self-preservation."

"You've lost your mind, Councilor." She gave out a nervous sneer. "Wanting to communicate with a siren doesn't make me one of them."

His hands patted the air as if trying to appease her. "Settle down, Detective. I've always known." Carefully regarding her, he scratched his beard. "Ruth told me when she adopted you. Why do you think I visited you so often when you were young?"

Surprise colored her expression, and she blinked, thinking about it for a moment. "You were assessing whether or not I was a threat."

"And you weren't… you aren't. Ruth raised you right. You care about others and you give everything for this nation. She wasn't your biological mother, but you are just like her, in every way that matters." His eyes glistened with tears.

A rush of emotions swam through Mera, threatening to engulf her, but she swallowed them back. "T-thank you. That means a lot to me, sir."

"She was so very proud of you. You even set Detective Dhay straight." With a shake of his head, the counselor chuckled to himself. "A remarkable feat, considering his nightblood."

A bitter taste laced her tongue. Bast's merits were his own, but she wasn't about to argue about it now.

"So, you know. About me, Queen Wavestorm... You know about all of it?"

"Yes. I know your biological mother was raised from the dead by Poseidon and that she killed Ruth." A certain fury swirled behind his otherwise calm stare. "I'm glad you killed that monster a second time. I owe you a debt for avenging our Ruthie."

Ruthie?

Now more than ever, Mera was certain that the councilor and her mom had shared something in the past, though she couldn't guess what kind of relationship they must have had.

"If you've always known, why am I still alive?"

"Ruth and I went through a lot together, more than you'll ever know. She trusted me, and I promised her that I would keep you safe should anything happen to her. You were the most important thing in her life."

Fan-fucking-tastic.

If Mera was precious to Ruth, and Ruth was precious to Adams, it meant Mera was precious to him too. That was good, in a way, because he wouldn't kill her on the spot tonight for being a siren, but bad because there was no way in hell he would let her risk her life to catch Azinor.

Engines revolved in her mind as she tried to think of a way out of that mess. A way for him to grab one of the two stamps on his desk and punch "APPROVED" on that damned form.

"Peter," she started, "my mom made me one of Hollowcliff's finest, even though keeping me alive broke the law. There was one rule Ruth always put above the city, and the country's needs —protect the innocent, no matter the cost." Her gaze shifted to the Clifftown nightscape beyond the glassed walls. "I promised myself I would honor her legacy, and that means I have to get to the isles. Atlanteans are innocent, and they might need our help. What if joining forces with them is the answer to keep Tagrad safe?"

"Atlanteans and Tagradians working together?" He laughed. "I could never pass a motion like that in the council, no matter how hard I tried." His gaze narrowed at her. "How are you certain your people haven't joined Poseidon?"

"Last time I saw him, he seemed to despise my uncle."

"Seemed? Not good enough." He leaned forward, interlacing his fingers on the wooden surface. "How do you intend on stopping him? According to your report, killing Poseidon isn't an option."

"I'll figure out a way. Look, I'm asking you to trust me. Besides, you said you owed me for killing Ariella Wavestorm, so…"

This was it. Her last shot.

The councilor was considering it, she could see it in his eyes. He considered it for maybe two seconds, then shook his head.

"Your plan is reckless at best, and terribly conceived at worst. Your vow to protect the innocent goes against my vow to keep you safe. I *am* in your debt, Mera, but I can't break my promise to Ruth."

Her lips pressed into a thin line. "This was a giant waste of time, wasn't it?"

"Not at all. We had a nice chat." He gave her a mocking grin. "I was hoping you'd give up eventually, but you certainly inherited your mom's stubbornness."

The councilor grabbed a stamp from his desk and slammed it against her form. Mera didn't need to read the big red letters to know what they meant.

DENIED.

CHAPTER 2

WHEN SHE STEPPED into her apartment, Mera found Bast standing in the living room, waiting for her with two glasses of wine. A wooden platter with ham and cheese rested atop the coffee table near the white sofa. She couldn't help but smile. No matter the hardships in their path, he would always be there for her.

Her perfect hart.

"How was it, kitten?" He handed her one glass, but didn't wait for an answer before stamping a soft kiss on her lips. "Is Julian feeling better?"

Bast's touch, his mouth, and his woodsy scent were fresh air to her.

"He's getting there."

Tonight, Bast's silky loose hair fell over the left side of his face. His vest was unbuttoned, and so was the upper part of his shirt, revealing a strong chest made for licking... and maybe a little biting.

By now, Mera's siren would've added something along the lines of *'Soft biting. Can't damage the goods,'* but her presence had dimmed since her encounter with Azinor.

Not that her siren was gone, of course. They'd always been one and the same, and that hadn't changed. They were simply more welded together, somehow. Perhaps, accepting her past had caused the change. Perhaps, it'd been something else entirely.

Shrugging it off, she clinked her glass with his before taking a sip. The wine tasted smooth and velvety as it went down her throat. "Hmm, this is good."

"It should be." He gave her a cocky grin. "It comes from the best vineyards in Lunor Insul."

Mera gawked at him. "You guys have vineyards?"

"Of course." Bast took another sip. "Why do you think Ben is an alcoholic? He took a nightbringer to Al Rhaelli last month, because they have a wine festival that's supposed to be *divine*. Last we spoke, he was having so much fun, he refused to come back."

"That seems right up Ben's alley."

"It is. The *baku* even told me he found his life's purpose: 'to become a wine maker in the warm, welcoming bosom of Al Rhaelli'." His free hand ran along her back. "He'll probably grow out of it within a year."

Smiling, Mera leaned her forehead against his chest. "You Dhays and your strikes of fancy."

He kissed the top of her head, his hand pulling her closer to him. "Despite my attempt to lighten the mood, something is still bothering you. Is it... Julian related?"

Worry and trepidation flowed from his side of their bond, even if Bast had nothing to fear.

"Jules is back at Emma's. I called her on the way here and she said he already fed a bit, so that's progress. But I wouldn't say I helped. Not nearly enough."

"Ah! There's my partner who carries the weight of the world on her shoulders." Hooking a finger under her chin, he lifted her face gently. "You did what you could. That's all any of us can do."

He had a point, but that didn't diminish her guilt. Mera stared at him, dreading what she was about to say next.

"Councilor Adams requested an urgent audience with me tonight. It took weeks for that damn form to reach his desk, and once it finally did…" She shook her head. "He was playing me. He wanted us to stay put."

Bast spun his glass in small circles, watching the liquid twirl. "So, he denied our request."

"He did, and also… he knows."

Mindlessly sipping his wine, he glanced at her while a frown marred his forehead. "Knows what?"

"That I'm a siren."

The crimson liquid caught in his throat, and he nearly spat it out as he glared at her. "What? Did you tell him? Why would you do that?!"

"Calm down. He's known since Ruth adopted me. It's the reason why he denied the request, actually. He's being overprotective."

Her *hart* still stared at her in a panic, his strong chest heaving. Even though he seemed terrified, Bast looked absolutely stunning.

Standing on her toes, Mera pecked his lips. She set both glasses on the kitchen counter, then kissed the curve of his neck. "You know, I had a long day."

His muscles relaxed, if only a bit. "You're trying to distract me."

"And you're thinking about murdering the councilor to keep my secret." Her teasing hands removed his open vest and tossed it aside, then went on to unbutton the rest of his shirt. "You forget our bond and our mind link."

"*Halle…*" He scratched the back of his neck. "Kitten, I have to keep you safe."

"I am. Councilor Adams won't talk."

A growl rose from Bast's throat. "Well, we can always go to the isles unofficially, but we would be arrested when we returned to Tagrad. We'd probably be charged with treason, too. Is that a price you're willing to pay?" he asked as Mara nibbled at his lower lip.

"Yes. You?" She tossed his shirt aside.

In return, Bast removed her black leather jacket, then pulled up her T-shirt and let it fall to the ground. His hooded gaze locked on her lacy black bra, and he licked his lips.

"How could I not join you, *min hart?*" His eyes glinted with something wild and untamed. "Being up to no good is a talent of mine, you see."

"It really is." Standing on her toes, she kissed the edge of his jaw. "Now, how about we practice some stress relief, Detective Dhay?"

Bast groaned, eyes closed while he relished her kisses. "Evil *akritana…*"

He undid her bra masterfully, then her pants, and faster than she realized, Mera stood there, fully naked.

Bast took a step back to admire her, a certain worship beaming from his eyes. "Mine. All mine."

Her hungry gaze took in his strong abs below a chiseled torso; the smooth, tanned skin she loved to kiss; and those wild, clear-blue eyes that watched her so lovingly.

Hers. All hers.

She licked her lips when she spotted the massive bulge inside his pants. Stepping closer, her fingers began undoing his belt, her eyes locked on his.

Bast caressed her hair while his free hand went down to her naked ass. "What you do to me," he breathed.

Once his belt was unbuckled, Mera pulled off his pants and underwear. Soon enough, there he stood, as naked as she was.

Beautiful. Feral. Hard as freaking stone.

Suddenly scooping her up in his arms, Bast winnowed them to her bedroom. He dropped Mera on the mattress, bridging atop her.

His mouth rained kisses along her neck, then her breasts. His tongue twirled around her nipples, before he licked his way down to her crotch. Spreading her legs apart, he glanced at her with eager, wicked blue eyes. Without warning, he sunk his mouth into her most intimate part, his tongue playing with the pearl between her thighs.

"Ah, Bast!" Mera gasped, arching her back as pleasure unfurled inside her.

He ravaged her with his mouth non-stop, barely giving her time to breathe. Heat pooled inside her, shooting up to her head while she clawed at the sheets. Soon, her fingers moved to his head, caressing his locks as he kept attacking her. Already, Mera's desire dripped down her skin to the bed, her core aching, burning to explode.

Bast's assault was violent, merciless, and too good for her to bear. She fought against the buildup, but it was useless.

Her eyes rolled back, and just like that, she came undone, roaring out his name as she shuddered harshly. Bast held her hips in place while ecstasy consumed her, his grip hard as steel.

Not willing to let go, his tongue kept twirling around the pebble between her thighs, making her see white. It felt like drowning and breathing at the same time.

"Aaah! You prick!" she bellowed as another wave of pleasure hit her, a scorching storm that swallowed her completely.

Once she returned to herself, Bast let go with a grin. His lips were coated in her juices.

Mera's body felt like jelly as he crawled up on her. Her *hart* admired her with complete devotion. "Hearing you scream like that is my favorite thing in this world."

She wrapped her arms over his strong shoulders. "Then make me scream again."

Leaning down, Bast kissed her so hard that his teeth scraped the tip of her tongue. Mera tasted herself on his lips, and a moan escaped her mouth, flowing into his.

His hips bucked, and with one hard shove, he plunged into her while drowning her in kisses that made her forget her own name. Gasps burst from her as he slid between her walls.

The muscles on Bast's back shifted with each slow, harsh trust, and Mera closed her legs around him, if only to feel more of him sliding in and out, in and out... Hell, she might scream again too soon.

"I love you," she breathed, cupping his cheeks when he increased the pace.

"You're my life." He bit the curve of her neck gently, his hips bucking in a frenzy. A resigned moan swirled in his chest. "Mera, you feel so fucking good... Ah..." He hissed through his teeth.

Bast rammed into her, making her bed creak loudly. In the bed's defense, it had withstood a great deal of lovemaking. Just yesterday, it nearly cracked as Mera rode Bast into his undoing, but much like Mera herself, the wooden frame was tougher than it looked.

Heat shot up to her head while he relentlessly plunged into her, making her see stars. As his hips slammed against her, Mera couldn't keep her ground; couldn't control...

"Bast, I think, I..." She didn't get to finish the sentence.

Once again, she exploded in a frenzy of desire and delight, losing her sense of self, of time and space. She faintly sensed her body thrashing as pleasure took over, her mind spinning.

"*Kura, min hart!*" Bast snarled with a grimace and let go, filling her womb with thick, warm streams. His muscles clenched and he shook slightly, unloading inside her, his pleasure only fueling her own.

Beautiful. Perfect.

Once they came to, their breaths slowed, but Bast remained

deeply sheathed inside her. He leaned down and kissed her lovingly. "I wish we could stay in this bed forever."

So did she.

"Let this be our forever, partner." She grinned mischievously. "But I have to say, I'm craving more 'forevers' tonight."

"Then strap in, kitten." His blue eyes shone with malice, and he gently bit her shoulder. "We're only getting started."

CHAPTER 3

MERA INHALED DEEPLY. The salty tang of the sea filtered into her core, urging her to sink under the waves and never return to shore. By now, she'd learned to tame those urges, but they always remained.

The ocean mimicked the sky's bright turquoise, and seagulls cawed in the distance. The beautiful day could only be a good omen to what she and Bast were about to do—even if she didn't believe in silly things like omens.

Faeries of all levels rushed around the port of Tir Na Nog, a vast marina that occupied half of the borough's shore. The port welcomed ships of many sizes and purposes—whether for export or import, tourism, leisure, fishing—the port of Tir Na Nog harbored them all.

Most ships moored there, however, were nightbringers. Their thick iron hulls were filled with mighty cannons, and sharp harpoons peppered the metallic decks. The floating fortresses were a must when crossing waters near Atlantea, even if there hadn't been an attack since the war ended.

Mera stood on a small sub-section of the port, waiting for Bast. He'd winnowed them there that morning—along with two small suitcases—before leaving to work on some "last minute details" with his brother, the Night King.

Mera shouldn't be surprised that Corvus was involved. Of course he could help them get to the Isles of Fog without official permits. Illegal and forbidden were words he knew well, even if he was king now.

A tall, wooden tower stood in the middle of the port's vast plaza. A golden clock topped the structure, and its bells reverberated loudly when the hands struck 8:00 a.m.

Mera sighed despondently. By now, her new captain would have realized she'd left Clifftown, as well as her duties as one of Hollowcliff's finest. Soon, so would Councilor Adams.

She hated disappointing her superiors, but she had to follow her gut, as Ruth had always taught her. Which meant that this time tomorrow, she and Bast would be declared criminals for abandoning their posts *and* attempting to engage with sirens.

No coming back from it.

That unavoidable fact left a bitter taste on her tongue, especially after she'd served the force for so many years.

Dragging Bast along didn't seem fair. She didn't want to be the reason why he lost his badge, but he refused to stay.

"My duty is to you," he'd said. *"If you attempt to do this alone, I will find you. So save us the headache, kitten."*

Bastard knew her well.

Now, Mera was abandoning her post and her career for a wild goose chase that might prove pointless. After all, she was a banished princess. She'd killed the queen, and instead of staying to survive a trial—a nice way to mask her death sentence—she'd decided to perish on her own terms by dashing into the forbidden zone, knowing it would kill her. The thing was, her suicide mission hadn't turned as suicidal as Mera had hoped.

Would her friends hate her for never coming back? Would they even listen to her now?

The words Professor Currenter had told her when he'd

"possessed" Madam Zukova, back when Mera and Bast investigated the Summer King's murder, awoke in her memory.

"Promise me you'll never attempt to come back. Grow strong, little fry."

Mera hadn't planned on returning, but something had seemed off back then. Considering what happened since... Yeah, she had to get to Atlantea. *Fast.*

When the air next to her cracked, she stepped aside, watching two portals that showed the night sky next to her—each the size of a stubborn nightling. Bast and Corvus soon jumped out from the gateways, and the portals disappeared.

The Night King fixed his spiky white hair, then his black suit. "Detective. A pleasure, as always." His mouth stretched into a wolfish grin. "I see you're up to no good, once again."

She crossed her arms. "Who are you to judge, *baku?* You're always up to no good."

"Precisely." He pressed his palm on his chest. "I meant it in the most respectful of ways. In fact, your goody-two-shoes nature had to give in at some point. Bast's influence, I suppose." He tapped his brother's back with a certain pride.

Mera rolled her eyes, but couldn't hide the smile that took over her lips. "Aren't kings supposed to follow rules?"

Glancing around as if searching for said kings, Corvus shrugged. "Not *this* one, surely. The Night Court doesn't follow rules set by anyone other than the Night King. We simply *pretend* we do." He leaned closer and winked at her. "Don't tell that to the council."

Mera chuckled. "Your secret is safe with me."

"Broer, will you get to the point?" Bast grumbled.

"Ah, yes." Corvus clapped his hands. "I've booked you a pirate, but not just any pirate. He's a warlock, and he might come in handy on your way to the isles. Captain Flint is his name." He pointed to a dark wooden ship with navy-blue sails approaching the port.

Winnowing to the isles was a no-go. The journey alone was five times the distance from Clifftown to Tir Na Nog. Not even Corvus, arguably the best winnower in the entire country, could get them there. Also, even if Bast flew them to the isles, he would need pitstops for a few nights—impossible without any land in sight.

So, a pirate ship it was.

"I did my due diligence, of course," Corvus continued. "Captain Flint knows his way around the isles, and he says he's even contacted some of your people, Detective. But truth be told, I think he might be boasting."

"Did he give you any names?"

"Yes, actually. One as equally amusing as Wavestorm. Someone named Tiderider?"

She nearly gasped. "Tiderider? As in, Belinda Tiderider?"

Corvus waved a hand in the air. "I suppose? Can't remember."

Bast's brows furrowed, worry taking over his face. "Do you know her?"

"Belinda used to be my best friend. I haven't seen her since…" Since Mera abandoned her and everyone else she cared about to cross the forbidden zone.

Belinda's mother had been a part of the resistance against the queen. She'd been captured and executed in front of Mera and Belinda herself, which prompted Mera to stand against the tyrant. The queen's death, Mera's arrival in Tagrad, and everything that happened after, could be pinpointed to that particular moment.

"I can't believe…" Mera turned to Corvus, her throat feeling as if it had been coated by sandpaper. "What did Belinda tell Captain Flint?"

"Difficult to say. There was a great deal of alcohol involved when I spoke to him. Pirates take their payment in coin and ale, you see." He clicked his tongue, then pointed to the approaching vessel. "You'll be able to ask him yourself soon enough."

Anticipation piled up inside Mera, but there was something else. An uneasy sensation that thrummed under her skin. Her own voice whispered in her ears, but Mera couldn't understand what it said.

"Hash, hash..."

"Something's wrong," she mumbled, narrowing her eyes at the horizon.

The ocean shifted, pulling and pushing Mera's essence in a thousand different directions, rumbling a warning into her bones.

Bast stepped closer. "What is it?"

It couldn't be. It simply couldn't be, and yet, every sensation in her body assured her she wasn't mistaken.

"I thought he would attack Atlantea," she muttered. "We ruined his plans for the mainland. How could he create... "

"Kitten?" Bast's tone was harsher this time. "What's going on?"

How? When she realized the answer, her heart skipped a beat. "The magic enhancer."

"What about it?"

"You lost it when you pulled me out of the water, back when we first faced Azinor."

"Yes, but you returned to the spot and searched for it. You said it must have been either buried deep in the sand or lost to the sea."

"I was wrong." Her body thrummed with the ripples that cut through the water. "He found it."

Her *hart* gulped, his nostrils flaring before he acquired a battle stance. "Let him come. He'll have no chance against the three of us."

Spheres of night bloomed from his hands, while an aura of darkness enveloped Corvus, both brothers preparing for battle.

"Corvus, you mentioned Lunor Insul has a magic barrier for emergencies," she noted. "A fail-safe in case waterbreakers broke through the protection zone."

He frowned, clearly not understanding where she was going with that. "Yes. Why?"

A thousand variables ran in Mera's mind. She pointed to Lunor Insul, which from the port, was as big as her thumb. "Winnow to Flint's ship, take him and his crew to the island, then activate the shield." She stepped forward, facing the ocean. "When the wave passes, return to this spot."

He chortled, showing her the port and the calm waters ahead. "What wave? Lost your mind, Detective?"

As if on cue, the ocean began receding toward the horizon, leaving a crowd of writhing fish in its wake and taking small boats along. Most nightbringers sunk slightly on the sloshy bottom, the people aboard them clueless to what was happening.

Bast's guard fell as he watched the water recede, and recede... and recede. "*Sakala mi...*"

With horror and panic trying to steal her common sense, Mera turned to her *hart*, perhaps for the last time. Yet, she wouldn't give in, wouldn't run. "Bast, you have to evacuate the borough."

Before he could oppose, she pulled her phone from her pocket and dialed Councilor Adam's number.

"Mera, what on all the realms were you thinking?!" His enraged voice reverberated into her ear the instant he picked up the line. "Return to your station at once, and we'll pretend this never happened. That's an order!"

Her gut tightened. "I can't go back. Tir Na Nog is under attack."

CHAPTER 4

SCREAMS ERUPTED throughout the port as faeries began to run around like headless chickens. They'd never seen an *ekrunami* in their lifetime—the last one on record had happened before the Great War—but like Bast, they'd learned about the signs in school.

Corvus exchanged one worried glance with him before winnowing away, and a certain relief washed over him. At least his brother would be safe.

Fisting his hands, Bast stepped closer to Mera, facing the horizon. "I'm not leaving you."

"Clifftown is sending help." She put her phone back in her pocket. "I've got this, partner. Go warn the fae councilor. We have a borough to save."

A growl erupted low in his chest. As a Hollowcliff detective, his duty was to Tagrad, but as Mera's *hart*, he would always put her first.

Country be damned.

"I'll never forgive you if you don't help them," Mera warned, knowing the impact that would have on him.

"Would you do the same if you were in my shoes?"

Her gaze left his. "I know I'm asking a lot of you."

She was, but they had no choice.

"Hang on. I'll be back soon."

His *hart* smiled sweetly, a certain sadness hiding in the way her lips curled. "I'll be here."

A sharp force immediately yanked him from behind, enveloping Bast in endless darkness.

He floated amidst the night sky, drifting past stars that blinked in the distance. It was hard to tell up from down, but by now he was used to it. His loose silver hair floated around him as a gripping cold bit at his fingers. It was like falling and not falling at the same time, hanging between two different realms.

Ahead, a slit cut through the darkness, showing an office made entirely of sandstone. Bookshelves lined the back wall, with hanging vines dropping from the top, cascading atop the heavy tomes and golden trinkets on the shelves.

A male with short auburn hair signed some papers on a cedar desk, completely unaware of Bast's presence on the other side. He wore a fitted white suit that must have cost a fortune, and even from the distance, Bast could spot the freckles atop his skin.

A magic barrier buzzed between him and the slit, thin and wavering. He pushed his palm against it, feeling the power thrum on his skin.

Too easy.

Bast's night and stars concentrated around his hand. His power clashed against the barrier's, fighting its resonance until the wall cracked like broken glass. He stepped into the councilor's office, surprised at how easy it had been to crack the magical protection around it.

"That barrier was a joke," he told Councilor Asherath—not Bast's captain, Fallon Asherath, even if Bast wished it were him sitting in that white leather chair.

The councilor was Fallon's cousin, Colin.

A stuck up, stupid suket.

"How dare you?" The Sidhe slammed both hands on his desk before jumping to his feet. His wide green eyes were filled with fury; a type of glare Bast had grown accustomed to given his talent for making enemies.

"You can be mad at me later, Colin. The borough—"

"You invaded my office and broke through the protective barrier around it! Have you lost your mind? I'm not just Fallon's cousin anymore, Sebastian. I've been elected councilor of the fae borough. Show some respect!"

Bast cocked his head left. "If anything, I've proven that you have terrible security. I did you a favor, didn't I? You're welcome, by the way."

"Oh, you fucking *baku!*"

"Listen, Colin. Tir Na Nog is under—"

He pointed a finger at him. "No! Your roguish ways may work on my cousin, but I'm not a push-over. There are laws we must respect, now more than ever after the corruption scandal this borough went through. Guards!"

Bast snarled, displaying pointy teeth that showed his temper was running low. "Oh, yes, I remember. If not for what Mera and I did, your corrupt predecessor, August, would still be sitting in *that* chair. The same predecessor who tortured Fallon before banishing him from the Autumn Court decades ago." Bast pointed at the *baku*, his wrath taking the best of him. "It is *you*, Colin, who should show some respect!" He slammed his hands on the table, but Colin didn't flinch. He merely watched him through cunning emerald eyes. "You did nothing as Fallon was exiled in shame. You watched him go down cowardly and in silence, which I suppose was good training for your role as councilor, wasn't it?"

Two bulky Sidhe burst into the office, but Colin raised his palm, stopping them. His mouth twisted downward in a bitter curve, his chin bearing an uncomfortable resignation. "You forget yourself, Detective Dhay."

No, he didn't, but in his fury, Bast had forgotten about the bigger picture. "There's an *ekrunami* heading toward the shore as we speak. You have to tell people to seek high ground through the emergency system."

"An *ekrunami?*" Colin chortled. "You must be hallucinating. Your nightblood has clearly taken the best of you."

"*Kura!*" Bast pinched the bridge of his nose, forcing himself to calm down. "Put your distaste for me aside and do as I say, you *shig*. Our people will die. This is not a joke!"

The councilor swallowed, seeming to think twice before finally nodding in agreement. "You better be right, or else... "

Colin made a circular move with his hands and closed his eyes. After a moment too quick to count, but that seemed to stretch like an eternity, an alarm wailed through town, followed by Colin's voice repeating, *"Ekrunami alert. Seek high ground immediately."*

The phone on his desk—a Tagradian requirement, even if most fae abhorred technology—rang loudly.

"Peter. Yes, I heard," Colin answered, then listened to what the other councilor explained. "My agents will be too busy with the evacuation. I don't think the machines you're developing with Lycannie can help, but I'll take anything you have." He listened again. "They're on the way? Good." He hung up the phone.

"What was that?" Bast asked.

"You should cover your ears," he warned before covering his own. His two guards did the same.

"Why woul—"

A loud swooshing sound burst from outside, as if the sky itself was being ripped in two. Bast jerked when the sudden shrieking pounded his eardrums, piercing his brain. The walls in the office shook violently.

Stamping both hands on his ears, he headed to the window to see two metallic, arrow-shaped things cutting through the air. Their sound dimmed the closer they got to the shore.

"Danu in the prairies," Bast mumbled.

Flying machines.

The human borough had flying machines.

CHAPTER 5

MERA'S POWER thrummed in her veins, following the rhythm of the waters. Taking a deep breath, she ignored the pit in her gut, and the fear pricking her chest.

She was going to die today. No doubt about it.

An alarm wailed in the distance, telling people to find high ground. Winged fae zinged toward the mainland, while those who couldn't fly kept hurrying away. Crowds disembarked the nightbringers half-sunken in the sloshy sand, soon leaving the iron beasts empty.

Mera's only purpose now, her only duty, was to buy Tir Na Nog time.

Raising her arms, her power expanded in a pulse that connected every bit of her being to the sea before her.

A school of fish swam peacefully on the far end of the horizon, unaware of the tidal wave that hurtled toward them. Miles beyond Lunor Insul, a forest of algae flailed violently as the tsunami rushed by it. Where the wave had already passed, far in the deep sea, turtles swam through the currents as if nothing had happened.

They were all stamped in her essence, for Mera was the ocean and the ocean was Mera.

Her eyes soon spotted a line rising above the edge of the horizon. It grew thicker while it approached Lunor Insul, and then the wave slammed against the invisible dome. Water piled atop itself, rising higher and higher, until it tilted over, engulfing the entire island.

Lunor Insul was inside the protection zone, an area covered by a spell that disintegrated any waterbreaker who dared cross it. Technically, a magic barrier wasn't necessary, but the Night Kingdom stood too close to the open ocean. Corvus' father hadn't trusted Tagrad to protect his people, and thanks to that, he had just saved them.

The same wouldn't work in the mainland, of course. Tagrad was simply too big, and even the most powerful of shields couldn't cover it entirely. Besides, the protection zone had been enough for centuries.

Until now.

Corvus' island disappeared under the wave, but the tsunami didn't lose momentum. It kept hurling toward Mera and the mainland, almost as if it had a will of its own. The wave rose into a mighty wall that had to be hundreds of feet high, with a shoulder that stretched as far as the naked eye could see, nearly following the entire shore.

The port was now empty. Silent.

The rush of water roared closer, along with the caws of seagulls flying above, trying to escape the ocean's wrath.

Mera's own voice split into several, whispering words she couldn't understand, except for one phrase.

"It's time."

Her muscles clenched when she pushed the ocean back. Saltwater droplets sprinkled atop her as the tsunami rushed closer, drenching the port in shadows and blocking the sun.

The wave was too massive, its weight too grand. She

couldn't do this. Mera was a puny ant holding back a falling tree.

She would fail.

Regardless, she would try.

Her power slammed violently against the water, creating giant ripples on the tsunami's wavering face.

At first, the ocean didn't listen, but when she let out a siren's shriek, the sonic boom slammed against the tidal wave. It spread throughout the length of the shore, bringing the tsunami to a halt.

Mera kept pushing her power forward as the shriek slowly died in her throat, her head pounding like it would explode. When she clenched her lips shut, the wave didn't move forward.

Panting, she looked up at the giant waterwall that halted a mere fifty yards from where she stood. For a moment, she wondered if she'd stopped time itself.

"It worked," she croaked, her breaths rushed and labored.

Her victory only lasted a moment, though.

A figure emerged from the crest of the sea; a man with no hair on his head. His strong, corded muscles spread across his body, and though he was a waterbreaker, he didn't have fins on his ears or gills on his neck.

Inky runes ran across his gray flesh, covering his entire trunk, chest, and arms. The dickwart wore black pants that clung to his skin; the same stretchy fabric Atlanteans used for their bodysuits.

Azinor wobbled slightly atop the streams that swirled underneath his feet.

"You never cease to amaze me, Daughter," he shouted, his deep tone reaching her as if he stood right next to Mera. He must have been using magic of some sort.

Mera's eyes narrowed to a green light blinking from a silver chain around his neck. It had to be the magic enhancer, but it used to have a red ruby encrusted in its middle. Now, it pulsed with lime-green light in the way of a beating heart, which meant the asshole must have synchronized his magic with it.

"You needed an enhancer to create a tidal wave, but I stopped you on my own." She sneered. "You're pathetic, Azinor!"

His proud smirk vanished. "Power isn't all that matters, especially if you don't know how to use it. Do not mistake your fleeting luck with victory. You have not won this battle, and you will not win the war, child."

Mera winced as the weight of the water tried to crush her to the bone, pressing into her power, eager to squash it.

"I must admit," he continued, "I do need you to take down your uncle's reign, not because you're essential, but because you would spare me a great deal of time."

Not essential. That was the story of her life when it came to *Father* and *Mother*.

Well, at least now she knew his plan. Azinor wanted to take Mera. Attacking the mainland was just a bonus.

"Fine!" she bellowed, even though she didn't have the need. The magic he used seemed to work both ways. "End the tsunami, and I'll go with you."

He shook his index finger. "There's no fun in that."

Dickface!

His plans suddenly unraveled right in front of her, and her heart skipped a beat. "You want to use me as bait."

He merely grinned while a second figure rose from the water next to him, breaking through the crest.

Mera blinked. *No.* Her eyes must have been playing tricks on her.

No, no, no...

A woman with russet hair and a scaled wine-red bodysuit stood next to the prick. She wore the Crown of Land and Sea atop her head, and when she spotted Mera, she shot her a hateful grin that seemed too big for her face.

Mother.

Azinor had rebuilt her.

Last time they'd clashed, Mera had turned the bitch into a mushy pile of goo, and yet, there she stood, looking better than ever. If not for the hole in her left jaw, which showed tendons and teeth, and the fact that her right hand was still made entirely of bone, Mera wouldn't have been able to tell she'd died... twice.

A sharp pain stole her breath, and tears swelled in her eyes. Ruth's death, Julian's painful transition into a vamp; they had been for nothing. Ariella was back. She was fine, and Ruth was gone.

"No," Mera spat through clenched teeth. Warm, angry tears strolled down her cheeks.

"Your uncle would do anything to save you, sweet *Me-ra*," Mother spat with that bitter, arrogant tone of hers; a voice that always made Mera's blood boil. "His weak heart will be his demise."

"I'll fucking kill you all over again!" Mera barked, teeth grinding as she continued to push against the tidal wave, yet her fury threw her off.

The tsunami rushed forward a few yards, but with a siren scream, she shoved it back. Tears freely streamed down her cheeks, and she clenched her jaw so hard that her skull pulsed.

"You won't last much longer," the queen stated the obvious.

She was right, but Mera's goal had never been to come out of this alive. She only had to keep them distracted; buy the people of Tir Na Nog time to escape the wave. And then, the massive water wall could crash upon her.

She doubted she would feel any pain.

Azinor's eyes narrowed, and he seemed to see right through her plan. "We've indulged her enough. Bring our daughter to me."

The queen began sinking through the crest, but stopped

midway when two loud booms exploded from the sky, the sound bursting into Mera's eardrums.

Two arrow-shaped devices the size of school buses lunged forward, hovering several feet above Azinor and his dead pet. Made of what resembled smooth, pearly silver, they circled the wave's crest non-stop.

Flying machines.

Peter had mentioned Clifftown would send help, but Mera had never expected this. She'd heard the rumors of course, but she still couldn't believe her own eyes.

The device's engines blew air at the crest, making the queen's locks flail in different directions. Their sound was deafening, as if thousands of buzz-saws had been turned on at once.

"This is a warning." A voice that seemed too neat to be human boomed from the speakers in the machine's wings. *"Surrender or face the consequences."*

Azinor merely watched, unfazed. Giving the aircrafts a ferocious grin, he yelled, "We'll face the consequences!"

The flying machines—Mera once read an article that called them *jets*—fired at the dickface and Ariella with thick bullets that resembled tiny comets.

When the bullets crashed merely a foot from Azinor, they splattered into oblivion, but not before showing the thin, blue plasma shield that protected him and the queen.

Only then did Mera notice the two metallic stingrays that swam just inches below the crest, their glowing blue eyes shining without a soul within.

Atlantean technology.

The stingrays were generating the shields.

"Fly away!" Mera bellowed, but whoever operated the jets couldn't hear her from so far away, especially with the engines humming.

The stingrays whirred a strange, thrumming sound, before shooting blue plasma streams toward the aircrafts. The jets exploded with a mighty boom that enveloped the crest in flesh-melting fire. Immense heat stung Mera's skin, and she threw a hand in front of her eyes.

Maybe that did it. Maybe the explosion had killed Azinor and Ariella, though that might have been wishful thinking.

As the heat receded, Mera's ears rang with a continuous, beeping sound. Teeth clenched, she fought to keep control of the tidal wave, her body on the verge of giving up.

She looked up to the sky to find the crafts completely gone, pulverized out of thin air. Nothing had fallen on land, not even a tiny piece of metal.

Azinor stood proud and unscathed at the top of the wave. Glancing down at her, he let out a mad, hungry grin.

"Where were we, child?"

CHAPTER 6

Azinor nodded at the queen, and the bitch sunk into the crest of the wave, her shadow swimming down the wall of water in the way of a Great White ready to feast.

Mera's magic surged forward, slamming against the wave as she attempted to shove it back. A sound that belonged to a wounded animal escaped her throat, but no matter how hard she tried, the tsunami didn't buckle.

Shadows of runes suddenly bloomed on her skin, forming words she couldn't understand. They tingled her flesh, buzzing with a gentle hum.

"*Gachun!*" declared a faint voice in her head; no, her own voice, but Mera had no clue what *gachun* meant.

"*Push.*" She couldn't tell how she knew, she simply did.

Her veins began to burn, as if lightning crackled inside of her, and Mera pulled from that heat, channeling the energy. Snarling, she rammed her renewed magic against the water wall.

The wave receded, but only by a few yards.

Damn it!

She couldn't send it back; she could barely freaking move.

The queen swam down to her eye level. Her head poked out of the tsunami's wall, breaking the flow of water. Ariella stretched a bony hand at her, and her emerald eyes shone with a hint of pity.

Mera must have been seeing things, of course. Mother had never pitied anyone. Ever.

"Come, child. Do not provoke him."

"Rot in hell!" she spat.

Hurt flashed behind the queen's eyes, but that too must have been an illusion. Ariella Wavestorm didn't care about Mera; she didn't know the meaning of the word.

Jumping from the water wall, the queen landed on the sloshy sand below. Once again, she offered her arm, even if Mera couldn't—wouldn't—reach for that monster.

Desperation gnawed at her gut. This was the end. Mera couldn't move, couldn't attack or defend herself. Every bit of her power was diverted into holding back the wave.

The queen knew that, of course, and she drew out Mera's agony by stepping slowly toward her. Once she reached the backshore and the stairs that led to the promenade, the game would be over.

"Damn you!" Mera barked, knowing the battle was lost.

From the crest, Azinor pointed his chin toward her, a clear sign for the queen to hurry. Just as the bitch boosted forward, a comet of darkness hit the ground next to her, sending a wall of wet sand flying upward.

Ariella halted as sand rained down on her, glaring at the spot near Mera, the spot Bast now occupied.

An aura of night and stars wafted around him, his eyes pitch-black and his fangs sharp. His silver wings spread wildly, roofing over Mera. "Touch her and you'll regret it," he growled.

The queen stepped forward, ready for the challenge, but Azinor called her from the top of the wave. Begrudgingly, she jumped back into the tsunami, quickly rising to the crest.

A sphere of thundering night enveloped Bast's hand as he lifted it, his wings disappearing behind him. With his free hand, he touched Mera's arm.

"You'll explode into a billion pieces before you winnow her out of here, nightling," Azinor stated calmly, his voice clear around them. "Even a powerful fae like you can't block my macabre."

Bast was one of the strongest Sidhe Mera knew, but there was a fair chance that the asshole was right. And if he was, she wouldn't be capable of blocking his attack. She was too weak to defend Bast.

"Let's go," her *hart* whispered next to her. "I'm faster than this *suket*."

It was too much of a gamble, and she couldn't risk Bast's life. Couldn't risk the rest of the borough, either. "I can't bet on that, partner."

He chuckled without any amusement. "Not your choice, is it?"

"Actually, it is. I can block your winnowing. I saw Ariella do it with Corvus once, and I'm pretty sure I can do it, too."

"Mera—"

"Has Tir Na Nog been evacuated?"

A mournful look captured his expression. "We did what we could."

"I'll stay for as long as I can." Her body shook from the effort of holding the wave. "You have to go."

Bast stared at her as if she'd gone mad. "Kitten, please."

"I have to buy your people time. Sidhe might have wings, but most faeries don't." Her attention turned to Azinor, even if her head felt too light, her thoughts blurring.

Hell, she might pass out soon.

"I'm not leaving you," Bast countered, his jaw set as he acquired a fighting stance. "If you stay, I stay."

Mera panted as if she'd ran a marathon. Droplets of sweat

fell in her eyes, her muscles shaking. She was about to pass out, and she would doom Bast, along with so many innocents... She had to pull through, had to keep standing, even if she wouldn't last long.

A portal of night and stars suddenly opened through thin air, right next to Bast, and out came Corvus.

"Just in time, *broer*," Bast smiled. "With you here, we might just make it."

The queen raised her hand, and Mera knew what she was about to do. She would try to macabre Corvus.

"Wait!" Mera bellowed, stopping her.

"Danu in the prairies!" The Night King gawked at the queen. "Won't you stay dead, you *slatch*?"

Mera had a tsunami to hold, and she couldn't protect two faeries from those assholes' magic. Sure, the three of them might have had a chance of beating Azinor and the queen, but only if Mera had been in good shape.

Maybe she was putting little faith in Bast's and Corvus' magic. She'd seen what they could do, should trust their abilities, but she'd also witnessed Azinor's colossal power.

Mera stared at Corvus, every inch of her body shaking. "Do you understand why I asked you to come back? This is *my* battle."

"But—"

She shook her head. "I can't hold on anymore."

The Night King faced the tsunami, watching as it began inching forward. He swallowed dry, a heavy resignation shining in his eyes.

Bast frowned. "What—?"

Turning on his heels, Corvus wrapped his arms under his brother's shoulders, then opened a portal behind them.

Horror shone in Bast's wide, blue eyes as he tried to reach for Mera, but he was already falling back with Corvus into an endless night.

"No!" he bellowed as the portal blinked out of existence, taking both of them to safety.

Hoping she'd bought enough time for the people of Tir Na Nog, Mera let out a long sigh.

"Get her!" Azinor thundered.

Ariella dropped through the wave again, and Mera knew there would be no offered hand this time. It didn't matter. The queen would never reach her in time.

Mera's arms dropped, and she let go of her last bit of magic. The giant water-wall rushed forward, towering over her.

In those last seconds, she wondered if she would see Ruth again. She didn't believe in an afterlife, but the thought brought a smile to her lips.

The tsunami roared as it crashed upon her, but Mera didn't feel a thing. Just like a forgotten dream, she was gone.

CHAPTER 7

"Cookie, you need to wake up." Ruth's voice rang everywhere around her, but Mera was surrounded by darkness, and couldn't tell where her mom might be.

"I don't want to," she grumbled.

"Cookie, wake up." Her tone carried a world of worry. "Now."

With a gasp, Mera sat up from her bed.

Ruth was sitting on the edge of the mattress, watching her with a certain panic. Her hair was light brown instead of grey, and she was missing a few wrinkles. She used to look like that when Mera was a merling, no older than fifteen.

Next to the window showing the night outside, a warlock in a long, black cloak watched her with his mouth slightly open. Tattoos covered his face and what she could see of his hands.

"Ruth, we should call the council."

"No," her mom snapped.

Blue light flashed wildly across the room, coming from somewhere near Mera. She wondered if there might be something off with the electricity. Maybe the warlock was there to fix it, though warlocks didn't usually fix wiring... *did they?*

Mera rubbed her eyes, feeling a bit sleepy. "What's going on?"

Only then did she realize that strange, black tattoos danced atop her arms. Maybe her ears were playing tricks on her, but she could hear the humming of electricity coming from *inside* of her. As if an electric field buzzed in her core.

Definitely not a problem with wiring, then.

A cold, crippling fear rose inside her. "Ruth?"

The light flickered atop her Ponyland poster on the left wall, and on the volcano she'd built for a school science project, which sat on the right side of her desk. Blue light flashed everywhere, coming from... her.

"It's okay, cookie. You're fine."

"Ashermath nin ha," Mera's own voice whispered, and her head snapped left, trying to follow the sound.

"Can you hear that?" Her voice cracked with fear, and soon more whispers joined in, all coming from her, all a part of her, uttering words she couldn't understand.

"No, cookie. We can't." Ruth swallowed dry as the sapphire bolts flashed across her terrified expression. "John, can you block it?"

"I-I can try."

Lowering his head, the man began murmuring. The tattoos decorating his hands and face glowed red as he chanted.

Slowly, Mera's crippling fear dimmed. The voices faded away, and so did the blue light that had been flashing around her room. She didn't feel a thing, and after a while, the warlock's chant slowed to a halt.

Moonlight peered through the windows, drenching her room in soft silver light.

"It is done," he confirmed. "She'll pass under any radar, and tonight's event will wash away from her memory. But Ruth—"

"Not here." She cupped Mera's cheek, then kissed her forehead. "How are you feeling, cookie?"

"Fine." Mera blinked, trying to center her thoughts. Something had just happened, but she couldn't remember what. "Did I have a nightmare?"

Her mom smiled sweetly at her. "You did. Remember you're safe, okay? You'll always be safe here with me. Now, try to get some sleep."

A certain relief washed over Mera, and she nodded as she lay back in bed. Ruth tucked her in, kissed her forehead one more time, then left the room. The warlock followed after her, shooting Mera an awkward glance.

'*She's lying,*' Mera's own voice whispered in her ears, a new presence formed inside her core.

One voice out of many.

Mera couldn't tell why she knew that this voice, this siren's call, was a part of her. She simply did. And so, she wasn't scared. Not even a little bit.

"I trust Ruth," she told herself.

Her siren chuckled. '*That means I do, too.*'

With that, they both fell asleep.

"Cookie, you need to wake up..."

Mera tried, but her eyes were so heavy. Under narrowed lids that closed too quickly, she caught glimpses of bubbles, rushing water, and a deep blue surrounding her. Sounds broke through her slumber, but Mera was still trapped in a blurry haze, with no sense of place or time.

"Bast..." she mumbled.

"She must recover if we're to use her." Azinor's muffled voice felt far, far away.

Mera tilted her chin down to see a strong, gray arm wrapped around her waist, carrying her along.

"Our daughter is a stupid wench," he growled. "So selfless and virtuous. It's appalling!"

The dickwart carried her the way one would carry a football. In her haze, Mera couldn't tell why she found that amusing. A weak chuckle birthed in her chest, yet it died when everything went dark again, and her body fell limp.

She stayed that way, drowned within a void, waiting for Ruth to tell her to wake up again, when a shrill tone awakened her instead.

"They found us!" The queen's voice carried absolute horror.

Music to Mera's ears, really.

A droning sound, like millions of engines whirring at the same time came from behind them. A sapphire dot shone against the navy-blue of the ocean, followed by another, and another. Small, neon-blue comets that rushed closer and zinged past them.

"Damned the trenches!" Azinor snarled, making a sharp turn. "I've used all my power, and the enhancer's."

"You must recharge."

"Obviously!"

The comets missed them by a few inches, boiling through the water. Someone was shooting at them.

Hissing bullets of light.

"Halt!" a woman's voice rang from behind, breaking through Mera's haze.

Water rushed past them as Azinor and his pet turned and twisted, making wayward paths through the sea.

"You're weak after your little stunt, you shrimp-brained batfish!" The woman shouted. "You won't escape this time!"

"Watch me, Officer!" he barked, his grip pressing Mera's waist harder against his left hip.

"It was a trap!" the queen shrieked. "They waited until—"

"Quiet!" he growled.

A trap?

They—Atlanteans, surely—had let Tir Na Nog drown, only to have a chance at capturing Azinor?

Mera's vision wavered between clarity and a blurred mess, and her mind spun, brain thumping against her skull. She couldn't move a muscle, even if she tried. She was so weak...

As more blue comets zinged past them, she spotted two muddled figures chasing after the asshole and the queen, but she couldn't see well.

"You'll hit Mera!" one of them shouted, a male voice so very familiar...

"I never miss," the woman grumbled, before shooting again.

They were getting closer. No, Mera was slowing down. Azinor's grip on her waist loosened.

Her gaze lifted to find a cloud of dark-red puffing above his neck. One green eye floated amidst the cloud, joined by a constellation of fractured pieces of skull and teeth. Bands of torn flesh floated casually as dark blood kept shooting from the open wound.

"No!" Ariella shrieked in horror.

As Mera began falling toward the ocean's bottom, she spotted one of the figures trapping circles of blue light around the queen's wrists.

Shackles.

"Ariella Wavestorm, you're under arrest!" the shadowy form shouted.

"That's Queen Wavestorm to you!" Mother seemed to thrash against her cuffs, but Mera couldn't tell for sure. Her form was already so blurred, so far away... Her vision tunneled, and her attention turned to the muscled, headless body falling right next to her.

Was he really dead? Had it been that simple?

As if on cue, the creep's hand twitched, and his body began moving on its own. To her left, the enhancer fell in spirals, and the headless corpse began reaching out for it. Another hand caught the chain just in time, a thin, long-fingered hand with cobalt skin.

"Not so fast," the blurred form taunted before shooting at Azinor, piercing a hole in his chest.

A ghostly roar shook the water around them, and in an eye-blink, a violent current took the prick's body away.

"Don't let him escape," Mera mumbled.

She had to wake up, had to gather her bearings and catch the bastard, but she was so tired... Her body continued sinking into the darkness below, until someone grabbed her wrist.

"Caught you, little fry."

She blinked at a blurry face with glassy pink eyes, a kind smile, and white hair tied in a tight high bun. Then, everything went dark.

CHAPTER 8

Bᴀsᴛ's ғɪsᴛ crashed against Corvus's jaw so hard that his brother toppled backwards. He opened his portal of night and stars and lunged forward, but before he could cross, Corvus trapped him in a chokehold.

"*Kura!*" Bast bellowed as he thrashed against his grip. "Let me go!"

"The detective would never forgive me!" Corvus tightened his grasp, but when Bast elbowed his ribs, he let go with a loud, "Ouch!"

"You left her behind!" he barked before jumping into his own portal, soon blinking out in the sky above the port. His silver wings flashed behind him, keeping him adrift.

The ocean had rushed miles and miles inland, the blue water turning a sloshy brown as it engulfed dirt, roads, homes... The port's high tower had completely disappeared underwater. So had everything else.

Bast's stomach fell upon itself as he watched the devastation below him. Boosting forward, he scanned for survivors, but the rooftops that stayed above water were empty. Either those near the port were dead, or they'd managed to escape to safety—Bast hoped for the second. And if those faeries were indeed safe, it had been thanks to Mera.

Desperation threatened to swallow him while he glanced at the rushing brown water, but he couldn't lose focus. Taking a deep breath, he closed his eyes and tried to reach her.

"Kitten, where are you?"

Nothing but hollow silence answered him.

Mera had to be alive. Bast couldn't consider the alternative, so he ignored his deepest fears. He had to, if he were to find her.

Fact: Azinor needed Mera, though for what, he couldn't guess. The *shig* wouldn't kill his own daughter if he needed her for his plans, whatever they might be, which meant Bast had a little bit of time, at least.

Turning to the open ocean, he balled his fists. He would get his *hart* back, and he would burn anything and anyone who stood in his path.

Corvus suddenly winnowed next to him, his pitch-black wings flapping frantically. Bast couldn't look him in the eye, not yet, even if he understood he'd only followed Mera's wishes.

"I know you're mad at me, but there's someone more deserving of your wrath." His brother pulled out a phone from his pocket.

"I thought you hated human technology."

"I do, but this little thing can be quite useful. I wouldn't have found the detective if not for this 'zellphone', back when you were kidnapped by the dead queen."

"It's called *cell phone*."

"Whatever." Corvus waved a hand dismissively. "See, if I hadn't found her, she wouldn't have been able to save your ass. So, I keep this *cell phone* for emergencies." He tapped the device mindlessly before showing it to him. "Speaking of which..."

Images of Mera holding back the *ekrunami* played on the screen. The camera hovered high above her and the crest of the wave, showing Azinor and Ariella Wavestorm. A red strip at the bottom of the display read, *'Detective Maurea: Hollowcliff's finest or siren spy?'*

Interviews with people from each borough followed. Many called her a double-agent, and others called her a hero. It was hard to tell where the majority might lie, though one thing was certain: her secret was out and nothing would ever be the same again.

"The *sarking* flying machines had cameras," he growled. "Wait. If you found Mera once using your phone, maybe—"

Corvus shook his head. "Already tried and failed. My guess is she's deep underwater by now. These things aren't exactly water resistant."

Bast grit his teeth, his fists balling. "Then there's only one thing left to do before we go after her."

A mischievous grin hooked Corvus' left cheek as he put the phone back in his pocket. "You've been there before, so lead the way, Brother. I'll handle the magic barrier around the building."

Within the next moment, Bast blinked into Councilor Adam's office, with Corvus following him.

Constructed in all white marble and sharp lines, the office reminded Bast of the temples of Danu, with a big, squared mouth that showed the city of Clifftown on the left. His shoes thumped on the marbled floor as he marched toward the mahogany desk at the end.

Councilor Adams watched them approach while holding a phone to his ear. "Samantha, I have to go. Increase the security measures on the shore. I'll update you when I return from the assembly." He hung up, his hazel eyes never leaving Bast and Corvus. "I didn't think you would be bold enough to waltz into my office, Detective Dhay." He nodded at Corvus. "Night King."

Bast raised an eyebrow as he assessed the office, listening to the silence around them. "Your guards should have barged in by now."

"They should have, but you didn't exactly use the front door, did you? Besides, you're both more powerful than most criminals in this country, not to mention skilled assassins. Flying off the radar is a sport for you." He crossed his arms. "Do tell me, how did you break the magic barrier around the building?"

Corvus wiggled his fingers as if saying 'hello'.

"You seem awfully calm for someone who betrayed Mera, Councilor." Bast stepped forward, hands behind his back. "Mighty brave of you, since you're alone in this office with me and my brother. You see, our nightblood makes us quite *unstable*." His lips curled to display pointy fangs that sharpened along with his rage.

The councilor showed no fear. "The jets weren't supposed to have cameras. It was an internal leak, and the person responsible is now in jail for breach of confidentiality, I can assure you."

"She was caught on tape, *Peter*," Bast spat, forgetting about décor and protocol. "You said Ruth was important to you, and that you would protect Mera. Instead, you exposed her to the world." He slammed a heavy palm on the councilor's mahogany table, resisting the urge to punch the *suket*. "You fucked up spectacularly!"

The councilor ran a hand through his blond-going-white hair, and his eyes glistened.

If Bast didn't know better, he would say the *shig* felt remorse, maybe even guilt. No. Politicians were incapable of both.

"Make no mistake, Detective Dhay." Adams stared at him. "I fully intend to fix that mistake."

"How? The entire nation is up in arms because of the '*traitor among us*'. That's what they're calling her on the news! A fucking traitor. After everything she's done for Tagrad. By Danu, she stopped an *ekrunami*!"

"An *ekru*... ah, yes, the tsunami. Forgive me, my Faeish has always been a tad lacking." The councilor scratched his trimmed beard. "Indeed. If not for Mera, thousands more would have died. We simply need to remind those who are calling her a traitor of that fact." He paused to consider something, then nodded at Bast. "Which is why you'll both accompany me to the emergency assembly. Right now."

"The council assembly?" Corvus blinked. "Are you serious?"

"Yes. It's actually fortuitous that you're here, Night King. I always thought Lunor Insul should have a seat at the table."

Corvus turned to Bast, eyes wide. "Brother, say what you will, but I like this *baku*."

Yet, Bast watched Adams with suspicion. "Say that once he fixes the shitstorm he's created."

"I fully intend to." The councilor pointed at Bast. "Go on, then. Do your winnowing thing. Time is of the essence."

CHAPTER 9

MERA WOKE up in a familiar place.

She lay inside a hole carved into the stone wall of a living room; a hole her people called a pod. Many sea creatures buried themselves in sand or hid in underwater caves to rest, and waterbreakers weren't any different.

Tiny specks of glowing yellow algae on the pod's ceiling shed a dim light on her, almost as if Mera was staring at a starry sky.

An old waterbreaker with hair tied in a high bun—a reminder of his time in the military, since all male soldiers fixed their hair that way—sat beside her on the pod's edge. He wore a skintight white bodysuit with silver engravings that resembled buttons on the side of a jacket, and a silver belt wrapped around his waist.

Maybe Mera was seeing things, but she could swear there was an empty gun holster attached to the left side of his belt.

Tears pricked her eyes. Truth be told, she'd never understood why waterbreakers cried. A remembrance from their human forms, she supposed.

"You're here." Her tone came out weak, broken. "You're really here."

She'd dreamt of this encounter for so long, endlessly hoping one day it would come true. Even now that it had, she still wondered if she might be dreaming.

With a sweet smile, he took Mera's hand and pressed it against his chest. "We meet again, little fry. Lie still, I'm almost done."

Only then did Mera notice the glittering wisps of light that flowed from his cobalt palm into her light-gray skin.

He was healing her.

Glancing down at her clothes, she noticed her white shirt fluttered slightly atop her torso, her jeans clinging to her skin. Somehow, she'd lost her leather jacket, which sucked above all else because it was Mera's favorite piece of clothing—a gift from Ruth when she'd graduated from the police academy.

"I've arranged for an alternative," Professor Currenter offered, seeming to have read her mind.

He nodded to a carving that rose from the living room's stone floor, shaping a round table. A black, scaled bodysuit hovered atop it, just inches from the surface.

"Thank you," she said, just as her attention drifted to the mouth of the cave.

A glittering city spread outside, circling a silver castle that seemed to stretch toward the surface. The underwater metropolis appeared to be protected by a nearly invisible energy dome, one that occasionally sparkled light blue. A round sphere beamed from high above, drenching the city in a soft glow similar to the moon's. However, with the profusion of neon, rainbow-colored lights blinking everywhere down below, the sphere seemed a bit unnecessary.

"Is that…?"

He nodded.

Atlantea. How much it had changed!

Her attention returned to him, her jaw hanging in shock. There was so much she wanted to ask, so much to tell the professor, but she only managed to notice the obvious. "You haven't aged."

He looked old, of course, but he'd also looked old fifteen years ago. It was almost as if time had stopped moving for him.

"I have aged, dear, just not enough for you to notice." Once he was done healing her, he tapped her arm. "Time flows differently for me." As if that explained it, he turned around and broke water toward the center of the room, a silent sign that he wouldn't dwell on the topic.

Mera sat up, her legs going over the edge of the pod. Waving to the cave, she smiled. "Well, at least nothing changed in here."

Most Atlantean homes had smooth curved walls of the brightest colors, thanks to luminescent technology within the paint. The ample, colorful spaces could often be peppered with repurposed corals, which were the base material for furniture and many appliances—such as ovens that worked on lava, fridges, and even cutlery. All of that had been normal back when Mera was a merling.

The professor, however, enjoyed sticking to older ways that seemed long forgotten. The only modern thing in his living room was the standing mirror at the edge of the space, which faced Mera, but even that couldn't be considered exactly modern.

Her reflection stared back at her with beady green eyes. Her nose was smaller than she'd grown accustomed to on land, and thin, nearly non-existent lips coated her mouth. Her russet hair hung heavier and fuller than usual, since minuscule red scales coated each thread.

The last time she had seen her reflection in that mirror, she'd been a child about to battle her own mother to death.

"You sound like your uncle Barrimond," the professor

pointed out. "I'm fine here. An old home is perfect for an old seal such as myself, don't you think?"

The fins rising from her earlobes poked through her red mane, twitching slightly as she scanned the space. "I like it. Always have."

He floated ahead, even if bodies didn't float easily that deep. "So much has happened, little fry. Where to start?"

"Maybe with how I'm here?"

"That's fairly easy. First, you must have noticed my attire." He motioned to his white bodysuit with a certain pride. "When your uncle became king, he named me commissioner of Atlantea."

Mera nearly gasped, even if she couldn't gasp underwater. "Commissioner? But you're a teacher!"

"A teacher with military experience." The gills on his neck inhaled a batch of water, then quickly let it out in a move similar to a sigh. "Not my preferred profession, I'll admit, but the king needed me, so a commissioner I became."

A commissioner implied the existence of a police force. "What happened to the queen's guard?"

"Still active, but the guard protects solely the king. They're not allowed to make arrests or go on investigations. That's the police department's job. You'll soon notice we're a quite democratic government, despite being a monarchy."

A smile spread on her lips.

"As to why you're here." The professor swam in circles, hands behind his back. "Our intelligence informed me that Poseidon had a magic enhancer. Shortly after, the bastard created a tidal wave, so we knew he would focus on land. We also knew he would be weaker after the attack."

"So, you let him go ahead," she countered bitterly. "Even though it would cost thousands of landrider lives."

"We didn't *let* him. The distance between Atlantea and Tagrad is considerable. We would never have reached him in time to stop his attack. And even if we could, the moment we entered the forbidden zone we would be turned to dust." He shook his head, a certain sadness and regret in his eyes. "Not that we could have stopped him, mind you. We're not as powerful as you are, little fry."

Some of the tension left Mera's shoulders. At least they hadn't chosen to let landriders die. "You assumed I would do the job, then?"

"Not at all. I should have, of course." He swam closer and cupped her cheek. "Sacrificing yourself for others is in your nature. I'm so very proud." Taking a shuddering breath through his gills, he turned away. "In any case, Belinda and I would only be able to intercept him on his way back, once he left the forbidden zone. Waiting was our only option."

"Belinda?" Mera's heart jumped from zero to sixty in a second, and she rose from the pod, too excited to sit still. "As in my best friend, Belinda?"

"Quite right. She's one of my most trusted officers."

"She's in the force? So am I!"

"I assumed that was the case when I contacted you through that seer. You work with a nightling, correct?"

"I do." Mera would eventually tell him about her adventures on land, but she still had much to learn about what happened underwater. "When you communicated with me through Madam Zukova, you told me to never come back. Was it because you feared Azinor might catch me?"

He nodded. "A moot point, wasn't it?"

Watching the landscape from the mouth of the cave, Mera scratched the back of her neck. Oval-shaped vehicles with glassed surfaces zinged by like tiny fish with translucent skin, but some of her people still rode orcas or giant mantas like she remembered. When the vehicles' headlights beamed past her gray skin, her hide edged toward the colors of the rainbow.

"It was just you and Belinda?" She turned back to him. "You

should have taken as many patrols as you could. He's too powerful."

"I agree, but Poseidon—as he's known on the streets—has many followers. I couldn't risk a leak. So we took a car and two other officers I trust. Now, don't you deem that to be lacking. It's been many moons since I've last been active, but this old seal still has a trick or two up his sleeve." He winked at her.

The image of Azinor's head vanishing in a cloud of blood flashed in her mind. Well, the professor certainly knew what he was doing.

Waterbreaking herself forward, she wrapped her arms around him. "I'm glad you're okay. You, Belinda, my uncle... you are okay, right?"

"We are." He hugged her back, his chin resting on the top of her head. "Your uncle is a great king. We've made remarkable advancements thanks to him, not only on a technological level. We're also a fairer society. I've always figured you'd like to hear that."

Uncle Barrimond had protected Mera from several beatings, standing between her and the queen when she was little. He would also sneak sweets to her when Mother wasn't watching, and he would tell her wonderful stories about brave warriors who once fought for Atlantea.

"With pride and honor, they fought for glory," he used to say. Words fitting a king.

"But?" she asked, swimming back a little. There was always a 'but.'

The professor clicked his tongue, making a croaking sound akin to a dolphin's. He always did that when he was nervous.

"Your uncle refused to conquer Tagrad, even if we could easily win a war with our technology. That made him fairly unpopular among certain groups, the same groups that used to support your mother." The professor watched her through mournful pink irises. "Poseidon saw that as an opportunity. He has been wreaking havoc around the kingdom for almost a year now, turning many of our people to his side. Atlanteans have always worshipped the God of the Sea, so his 'legend' certainly didn't help. Too many see him as a deity risen from the trenches, not a maniac who happens to be immortal."

"How can Atlanteans believe he's a God?" she asked bitterly. "He's just a psychotic asshole who took Ariella against her will."

Shock rippled across Professor Currenter's face. "She always called you Daughter of Poseidon. I thought she was going mad..." His hand cupped his forehead, eyes growing wide. "By the darkest depths of the trenches, does this mean you're his—"

Mera nodded, a sour taste trickling down her throat.

"Oh, my dear princess. I'm so, so sorry."

"It's okay." Though, it wasn't. It never would be until she put 'father of the year' six feet under.

The professor suddenly trapped her in a nearly suffocating hug, but Mera wouldn't complain. *How she'd missed him...*

"You're the strongest merling in the seven seas, you know that?"

She chuckled. "I'm not a merling anymore."

"You'll always be a merling to me." He lifted her chin slightly. "The king has asked to speak to you. Perhaps on the way, you'll tell me about your adventures in the world above?"

THE BLACK BODYSUIT the professor had given her fit Mera perfectly. The fabric didn't cling to her shape as much as she remembered. If anything, it felt light and easy to wear, almost like a second skin. It even had small pockets near her torso and hips, though she couldn't fit much inside them.

As she followed her old mentor through the castle's halls, she couldn't help but feel puzzled.

Everything had changed.

When she was a merling, Mera had hated the palace's gloomy and empty stone rooms. She'd hated the shiny silver that coated its façade, a veneer of beauty that hid the rotten decadence within it.

Memories came to mind, impressions of silent servants, endless beatings, and her own screams sinking into the stone walls; the eternal reminders of the horrors she'd experienced there.

She'd always wondered if the palace's harsh, cold halls had been built that way to mirror her misery, but it was wishful thinking, of course. Mera had never been that important to the queen.

To her surprise, however, Uncle Barrimond changed every inch of the place. He might as well have demolished the entire palace and rebuilt it from scratch.

A white and pearly surface now covered every wall and floor. The glowing yellow corals attached to the baseboards gave the space a warm, welcoming aura. Tiny golden orbs floated near the arched ceilings, as if thousands of fireflies lit the palace with their glow.

The wisps of light reminded Mera of Lunor Insul, and her heart shrunk to a dot. She couldn't feel Bast through their bond, nor through their mind-link, thanks to the distance between them.

"Is there a way to contact the surface?" she asked casually while the professor led her through the bright and polished halls.

"I'm afraid not. We can't hack their networks since they're built on completely different materials than ours." He seemed to consider it twice. "We could find the old sea-witch, Ursula, later and ask her to send a message to your psychic friend, if that helps?"

Mera had no clue if Madam Zukova was still in Tir Na Nog,

let alone alive after the tidal wave, but she didn't have another option.

Professor Currenter turned left, leading her to an indoor garden. The fake moon shone brightly up above, shedding light into the open square.

Corals of all colors, shapes, and sizes spread around the garden, matching the fluttering algae that danced gently against the currents. Schools of colorful fish swam in large groups, twirling around a silver statue at the center of the space.

The professor swam toward it, floating right above the bright and colorful corals. Mera followed after him, scaring away the small fishes in her path.

The statue depicted a merling who looked strangely familiar. She seemed proud, defiant even, with brave and feral eyes that caught Mera's attention. The merling couldn't be older than thirteen, but she was dressed for battle, with war corals too big for her tiny frame and a trident that was twice her size. She seemed so small, so scrawny, yet so fierce.

"It's me," she whispered, a mellow sensation knotting in her throat.

"Your uncle and I built it after you left. We wanted to honor you in our own way."

Mera bent down to read the inscription on a square plate under the girl's feet.

"Princess Mera Wavestorm, freer of her people.
With pride. With honor."

She'd promised herself to never cry again within those walls, but right then, it was a promise too hard to keep.

"With pride. With honor," she croaked. "Like in the stories Uncle Barrimond used to tell me."

"You remember?" A heavy, familiar voice asked from behind them.

Mera turned to see none other than her uncle, standing under an arch that led inside the castle.

The same wide smile she'd missed graced his lips, the same kind, beady brown eyes and hair, the same caramel skin. He looked nothing like his cruel sister, a luck Mera didn't have— she was Mother's spitting image.

Uncle Barrimond looked absolutely regal in his white bodysuit with golden embroidery, and a golden crown around his head. Once he opened his arms to her, Mera couldn't help but rush toward him.

"I'm so glad you're safe," he confessed, squeezing her as fiercely as the professor had a few hours ago. "When Harold told me you were alive, I could hardly believe it."

Harold?

Since when did her uncle call the professor by his name? *Harold* was like a father to Mera, and still, she would always call him Professor. Force of habit, she supposed.

"You erased the queen from this place," Mera noted quietly, her cheek pressed against his strong, bulky chest. "Thank you, Uncle." She floated away to find him wincing, as if he was about to cry.

"The things she did to you... I wanted her gone from here, but not you." He pointed to the statue. "You had to stay."

"You did a fine job, my king," Professor Currenter bowed his head at him. "Now, the rightful heir has returned."

"Oh, no." Mera shook her head. "I'm not an heir."

"But you *are* a princess, my dear," her uncle countered. "The laws at the time you left were ghastly, but I've implemented many changes. You're safe now, and you will face no repercussions for taking your mother's life. You're the rightful queen, Mera, and I will be happy to abdicate the throne for you." Uncle Barrimond swam closer to her old mentor. "Having said that, I would be glad to help you run things from behind the algae-curtains, if you deem it necessary."

"Uncle, please. I won't entertain this idea."

"But you must. If not now, eventually. I don't have any descendants." He gave the professor a mournful glance. "You're bound to become ruler, one way or another, my dear."

Reluctancy grew inside her, and Mera bit her thin lower lip. "The thing is, I haven't been a princess for a while now. I'm much happier being an officer of the law, like my mom before me."

Her uncle seemed confused. "My sister was never in law enforcement."

"She doesn't mean Queen Wavestorm," Professor Currenter explained. "She means her real mother, the human who raised her. Ruth Maurea, was it?"

Mera nodded.

Uncle Barrimond blinked, still seeming confused. "I suppose there's much you have to tell me."

"She will. At dinner tonight," the professor answered for her. "But first, I should escort the princess to the dungeons. I need her help with an interrogation."

A weary sigh left the king. "Are you certain this is the right time, Harold? She only just returned."

"There will never be a right time, my king."

"The dungeons?" Mera frowned. "Who are we supposed to interrogate?"

The professor clicked his tongue, never looking her in the eye. "The queen, little fry. I think you should see her."

CHAPTER 10

Mera followed Professor Currenter into the glass elevator that would take them down to the dungeons.

As soon as he pressed the down button and the doors closed, a square blue screen popped up on the elevator's glass door, showing a female waterbreaker with a red bodysuit that matched the color of her short hair. She looked at the camera while reporting the news around Atlantea.

"The new waterball stadium is complete," she announced. *"The inauguration will happen tomorrow at six, with a match between the Reef Sharks and the Rainbow Grouts. In other news, Ariella Wavestorm has been captured. We have no confirmation from the palace or the commissioner, but if the reports are accurate, then Poseidon has received a mighty blow."*

"Calling him Poseidon only gives him power," Mera grumbled.

"Indeed, but it's great for ratings, and reporters can be greedy bastards. You must admit it's a rather memorable alias."

Mera touched the screen, watching the reporter go on. "Well, at least things improved around here. Now the people have a voice."

"They do, thanks to you," Professor Currenter offered with a certain pride, though he hadn't been a professor in a long time.

Commissioner Currenter.

"I remember your wedding to Mr. Maelstrom," Mera blurted, though she couldn't tell why.

"You do?" He chuckled silently. "You were nothing but a little fry back then. Quite literally."

Mera smiled. "I remember an arch of colorful sea flowers. You looked dapper in a white bodysuit and golden war corals. Mr. Maelstrom dressed in the same way, only his corals were silver."

He stared at his feet. "You do remember."

"Mister Maelstrom had always been so kind..." The words left her for a moment. "How do you bear looking the queen in the eye, knowing what she did to him?"

Professor—*the commissioner*—seemed to think about it for a while. "I cannot hate a shark for biting me. It is an animal. It's simply following its instincts."

Mera blinked, taking that in, and her eyes tingled with tears she didn't shed.

"That's big of you, but Ariella made my life a living hell. She killed my friend Julian, and if he hadn't been turned into a vampire, he would have been gone. She also blew Ruth to pieces and nearly killed Bast, Commissioner." Mera swallowed, looking away. "Ariella isn't just an animal. She's a rabid beast that needs to be put down."

"First, you can keep calling me Professor. It feels odd when you don't." He watched her through wise, pink irises. "Second, I trust you to do what you must, and I'll respect your choices, no matter what they are. But could you try to extract some information from her before you, hmm, 'put her down'?"

Just as he said it, the elevator came to a halt and the doors opened.

The palace had changed, but the dungeons had stayed the

same. The cavernous space still seemed carved entirely from dark stone, and the bars closing the cells were made of shiny, smooth silver. The dungeons had no windows that showed the outside, except for small, barred gaps on each cell's back wall.

Small floating orbs lit the pathway. As they moved ahead, Mera tried to ignore the childhood memories that came afloat. Memories in which she was trapped behind those silver bars for days without any food, only because she'd dared say a word that displeased the queen.

"Are you all right?" her old mentor asked, watching her with worry as he led the way.

"I'm fine," she lied.

Offering her a supportive nod, he continued his path.

They passed by empty cells, and then not so empty ones. The waterbreakers behind bars gasped when they saw her, muttering Mother's name. Not a surprise, since Mera was her spitting image.

Most of the prisoners had gray skin, shaved heads, and wore identical moss-green bodysuits. It was odd how similar they looked to one another, like they'd lost everything that made them unique.

"Pay them no mind," Professor Currenter urged, stopping before a cell just ahead. "They're Poseidon's followers. Water-breakers out of their godsdamned minds." He nodded to whoever stood inside the cell, and her stomach turned.

The queen must be behind those bars...

Even if Mera couldn't see her from where she floated, it was as if her entire body had frozen in fear—a natural response when it came to Ariella Wavestorm.

"Make no mistake, Currenter," the queen's cruel tone came from inside the cell. "Regneerik is coming. You and my pathetic brother have limited days in this sea. Poseidon will catch you," she crooned.

"Azinor," Mera corrected, swimming closer and coming into

view. Trying to control the anger rolling down her veins, she faced the queen. "His name is Azinor, and he isn't a god, you fucking bitch."

Ariella's mouth contorted into a bitter curve. "So much spite and disrespect in the way you speak to me, Daughter. I doubt you ever addressed Ruth Maurea in this way."

Mera's hands fisted and her gills filtered water madly, but she never broke eye contact with that monster. "You might have given birth to me, but you were never my mom. I wish you had died instead of Ruth. Do I make myself clear, *Mother*? You don't deserve respect. You don't deserve love or adoration, only pain."

Maybe Mera was losing her mind, but Ariella seemed hurt.

Nonsense. The queen had never cared about what Mera thought of her.

Crossing her arms, Ariella looked away, showing the hole in her cheek as well as the tendons and teeth behind it. Her hair floated lazily around her. "What's the point of this visit? Is it to boast? You caught me, congratulations." She craned her neck left, watching the professor, who floated behind Mera. "Rejoice in your victory, Currenter. It won't last."

Mera turned to him, wondering the same. What was the point of this visit? The queen clearly wouldn't talk.

Recognition flashed in his eyes, and he seemed to catch her silent question. "I figured Ariella would be more willing to cooperate if you were here, little fry."

Mera chortled. "You're losing your memory, Professor. She won't tell me a thing. She despises me."

Professor Currenter cocked his head to the side. "Does she?"

Was he going senile? Had he forgotten everything they'd been through?

Rolling her eyes, Mera turned to the queen. "Tell him. Tell him that out of all the children who had the misfortune of leaving your womb, I was the one you hated the most. Tell him my presence here makes no difference; that it never did."

Ariella stared at her own feet. "I killed your brothers and sisters because they came from bored lords and humble servants who adored me. They were created out of love, even if one sided, and thus, they were weak." The queen appeared lost in her own thoughts. "I was their whole world. They were nothing."

The fucking monster...

Mera turned to the professor, raising one eyebrow that silently said she'd proved her point.

"*She* told me how wrong that was, back in the world beyond," Ariella muttered absently. "She said your love was a miracle, and that she was sorry I only knew your hate."

Mera frowned. "Who are you talking about?"

The queen blinked, coming to herself. "Hate fuels us, Daughter. Love is for the weak." She winced, as if her own words were hard to swallow, which made no sense whatsoever. Hate had always been the driving force in that monster's life.

"What's wrong with you?" Mera narrowed her eyes at her. "Did your *boyfriend* put your pieces together backwards?"

"Maybe he did, just to spite me. He needs me, but the order of factors doesn't alter the result." Mad laughter cackled out of her lips.

What in the seven seas had happened to her?

Back when the tsunami hit, Ariella had seemed mostly sane, though to her own credit, she hadn't spoken a lot. The queen didn't seem to be very talkative when Azinor was near.

"Where is he right now?" Mera pushed. "Why does he need you?"

"I'm his soulmate. I help him channel his power, and he hates and loves me for that." She nodded to herself, swatting the water as if swiping away a nagging seahorse. "That's why he brought me back. It was out of love, but mostly, it was out of need."

A certain horror took over Mera as pity grew in her chest,

something she'd never imagined she could feel towards Mother. The bitch didn't deserve her compassion, and yet, she had it.

"Even your soulmate doesn't care about you," she muttered.

The queen shook a bony finger at her, ignoring the remark. "Your power, your hate... they are stronger than Poseidon's. Stronger than mine. I raised you well."

"You did what?!" Fury took over Mera's pity, and she swam forward, clawing at the bars. "When I was little, I craved your approval, your love, but you hammered me with your fists and your cruel words day in and day out, until you destroyed me. You didn't raise me, Mother! Ruth did. She saved me from your fucking shadow!"

By the old gods, how Mera wished she could snap the bitch's neck right there and then.

The queen stared at her as if she was proud, which made no sense. "I did *something*, child. Your siblings were weak, yet you... you are the product of Poseidon's assault on me. You were made of pain, sadness, and rage; you were a sharp blade that I never saw coming. Unlike your brothers and sisters, you survived me, and maybe, you'll survive him, too."

"To hell with you." Mera turned to leave, unable to stand there any longer. "She will never betray him. Azinor is more important to her than her own life. Her own sanity, too."

Professor Currenter watched her intently. "What about rabid animals and the need to put them down?"

Mera shrugged, refusing to think about it, at least for the time being.

"Wait!" Ariella called after her.

Mera stopped in her tracks, but didn't look back.

"Return another day, child. Entertain me with your presence, and I'll tell you where to find him. He's weakened. You'll never get a better chance."

"Pass." Mera turned to her slowly. "You won't tell me shit."

"I promise you. Come see me again, and I'll tell you where

he's hiding." She offered Professor Currenter a tiny grin. "Your best officers haven't been able to locate his remains, yes? He *will* regrow, it's only a matter of time."

The professor didn't need to confirm it. The look he sent Mera said it all.

Troubled, she watched the queen for a moment. Mera didn't believe a word that came out of her mouth, but it wasn't like she had any choice. "If we're doing this, you better have more to offer."

Ariella bit her thin, bottom lip. "The voices. You can hear them." Not a question, but a statement.

"How do you know—?"

"Come back and I'll help you understand."

Mera's hands fisted, anger bubbling up again. Taking a deep inhale through her gills, she steadied her nerves. "Tell me now. Why wait?"

The bitch simply waved her goodbye.

CHAPTER 11

Bast stared at the large, emerald structure ahead of them.

The capitol building.

Thick pillars supported a veranda that lined the grand construction, and a triangular roof made of jade stone glinted when the sun touched it. The entire thing reminded him of mighty temples from ancient times, the ones he'd only seen in books.

The capitol building was located in the center of Tagrad, inside a neutral zone that bordered all five states. Though the boroughs of Hollowcliff didn't border one another—they were the capitals of each state—the states themselves shared frontiers around the neutral zone.

Access to the capitol was restricted, which explained why the magic barrier around it had been tough to pierce. Nothing Bast and Corvus weren't able to tackle together, of course. And now, there they stood.

Green staircases led to the entrance of the building, almost like a tongue sticking out. Bast and his brother followed the councilor as he went up the steps, soon reaching the roofed porch.

Two bulky wolfmen stood guard at the gates, each in their furry, beastly form. They moved to protect the councilor, but Adams raised his palm, stopping them in their tracks.

"They're with me." That was all he said before walking inside the building.

Bast followed after him, ignoring the wolfmen's suspicious glares, but Corvus turned to the tallest of them and bit the air mockingly. The wolf growled, showing sharp teeth ready to bite.

Rolling his eyes, Bast pulled the *baku* along before he could get them in trouble. "*Halle*, Corvus. We're walking on thin ice. Try to behave."

"I can't do that." His chin rose with a certain pride. "It's not in my nature."

They went on, crossing jade-colored halls with high, arched ceilings that felt out of this world. Bast had never seen a construction like it, though he'd seen plenty in his lifetime.

Their steps clacked against the polished floor and the sound crawled up the walls, breaking the deep silence that filled the space.

"Faster, will you?" Adams called out from ahead, and Bast promptly rushed closer with Corvus.

A big, wooden door with golden carvings that depicted a map of the five boroughs stood in their path. However, the councilor never slowed down. He might have slammed head-first against the surface, if the door hadn't suddenly opened with a loud, lazy creak.

"Danu in the prairies, this place is strange," Corvus muttered. "Was that magic or technology?"

"I don't have the slightest clue."

The buzzing hum of magic didn't tumble in the air, but Bast couldn't tell how technology could have sensed their approach. Then again, he hadn't thought flying machines were possible until that day.

Humans had many cards under their sleeves, it seemed.

The heavy door opened to a vast, round room with a domed glass ceiling. Daylight beamed atop a round, white table at the center, the only piece of furniture inside the space.

The werewolf councilor—a bulky male with caramel skin, and thick, bushy eyebrows that matched his night-black hair—talked to the witch councilor seated to his right. Bast caught mutters of the words "war" and then "Atlantea" as they got closer.

"Sirens clearly have technology far more developed than ours," the wolfman stated, paying them no mind. "Either we strike first, or we'll be defeated."

The witch, a petite thing with curly blond hair, seemed to be warming up to the idea. Yet, the female with red hair and yellow eyes on his other side, the vampire councilor, not so much.

"Going to war would hinder the nation's finances," she argued. "It's not smart."

"Yet, necessary," the wolf countered.

A screen blinked into thin air, coming from a small device on the right side of the table. If Bast recalled correctly, Mera had once called it a projector.

The screen showed Colin on the other side, his image wavering as if stricken by interference. He seemed to be rushing somewhere, and a curl of red hair slipped to the center of his forehead.

"Is this thing working? Can you see me?" His voice came out chopped and uneven. The fae councilor turned to his left and told one of his people to assess the damage on the east side of Tir Na Nog. He then shook the device he was using, and his image shook with it. "*Kura!* Damned this stupid technology. Can. You. Hear. Me?"

"We hear you fine, Colin," the bulky werewolf replied, only then turning to Adams, who'd moved next to Colin's empty seat. He nodded to the human councilor in a silent greeting. "We're discussing going to war with Atlantea. Peter has just arrived and he brought company."

Colin grumbled as his screen turned to Bast and Corvus. "Honestly, Peter? Of course you brought these two *shigs* to the assembly. Need I remind you that's against the rules?" He gave out random orders to someone on his right. "This meeting has to be quick. I must attend to my people."

"Quick it shall be, then," Adams said as he lowered onto his seat. "Councilors, going to war would be unwise. Sirens are no longer our enemy. Poseidon is the real threat."

"Is there a difference?" the witch councilor asked mockingly, fixing a blond lock behind her ear. "He's a siren, therefore, he represents Atlantea."

"Are you saying your worst criminals should represent Evanora, Mia? That all witches and warlocks should be judged based on the crimes of a few?" Adams argued, and Bast couldn't help but grin as the witch shifted uncomfortably on her seat. "Sirens can't cross the protection zone. Poseidon can. He's like nothing we've ever seen before."

"Poseidon *and* Mera Maurea," the werewolf councilor corrected, a low, beastly growl in his tone. "Both of them broke into the protection zone, which begs the question: How did they do it?" At that, he turned to Bast.

"Why the fuck should I know?" he lied.

The wolf's eyes shone a bright gold. "Language, Detective!"

"Order, please." Adams raised his hand. "Sebastian, I'll remind you that you're a Hollowcliff detective, and that you must address Tagradian authority with respect."

"You all seem to forget that my borough has been struck by an *ekrunami*," Colin cried out from the screen while he watched something beyond the display. "Tir Na Nog can't go to war right now. We must recover first, but once we are back on our feet... I agree that Poseidon's actions call for retaliation."

The werewolf councilor slammed his hand on the table with

glee, as if he'd won a battle that had barely started. "It's decided, then. Sirens have infiltrated our country, and we must go to war as soon as Tir Na Nog recovers. Who knows how much information Mera Maurea has already passed on to the other side? If she ever enters the country again, she must be killed on the spot. That is the law."

"You can't be serious!" Bast stepped forward, losing his last bit of restraint. "Mera saved Tir Na Nog twice! In the best-case scenario, she's been kidnapped, and in the worst…" He couldn't bring himself to say it out loud. He pointed at Colin's screen, a knot settling in his throat. "You should be thanking her for helping your borough, you ungrateful *shig!*"

"Peter, your guest forgets himself," the witch councilor snapped. "He has no seat at this table. If he does not respect this assembly, then the guards will have to remove him."

Bast growled at the witch, his nostrils flared. A flash of fear passed by her semblance.

"Sebastian…" Councilor Adams called out, a silent plea for cooperation in his hazel eyes.

With a grunt, Bast stepped back, standing closer to Corvus. His nightblood boiled in his veins, ready to take over, and that could only end in disaster.

"These are Detective Sebastian Dhay and the Night King, as you all know," Councilor Adams said. "They don't have a seat at this table, but their voices should be heard. After all, Lunor Insul was attacked, yet it sustained no damage because the Night Court had better measures in place. I say that earns Corvus Dhay a seat in this council, and why not a borough of his own?"

"That's preposterous," Colin argued from the screen. "Lunor Insul is under Tir Na Nog's jurisdiction."

"Now is not the time for a vote on the matter." The vampire councilor curled her red lips. "I do agree that this issue must be addressed later on, especially considering Lunor Insul has an advantage. For the time being, we must decide on the next steps regarding Atlantea and Mera Maurea. Unanimously."

"Fine." Councilor Adams motioned to Bast. "Tell Detective Dhay, then. Tell a national hero that you'll declare war on his partner's people. Tell him you'll put a bullet in Mera's head because she's a siren, even though she saved thousands of Tagradian lives today."

"Mera Maurea spent years on land *illegally*," the vampire argued, her fangs on display. "You must admit such a deed must be punished."

"Fuck you," Bast spat, stepping forward. "After everything she did for this country, this is how you repay her?"

The werewolf's chair slid back harshly when he stood. Only then did Bast notice how big he was; like a mountain rising from the ground. The *shig* fixed his yellow tie, which clashed against his light gray suit.

"Detective Dhay, I appreciate what you've done for my borough. Bruce is a good friend, and you saved his life. Lycannia is indebted to you, but your partner is a traitor who needs to answer for her crimes."

Heat rushed to Bast's head. He wanted to cut the *shig's* tongue right there and then, but it was the thought of Mera what calmed him down; the certainty he would see her smile again that appeased his wrath.

"Mera stopped the *ekrunami* on her own, and prepared to give her life in doing so. If not for her, thousands more would have died." He turned to Colin's screen, waiting for him to jump in, but the *malachai* was too busy reading a report. Huffing, Bast turned to the other councilors. "She and I have dedicated our lives to this country. If you banish her, then I say *you* are the traitors."

The councilors' outraged voices rose in a flurry of sentences he couldn't understand.

"Enough!" Corvus yelled, an aura of darkness rising from his skin. "Detective Maurea is the reason why Lunor Insul still stands. We will not stand against her, or her people."

"That's sedition!" The vampire councilor declared. "And a reason for war!"

Corvus' dubious brow arched at her. "But you can't focus on two wars at once, can you? You don't have the *mo-ney*."

Right then, Bast couldn't be prouder of his brother.

"A lot hangs on the balance, ladies and gentlemen," Councilor Adams interjected, lowering his hands in a request for silence. "Let's also remember that Detective Maurea is powerful, as we've seen in the leaked footage. She might be our only chance of defeating Poseidon."

"She might also be our doom," the werewolf added.

Adams ignored his remark, then turned to the floating projection. "Colin, you've been awfully quiet."

"Kind of busy here, Peter."

Oh, the *shig*...

"A first vote then!" The werewolf councilor clapped his hands. "All in favor of banishing Mera Maurea?"

Banishment. A "nicer term" for execution-upon-sight if she ever returned to Tagrad.

The *suket* raised his hand, and so did the witch councilor. However, the vamp representative didn't move, neither did Adams, or Colin.

A fucking relief.

"As much as I hate it, I am indebted to Detective Maurea," Colin stated. "If not for her, many more of my people would have perished. So, I say yes to a preparation of war until further attacks, and yes to granting her a fair trial once she steps on land."

"A fair trial?" Bast laughed. "Are you joking? She doesn't need a trial, she needs to be exonerated and rescued!"

"Kazania agrees with the councilor's suggestion," the vampire declared. "Mera Maurea shouldn't be executed if she returns to Tagrad, not without a trial first. In the meantime, we must prepare for war."

Shock and disbelief burned through Bast, and he blinked, unable to believe what was happening.

The witch councilor shrugged. "Evanora agrees to raising our defenses and preparing for war with Atlantea. We agree to a trial for Mera Maurea, should she step on land again." She gave Bast a mocking grin. "We certainly do *not* support a rescue mission for a siren who lied about her nature and infiltrated our country."

Bast's hands fisted, but only Danu could explain how he didn't lunge at her.

"Lycannie also agrees to a preparation for war, and a trial for Mera Maurea," the wolf councilor added, seeming rather disappointed.

Adams let out a weary sigh, then gave Bast an apologetic glance. "We can't go against the council. Preparation for war it is, but let it be noted that I stand against any option that's not an immediate pardon for Detective Maurea."

"Noted," the councilors replied in unison.

Fucking *shigs*, all of them.

"You should all be ashamed." Bast turned to his brother. "Let's go. This was a waste of time."

With that, they blinked out of the chambers, and back into the halls of the Night Court's palace.

A man stood in the center of the throne room. He had ginger hair, an eye-patch over his eye, and a few missing teeth. The strange man wore a black doublet with silver inscriptions, which matched his black pants and boots. His sleeves were drawn up to his elbows, showing runes tattooed on his forearms, and the black hat with a plump, red feather on the side seemed awfully big for his face.

"I hope ye don't mind," he offered, approaching them. "Yer assistant told me to wait for ye here."

"Yes, I asked her to fetch you before I went to my brother." Corvus nudged his chin toward the man. "Bast, this is Captain Flint. You can guess why I summoned him here."

Bast grinned. Not all was lost, not yet.

The captain flicked his hand, and the tattoos on his right forearm beamed a bright golden color until magical sparks rose from his fingers. "Pleasure to make yer acquaintance. Name's Flint, warlock of the seven seas, at your disposal. For a fair price, that is."

"Oh, really?" Bast raised one eyebrow. "I thought my brother had already paid your fees in advance."

"That was before a tsunami swallowed half of Tir Na Nog, mate."

"What's the price now, Captain?" Corvus asked mindlessly as he headed to the wine cabinet and pulled out three glasses.

"Double. Also, I wouldn't mind having one of yer ships, since mine is gone. That magic dome of yours shielded yer fleet nicely, aye?"

Corvus watched him for a moment before laughing. "You're my kind of *baku*, Flint. I'll give you half of the new rate before you leave, the other half when you return the ship to safety. Agreed?"

He shrugged. "Aye. Seems fair."

Opening a bottle of wine, Corvus filled the three glasses he'd set up on the top of the cabinet. "You may choose the ship you want and it will be yours, as long as you follow through with the original plan."

Flint frowned at him, then at Bast. "Yer still going to the isles?"

Bast nodded. "We sail as soon as possible. Corvus, will you join us?"

"I wish I could," his brother handed him and Flint their glasses with a certain dismay. "Unfortunately, I have an island to take care of. Plus, I doubt the council will leave me alone after that disaster of a meeting. They need Lunor Insul, especially if they intend on going to war with Atlantea."

Bast shot him a pleading glance, a silent message that his brother quickly understood.

"Yes, yes." Corvus nodded, raising his glass. "I'll stall them as much as I can."

"All right." Flint tapped his chin twice. "With the right crew and some wind magic, I could get ye to the isles in three days, give or take."

"Let's get started." Bast raised his glass in a silent cheer, then took a long gulp. "We have a siren to rescue."

CHAPTER 12

As Mera roamed the streets of Atlantea from above, she couldn't help but admire the modern buildings that towered over her path. Though the city didn't technically have streets—waterbreakers could swim in any direction they wanted—the gaps between the constructions formed dimly lit paths down below; paths that guided her.

She swam past big, glass surfacebreakers all too similar to the skyscrapers from Clifftown. Narrowing her eyes, she spotted spacious offices inside the buildings, with busy sirens rushing around. On the floor below was a crowded gym, followed by fancy restaurants, shopping malls, and much more.

In many ways, Atlantean society mirrored the one on land, and in many others, it was completely different. So much had happened since she left; so much she had yet to discover about her home.

Uncle Barrimond and Professor Currenter tried covering some of it during dinner the previous night, but a few hours hadn't been enough.

Mera did learn that the fake moon floating above town was a source of energy that drew its power from the heat of the lava pits. It was Atlantea's main power source, which fed into industries, buildings, and even the orbs of light that floated throughout the city—after taking one in her hand, she realized it felt squishy and membranous, as if made of jellyfish skin.

A hologram suddenly popped up next to Mera, startling her. She swam back, her heart racing while she stared at the image.

Unlike the wavering, chopped holograms on land, the neon-blue figure looked like a living waterbreaker floating right next to her. He wore a fancy bodysuit engraved with squared patterns, and he moved as easily as any real creature would.

"Good day to you, fellow Atlantean!" He beckoned her closer. *"Here at Davinor's dealership, we want your old car."* He stepped aside to reveal a holo-parking lot filled with floating, pill-shaped vehicles with translucid chassis. *"Come on down and buy a brand new one! It'll be a bargain, guaranteed! Find us at the intersection between Coral Avenue and Tide Street!"*

Mera's jaw dropped as she watched him and the parking lot. She tried touching his face—it looked so real—but her fingers plunged into his non-existing cheek, making whatever generated him waver. The holo-man didn't seem to feel a thing, and soon blinked out of existence.

"The commercials can be quite a nuisance." Professor Currenter called out from ahead, his arms crossed. They'd agreed to meet at that spot, and Mera was happy to see she could still find her way in Atlantea. "Your uncle is about to pass a law to limit their frequency."

"He's good at that, isn't he?" She broke water toward the professor, zinging high atop the empty streets below. "Improving things, I mean."

During their dinner, her uncle had explained that he'd changed many laws to help the people, including the rules that said Mera had to answer for the queen's murder.

"You were only a merling back then..." He swallowed a big chunk

of tuna wrapped in seaweed. "You're safe, dear, and officially off-the-hook. Which means we can announce your return."

"I'd rather not. For now, at least. It would be a shock for the people, and we have enough on our hands, don't we?"

He watched her as he chewed, a frown marring his forehead. Her argument clearly hadn't convinced him, not one bit. Still, he'd agreed. "As you wish, but eventually, Atlantea must know its princess has returned. Maybe word of your arrival could hinder Poseidon's efforts."

"Maybe," she'd replied, though she didn't think it would, especially since she'd left her people all those years ago.

Why would they trust her? Why would they follow her?

"Ready?" The professor asked once she reached him, pulling her from her memories. When she nodded, he turned and broke water forward, leading the way.

"Why didn't you pick me up with a car?" she asked from behind as they zinged through Atlantea. "Waterbreaking can be tiresome after a while."

"I'm an old seal, remember?" he chuckled, not bothering to turn back. "Some say that using cars is lazy, others call it innovation. I say it's a bit of both. Same for the automatons."

"Automatons?"

As if on cue, he nodded down to a figure walking at the sea bed, venturing through the empty streets with silver skin and neon blue eyes that seemed to pop against the darkness.

Driven by curiosity, Mera dove in an arch, and when she reached the bottom, she couldn't believe what she saw.

The automaton was shaped like a waterbreaker, but it was made of smooth silver plates with engines and cogs whirring underneath it. A blue plasma core shone dimly from the inside, light escaping through the gaps of its metallic skin.

She watched the thing's hollow, bright blue eyes. "This is insane."

The automaton carried two bulky metal blocks over each shoulder. The thing's movements were slow and jerky—almost akin to an old clock—but it kept trudging along at its own pace. It suddenly stopped and whirred its head toward Mera. The tiny cogs in its jaw spun, opening its mouth.

"Good morning, madam," it greeted without moving its lips, its voice a metallic, droning sound that perfectly fit the owner.

"Good morning."

The automaton snapped its jaw shut, then kept walking as if nothing out of the ordinary had happened.

Mera boosted up, and when she reached Professor Currenter, she couldn't help but shout in excitement. "You have robots!"

"Is that what landriders call their automatons?"

Mera laughed. Until recently, they didn't even have jets.

"We have algorithms and computers, but robots like *that*?" She blew water through her gills. "I used to read stories with them in science-fiction magazines when I was younger, but I never expected to see one in the flesh. I mean, in the metal?"

"I suppose automatons were the logical step after the stingrays." He shrugged. "Atlantea grew quickly, little fry. We'd originally designed them to help with construction, since the city's growth was too much for the whale trucks, but the automatons are quite useful everywhere. We're even testing a prototype for law enforcement." He winked at her before boosting up, following the façade of a sleek, onyx structure that had to be at least fifty stories high.

"Freaking robots," she muttered to herself, swimming after him.

Her people might have been known as Sea Fae once, but they certainly weren't afraid of technology; not like the fae of Tir Na Nog. Maybe it was because iron limited their power, and there wasn't a lot of it underwater. Or maybe, the fae on land were simply stuck in their old ways. Hard to guess, really.

They soon stopped before a large balcony with an open entrance. Neon orbs of all colors floated around, mimicking the rest of the rainbow city. Yet, as they ventured inside the building, the orbs turned a bright gold. They hovered near the ceiling, drenching the entire space in daylight.

A siren's vision adapted to the darkness of the ocean, but Mera supposed the lights' purpose was the same as the cars'.

Convenience.

Waterbreakers rushed around the vast space, wearing black bodysuits with silver embellishments on their chests that mimicked buttoned jackets. The metallic, silver belts around their waists carried sheaths for daggers, and holsters for guns that appeared different from the ones on land, though Mera didn't get a closer look.

The sirens wore silver bracelets around their wrists, but she couldn't say what use they might have other than esthetic.

Some of the people at the back had little black dots attached to their ears, and they seemed to be speaking to no one in particular.

Phones. They were on the phone!

"This is a precinct," Mera mumbled to herself, the set-up of the open space looking incredibly familiar.

"The main precinct in Atlantea, actually." The professor broke water forward, floating gently toward a crowd on the right. "She'll find you. Listen to what she has to say, yes?"

"Who?"

He couldn't answer. A swarm of officers had already fallen upon him, asking thousands of questions. Their silver wristbands projected blue images into thin water, showing him reports and file cases.

Ah, so that was what they did. Not just for esthetics, then. Mera made a mental note to fetch one of those handy little devices later.

She watched the officers come and go around the vast precinct, but none of them seemed to notice her presence. They passed by mindlessly, too wrapped up in their daily business.

"Fancy seeing you here," a familiar voice said from behind, but she couldn't guess to whom it belonged.

When she turned around, her eyes widened. Even though years had passed, she would always recognize her best friend.

Belinda still looked jaw-droppingly beautiful. Her blond hair was tied in a low pony, the tail fluttering slightly along the gentle currents inside the precinct. Her pinkish hide matched with the bright purple of her almond-shaped eyes, and she looked regal and proud in her black uniform.

Mera jumped at her, trapping Belinda in a hug. "It's you. It's really you!"

At first, her friend didn't react, but eventually she hugged Mera back, her arms tightening around her waist.

"I thought you were dead for so long..." Belinda's voice broke, and she cleared her throat, her arms squeezing harder around Mera. "I thought you were gone when the wave crashed, but then the bastard left the forbidden zone, carrying you, and I knew we couldn't fail."

"Thank you." Letting go, Mera swam back. "You're the one who shot him in the head, right?"

Belinda gave her a proud grin. "It didn't stop the dickweed, but at least he'll need time to regenerate." She nodded to a corner of the space, far from the officers and the noise. A silent cue for Mera to follow.

Once they reached the empty spot, near what seemed to be an abandoned elevator shaft, Belinda leaned closer. "That dirty anglerfish has too many lackeys around town. There are spies in the force, too, so you have to watch what you say around here." She narrowed her eyes at the officers ahead. "Poseidon's numbers are growing."

Mera nodded. "I've faced a similar situation in Tir Na Nog with my partner. It was tough, but we managed to fix it. You and I can do the same here, Bel."

"That would be nice. Wait, did you say 'partner'?"

"Yeah. I'm a detective, but now I'm pretty sure I'll be killed if I ever return to land."

"Why?" Her pink brow furrowed. "You held down a giant tidal wave, and saved hordes of landriders. They should be congratulating you."

"Maybe, but waterbreakers aren't allowed to set foot on land. That's a big taboo in Tagrad."

"Sure, we aren't 'allowed'. Except, anyone other than you and Poseidon would disintegrate before reaching the shore." Belinda rolled her eyes, then nodded to the front of the office, toward the group gathering around Professor Currenter. "The commissioner is busy, as always. He told me to look after you today, so, want to go for a bite? Old Sue still has her stand."

A warm giddiness bloomed inside Mera at the thought of eating Old Sue's fish sticks, just like they used to do after school.

"I'm in!"

Breaking water toward the balcony, Belinda zinged into the middle of Atlantea, and Mera followed. She couldn't get enough of the colorful, glittering city that extended below and everywhere around them, but as they ventured further downtown, dodging incoming vehicles became a serious problem.

One car zinged right past Mera's head, and then a male riding a dolphin nearly slammed into her.

"Watch where you're going!" he shouted before continuing on his path.

"Follow the breaker lanes, Mer!" Belinda yelled from ahead, motioning to the neon-yellow lines that flanked her left and right, going up and down the water like a rollercoaster. "Traffic downtown can get crazy, so the DMV put up some tracks to organize the flow a few years back."

A stinging feeling bloomed in Mera's chest as Belinda called her 'Mer', the way she used to when they were young. The same way Julian used to call her... She ignored the sensation, deciding to focus on the now.

They soon left the chaos behind and reached a small complex over a dozen stories high. Unlike the modern buildings downtown, this one was made of pure stone with glowing neon corals of all colors peppering the façade.

Belinda descended onto the roof, where a chubby lady with gray hair and night-black skin floated behind a metallic stand. The pink letterhead read, *"Old Sue's Fresh Salmon Sticks"*.

Old Sue still wore a white bodysuit with baby-blue stripes from when Mera was a merling.

"Certain things never change," she muttered to herself, settling behind Belinda.

Her friend motioned for two, and Old Sue promptly prepared their sticks, wrapping them in seaweed.

The old lady suddenly narrowed her eyes at Mera while she handed a device to Belinda. "Your new partner looks like the dead queen, Officer Tiderider."

"Yeah. She gets that a lot."

From a hidden pocket in her bodysuit, Belinda pulled out a nearly transparent card with neon green lines, which she promptly swiped into the device. Once the payment was approved, Belinda snatched their sticks, bid Old Sue goodbye, then swam up toward the roof of another structure. It showed them an amazing view of downtown Atlantea.

Her friend sat on the ledge, her feet swinging above the busy chaos of rushing vehicles, waterbreakers, and sea creatures.

"Old Sue didn't remember me," Mera remarked quietly when she sat next to Belinda. "She remembered the queen, but not me."

"Everyone thinks you're dead. Also, Old Sue gets tons of customers every day. One is bound to forget some faces when they're that busy, especially since you haven't been around for what? Fifteen years?" She handed Mera a stick. "It's for the best, Mer. Announcing your presence might weaken Poseidon's efforts, but it might also backfire—a lot. Not that we have many choices. He'll be sending his lackeys after you, which is why I'm in charge of your security."

"Wait, what?"

"Commissioner's orders. I know you can take care of yourself, but I'm pretty good with one of these." She tapped the gun in her belt's holster.

"Well, he couldn't have made a better pick." Mera felt her teeth sharpening, as was always the case when a waterbreaker was about to feed. "You shot Azinor in the head. That's a lot more than I've managed to do."

"Doesn't make any difference. The prick can regenerate like an octopus, no matter where you hit him." Belinda took a bite of her food, chewing slowly. "His lackeys tried to raid the precinct a few months ago. We taught them a lesson, but they killed my partner, Bluefin." Her mood darkened, an awfully familiar sensation for Mera.

"I lost my first partner, too," she offered quietly, chewing her food. "It's not the same, of course. We turned him into a vampire, but it was touch and go for a while."

"Guess you're a better partner than I ever was. He's still *somewhat* alive, right?" Belinda seemed to blink away incoming tears while she bit another piece of wrapped salmon. "Bluefin had a kid."

Mera's chest constricted, and her hand rested on her friend's back. "We'll make that prick pay for all he's done. I promise."

"Bluefin promised that, too. Didn't turn out so great for him."

They kept eating and watching the view, a heavy silence hanging between them.

"Poseidon is my father," Mera blurted, "but I prefer calling him by his true name, Azinor. Makes him less... almighty, I guess."

"What?"

She nodded to herself, a bitter taste going down her throat.

"The prick raped Ariella when she went into the trenches, and I was the product. I think that's why I didn't disintegrate when I entered the forbidden zone. Maybe it's also why I was able to hold back the tidal wave, but I can't explain how."

Belinda stared at her, her eyes so wide that Mera spotted her own reflection in her glassy purple irises. "Cursed mackerels. That's why the queen used to call you Daughter of Poseidon." She shook her head, hunching over her knees. "Life handed you a shitty deck of jellycards, my friend."

A weary chuckled reverberated inside Mera's chest. "Sure did."

They stayed in silence for a while, but Belinda soon broke it. "Wait, so the queen follows him, even after everything he's done to her?"

"Don't ask me why. Their dynamic is beyond deranged."

Mera took another bite of her fish, watching her friend. A smile sprouted on her lips as she went back to the time when they were little merlings, exploring the ocean together, going on mighty adventures, and riding waterdragons they couldn't save. "Remember when we lost that waterdragon to the trenches?" she murmured. "I was devastated."

"Gods, we really messed that one up, didn't we?"

Mera's attention fell on her half-eaten salmon stick. "When I first faced off Azinor, he thanked me for sending him the water-dragon. He said he drew power from those who ventured in the trenches, until eventually he amassed enough to break free. I guess the waterdragon helped him a lot."

Belinda seemed to consider it, her lips pressed into a line. "The dickweed can do whatever he wants with his magic, even raise the dead. It's insane."

"There are limits, though. He can raise the queen, but he can't raise other dead without a drug that can only be produced on land. He tried that in Clifftown, but it didn't work." Finishing her salmon stick, Mera wiped the edge of her mouth. "So, what's the plan to stop the prick?"

Her friend didn't hesitate. "We'll chop him in a thousand pieces, then scatter them across the seven seas. That should do the job."

"Hopefully." Mera took her stick and Belinda's, then headed to a nearby trash can. The can opened its mouth and sucked the sticks inside, quickly snapping it closed. "Can I ask you something?"

"Always."

"Do you think I haven't figured it out yet?"

"Figured out what?"

"That you are using the queen as bait."

Her friend blinked, her jaw hanging open. "Mer, we thought—"

"You and the professor are trying to protect me, I get it. But considering what the bitch and Azinor put me through, I think I should be kept in the loop. Don't you agree?"

"Absolutely. In fact, since you're back in Atlantea…"

She pulled out a shiny silver weapon from the holster attached to her belt. The device was shaped like a pearly, round-edged gun, with three blue blinking dots on the sides. The mischievous grin Belinda shot Mera was terrifying.

"It's time you learned how to use a phaser."

CHAPTER 13

MERA COULD GET USED to this. Being back home with the professor, Belinda, and her uncle felt right. Her friend had showed her so much the other day, that her head hurt.

From her room in the palace, Mera watched the rainbow city ahead. If she narrowed her eyes enough, she could almost spot the parts of the dome that went blue in the distance. Belinda told her that the dome protected the city from strong currents, and that the blue sparks came from big fish that occasionally hit the shield head first, only to swim away.

Breaking water to the center of the room, Mera observed the pearly curved walls, and the golden corals that peppered their surface. They matched the bright wisps of light that hovered near the room's ceiling. The queen-sized bed rested against the left wall, rising from the white floor.

A chill ran down her spine as she remembered the cold, dark stone underneath what her uncle had built; the legacy that tainted those immaculate walls. Rubbing the bridge of her nose, she reminded herself that the past was the past, the castle had been rebuilt, and that Mother couldn't hurt her anymore.

A few knocks came from her door, and Mera opened it to find none other than Belinda.

Her friend showed herself in, dashing to the center of the room. Twirling around, she assessed the space, her jaw hanging. "I haven't been here since... it looks so different."

"It really does." Mera held her hands behind her back. "What's the plan for today?"

"How about you help me clean the city a bit?" She nodded toward Mera's nightstand, which rose from the floor next to her bed. A silver phaser rested atop it, close to a metallic belt with a holster—a gift from Belinda.

The silver weapon dimly reflected the golden wisps of light hovering near the ceiling. *Beautiful and deadly as fuck.*

Phasers packed a lot more heat than human weapons, Mera had seen it firsthand when Belinda blew off Azinor's head with a single shot, and then again when she took her to the firing range the previous day.

Without hesitating, she picked up the belt, tied it around her waist, and placed the phaser gun in its holster. "I'm in."

Her friend eagerly rubbed her palms together. "Let's float."

"Will Professor Currenter be joining us?"

"Of course not, silly. He's the commissioner. Plus, he's in a meeting with the king." Belinda raised her brow knowingly.

Mera stared at her, not knowing what to make of that, or perhaps, making too much of it. "Do you know why my uncle calls the professor by his first name?"

Harold.

"They didn't tell you?" Seeing that they obviously hadn't, she fidgeted with the silver bracelet around her wrist. "Ah, crab's pinchers. I'm not sure if it's my place to tell, Mer."

Crossing her arms, Mera sent her a defying glare. "I'm not leaving until you do."

"Ugh, fine." Belinda rolled her eyes. "You see, the commissioner isn't just the commissioner. He's also the crown prince."

"What?" Mera gasped, not knowing how to feel about it. "The professor married my uncle?"

"They found each other after you left. They grieved together for so long... Come on, you have to admit it's kind of heart-warming."

"Yeah, but it's my uncle *and* Professor Currenter." Slowly, however, her shock began shifting into something warm and giddy. "Why didn't they tell me?"

"My guess is guilt." Belinda shrugged. "After Bluefin's death, I felt terrible when something good happened. As if smiling or being happy was an insult to his memory. Same principle."

Her chest stung at that. Mera wanted them to be happy, and she was glad they'd found each other. Her two favorite people in the world, together. Something good had come out of all the bad that happened to her. They shouldn't be ashamed of that, and Belinda shouldn't grieve her dead partner forever, either.

Leaving the topic behind, her friend pulled a little device shaped like a dot from a pocket in her bodysuit, then handed it to her. "This is a comm. We'll need them to talk." She picked another dot and fixed it on the space where her earlobe turned into a fin. "Ready?"

Once Mera fixed it the same way, she tapped to check if it worked. "You bet." Yet a sudden ache spread inside her, and she halted before they left the room. Maybe she was losing her mind, but Bast's presence awoke inside of her. He felt... closer.

Impossible.

She must have been imagining things, but the dreadful longing kept spearing her heart, threatening to drown her.

How she wished he could be there, next to her.

A worried frown marred Belinda's forehead. "Everything all right?"

Mera nodded mindlessly.

"*Bast?*" She pushed the thought through their bond, but her words met a void. She still couldn't reach him.

There was nothing Mera wanted more than to cross the seven seas, if only to touch him again, but she couldn't leave, not yet. Once Azinor took the bait and came for the queen, Mera would defeat the dickwart. Only then, she could finally return to her *hart*.

Her gills inhaled sharply when she turned to Belinda. "Let's go."

Swimming through the streets of Atlantea with her friend felt awfully similar to patrolling Clifftown with Julian back in the day.

Glass buildings towered over them, but stone constructions peppered by colorful corals—a memory from the old Atlantea—still broke through the modern landscape every now and then.

"You should see what they did with the old fun park," Belinda said while they broke water, dashing between constructions as big as stone krakens. "They made a gallery with holo-recreations of the giant ones, the beasts of old that used to roam the sea. They have their bones on display, too."

"No way! Can we go there when we're done?"

"Of course. In the meantime, tell me more about your life up above. I need details!"

They followed a current upward, then made a U-turn, passing by a waterbreaker who rode a narwhal. He carried a red squared backpack that read, *"Saul's Food Delivery".*

"A car would be faster," Mera pointed out.

"It would, but cars can be a little expensive. Besides, if you've spent months training your seafriend, you can't dispose of it just like that. There's a bond created, though I wouldn't know. Never had a seafriend, especially after we sent that waterdragon off to the trenches…" She shook her head. "Anyway, stop diverting. Tell me about your life as a landrider in disguise."

"It's such a long story."

"We have time." Belinda gestured to the city ahead. "It's why I didn't take a patrol car, you know. I wanted to catch up."

Clever girl.

Continuing their path, Mera told her about Ruth, and how she'd been her true mother. Her *mom.* She explained how she'd taught Mera everything about duty and protecting the innocent; everything that made her who she was. She also spoke about the delicate political balance governing Tagrad, and about her cases with Bast.

Once she was done, Belinda blew water through the gills on her neck. "Landriders can be so thickheaded. Also, I'm sorry about your mom."

"So am I."

Her friend swam closer, narrowing her eyes at Mera. "Do you realize you grin like a smiling fish when you mention your partner?"

Mera chuckled. "He's not just my partner."

"Gotten a piece of landrider meat, have you?" Belinda's tongue stuck out as if she'd tasted a rotten fish.

"It's a fine piece of meat, trust me." She glanced toward the surface, past the shining orb floating atop the center of Atlantea. "He's probably worried sick by now."

Belinda suddenly turned forward, scanning their surroundings. "Quick update: I hid the magic enhancer in a warehouse on the south zone." She pointed to a section of the city before them. The light of the moon orb seemed to only reach the area partially, illuminating it less than the rest of Atlantea. "Problem is, someone tipped off Poseidon's lackeys. Word on the street is, they're planning on getting the enhancer so that the rotten oyster can recover faster."

Mera pulled out her gun. "Last time he had a magic enhancer, he created a tidal wave. Who knows what he could do next."

Her friend nodded. "From here on, we need to stay sharp."

They turned toward a clearing, and Belinda suddenly yanked her to the side. Hiding behind a construction peppered by blue corals, she cursed under her breath. "Blasted barnacles. They already have the enhancer."

Mera glanced at the clearing from behind the side of the building, watching two male waterbreakers discussing with each other. They wore moss-green bodysuits, and had no hair on their heads. Their dark-grey skins looked eerily similar to Azinor's, and by the scratches and wounds on their faces, they'd gotten the enhancer at a high cost.

"Starwave, do you copy?" Belinda whispered as she tapped her comm. After a while, she clicked her tongue. "The patrol guarding the enhancer isn't answering."

Crap.

One of Azinor's lackeys held a dark-silver pin shaped like a hexagon with an emerald encrusted in its middle. The other carried a beeping device that flashed to an increasing tempo.

Mera gasped through her gills. "Is that a bomb?"

Belinda leaned over, observing the two. Nodding, she pulled out her phaser before boosting forward, aiming at the criminals.

"Police! Stay where you are!"

Mera followed with her phaser in hand, but the men made a run for it. Belinda fired, and a blue, shining orb left her phaser, burning through the water, yet the siren holding the enhancer dodged the blast too easily.

Her friend couldn't have missed, though. She was an excellent shot.

"It's the enhancer!" Mera shouted as she boosted after them. "He's using it to amplify his powers!"

She and Belinda zinged through town, dodging passersby, cars, and buildings as they tried to catch the assholes. They shot at the slowest one, but when the blasts slammed against a magic shield, Mera knew his partner was using the enhancer to cover his friend's back.

"Monkfish shit!" Belinda pointed to the access tunnels on the seabed, which led to open ocean and the outskirts of town, passing right under the dome. "They're heading to the tunnels!"

Once the criminals were out, it would be hard to locate them, especially if they caught the warm, middle streams of the gulf. Not to mention that the tunnels were packed with water-breakers coming in and out of their daily business. Also, the pricks had a bomb.

Suddenly, their plan became frighteningly clear.

A current buzzed under Mera's skin, like lightning coursing through her veins, warming her body from the inside out. She looked down at the criminals making a downwards loop. Soon they would reach the access tunnels.

Her own voice whispered in her ears, then split into a thousand voices, all belonging to her. Even though her bodysuit covered her from neck to ankles and she couldn't see the runes, their tingling hummed through her skin.

"Mallak, mallak!"

The voices bloomed from her core, as if her soul tried to speak to her. She couldn't understand how she suddenly understood what *mallak* meant.

Aim.

"Mer!" Belinda shouted through their comms, making a sharp dive ahead of her while she followed the criminals. "Hurry!"

Instead of obeying her friend, she put the phaser back in its holster and raised one arm. Energy crackled under her skin.

Aim.

Closing one eye, Mera focused on the bandit holding the enhancer. Her movements felt both like her own and someone else's at the same time. It was almost as if she were in a sort of trance, yet somehow perfectly aware.

A bolt of blue lightning burst from her palm, heating the water around her. It dodged Belinda and plunged forward, slamming against the miscreants' shield. The bolt broke through the magic barrier that had withstood several phaser attacks like it was nothing. Her power bulls-eyed the siren in his chest, and his body went limp.

Through her magic, Mera felt his heart stopping, and then, just like a whisper or a blowing wind, he was gone. The criminal's hand released the enhancer, sending it twirling down in a spiral.

The second lackey glared at Mera, his eyes wide with terror. "Soulbreaker."

Belinda rushed toward him, but he dropped the bomb, quickly breaking water to escape. The beeping gadget plunged toward the access tunnels and the crowd down below. Her friend couldn't catch the bastard and save all those innocents at the same time.

"Red-lipped batfish!" Without hesitation, Belinda shot at the bomb, brave idiot that she was. And she never missed.

The blast stretched into a burning, yellow plasma sphere about to engulf her friend.

Mera's power charged from her core, breaking through the distance between them in less than a second. It wrapped Belinda in a crackling ball of blue lightning just as the explosion washed over her friend. Golden light burned brightly, blinding Mera. The loud boom resounded in her ears, and a shockwave slammed against her, sending her toppling backwards.

Her core sizzled with the heat of the blast; the heat that swallowed the shield she'd wrapped around Belinda. She felt her friend's heart thumping in her magic, her breathing rushed.

Mera rolled through the city for a moment until she managed to stop. Just as she did, the shield zinged past her.

"Bel!"

Pulling her magic back to her core, Mera forced the shield down to a stop, her teeth grinding and head pounding. Her vision blurred when the power returned to her, setting Belinda free.

Her friend patted her own body, clearly wondering how the hell she was still alive while the brightness of the explosion slowly faded, leaving a cloud of bubbles in the water.

The crowd near the access tunnels watched with fear and awe. Mera couldn't explain how she heard their *'oohs'* and *'aahs'* from so far away, yet she did. Everything around her seemed sharper, clearer.

Apart from a few broken windows on nearby buildings, and some smashed cars, there didn't seem to be any great damage around town.

A relief.

Belinda turned to Mera, her gills working madly to filter water. "Plasma lightning! How in the seven seas did you do that?"

She would explain if she could, but Mera had no clue either. Her body began to feel heavy and weak. Blinking, she tried to center herself while her own voice whispered one last time.

"Aller."

Rest.

Darkness took over, and the lackey's panicked voice lullabied Mera into oblivion.

"Soulbreaker."

CHAPTER 14

WIND TOUSLED Bast's hair and saltwater sprayed his face as the boat dashed across the sea.

Corvus had given Flint his fastest frigate, the Marauder. The black vessel had onyx sails engraved with a silver half-moon that was crossed with a curved dagger—the Night Court's crest. Unlike bulky nightbringers, the ship would take them to the Isles of Fog in a third of the time, but because it was so light, the Marauder didn't have any defense systems. Since they'd left the protection zone the day before, the frigate was now an easy target for rogue sirens.

Not an issue with Bast on board, of course.

"Fret not, lad!" Flint shouted from the bridge as he steered. His crew—twenty nightlings, plus one warlock who was Flint's first mate—worked the sails and the deck. "We'll find yer lass and get her to safety."

The captain whistled to himself, and the merciless wind propelling the Marauder intensified.

"Captain, that speed might rip the sails!" his first mate warned, pulling at some ropes, but Flint only laughed maniacally.

"Then you better hold on tighter, Mr. Snipes!"

Griping the rails while the ship veered, Bast focused on the horizon.

Soon, min hart.

He closed his eyes, trying to reach Mera. He could feel her stamped against his magic, her presence so very weak. She was alive, but he couldn't pinpoint her location. Frustrating, but he called it progress, nonetheless.

"Kitten, answer me."

Nothing.

When he opened his eyes and looked down at the water rushing past the Marauder, he spotted a smooth-skinned creature breaking the surface in small arches like a dolphin. It matched the ship's speed, which was remarkable to say the least.

The gray-skinned male was hairless, with long fins stretching from his earlobes. He wore a moss-green bodysuit from neck to ankles, and when he glanced up, his glassy black eyes locked on Bast's. A sharp-toothed grin stretched his mouth, brimming with bloodlust.

Halle.

"We've got company!" Bast yelled before shooting a sphere of night and stars at the siren.

His darkness splashed against the surface, sending a wall of water upwards. Bast couldn't see the *akritana* for a moment, until his body floated to the surface. The ship left it behind all too quickly, but soon, ten more heads popped from the water, dashing closer.

"Battle stations!" Captain Flint yelled, just as a siren jumped from the water and landed on deck.

"Cover your ears!" Bast shouted.

The siren opened her mouth, and Bast heard the first shrieking tone before his darkness wrapped around his ears, blocking any sound. He turned back to see that Flint and his first mate were using a similar type of magic, so were most of the nightlings, but one of them crouched on the deck with his hands stamped on the sides of his head.

The siren stomped toward him, ready for the kill. Taking momentum, Bast whipped his darkness in a line. It wrapped around the siren's ankle and flung the *slatch* overboard.

The nightling exchanged one grateful glance with him before his own darkness protected his ears, and he acquired a battle stance. Soon, two more sirens jumped onto the deck, giving them no time to breathe.

Who knew how many more followed the ship from underwater. Could be a few, could be a hundred.

"Hang on, lads!" Flint's voice echoed in Bast's mind through some sort of spell.

He grabbed the rails, and so did the rest of the crew, just as the ship turned abruptly into a sharp curve, sending the sirens tumbling overboard.

It wasn't enough.

More *akritanas* jumped on the Marauder, their pointy teeth eager to rip flesh apart. Carrying rough-edged swords, they hurried toward the crew.

Flint raised his arm, and the tattoos on his skin shone a bright yellow before golden lightning struck one of their enemies. Meanwhile, Mr. Snipes muttered a spell that made a siren's body twist in unnatural directions—especially the *shig's* neck.

As the nightlings clashed against the invaders, Bast's wings flashed to life. He felt the pressure of the macabre trying to burst him from inside out, but his magic was much stronger than that of the sirens trying to kill him.

A couple of nightlings on the deck weren't so lucky. One's head exploded, along with another's chest, their remains splashing on the wood.

Raising his sword, Captain Flint jumped from the bridge and into the battle. "No mercy!"

He charged forward, swiftly beheading a siren before sending a lightning burst toward another, while Mr. Snipes fought at his back. Dreadfully, the *akritanas* kept jumping on deck, so Bast winnowed underwater.

He faced a group of twenty sirens zinging toward the Marauder. Winnowing again, Bast appeared behind two of them and grabbed them by their ankles, transporting himself to a spot high in the sky.

The sirens glared at him and his silver wings for a moment before he let them go with a smirk.

Shrieks filled the air, escaping the *shigs* that free-fell, but their cries died out when Bast engulfed them with a smoldering tongue of night and stars. He couldn't risk them using water to ease their fall.

Within a second, his power dissipated, leaving only the sirens' ashes and charred bones that plopped into the shy waves.

On and on he went, plucking *akritanas* from the deep like daisies, only to burn them to crisps in the sky. A preventive measure, of course. They couldn't reach the deck and attack the crew if they were dead.

One siren broke water too quickly, though. She wrapped herself in a bubble and escaped his darkness. Bast was getting weaker, as was always the case when he winnowed extensively, so he had to tread carefully.

The woman landed on the Marauder's deck, then raised an odd-looking silver gun with three blinking blue dots, aiming at the crew. "For Poseidon!"

When she pulled the trigger, something that Bast could only describe as blue, beaming stars shot from the nozzle, slamming against two nightlings nearby.

Their gazes fell to the gaping holes in their chests, and then they collapsed. The skin around the wounds was charred with remarkable precision.

Kura!

Bast landed on the Marauder, his wings vanishing behind his back as he glared at the siren with a murderous anger. Flint was faster, though. He sent a jolt of lightning at her, making her thrash in pain. The siren tried shooting at him, but the blast slammed against Flint's strong magic shield.

"Clear the water!" he yelled at Bast, just as another siren jumped on deck.

Taking a deep breath, Bast jumped into the sea. The moment he plunged, a thrashing current hit him, sending him deeper underwater.

A bald *akritana* rushed closer and grappled with him. His hands wrapped around Bast's neck, which was overkill, really. He thought about winnowing, but he had to save his energy.

The water around them bubbled as Bast's night and stars jolted at the siren, engulfing the *shig* completely. His companions charged closer, but Bast's power expanded, enveloping them in his magic until the ocean became the night sky.

Horrid screams echoed through his darkness, but they quickly died. Satisfied, he withdrew his magic to reveal an empty ocean ahead, except for the burnt pieces of bone that spiraled toward the bottom.

Using his power to propel himself, Bast broke the surface and landed aboard the ship.

"Cleared!" he shouted, barely catching his breath, his wet silver hair sticking to his face.

Blasts thrummed in the air, coming toward him, but his magic was quicker. Circles of night and stars popped to life around Bast, swallowing the blue shots before they hit him—his own version of a shield.

Quickly finding the shooter, he lifted his arm. A whip of darkness appeared around his palm while the *akritana* kept pulling the trigger—pointless, considering Bast's shield.

His whip lashed at the attacker, wrapping around the *shig's* ankle and burning the flesh it touched. It quickly cut through the siren's calf, toppling him backward.

As the *akritana* went down, Bast snatched his gun, then aimed at his head. His patience was wearing thin, his nightblood getting the best of him.

"Where's Mera?" he barked.

Mad laughter escaped the bald siren. "You can't save the princess, landrider. She's ours!"

Bast saw red and fired. The weapon's kick pushed him back, but he held his ground.

Halle.

From one moment to the next the *suket's* head was gone. Nothing remained, except for a charred circle on the Marauder's deck.

"Danu in the fucking prairies..." Bast glared at the gun with the kill-power of a tiny sun.

"Night Prince!" Mr. Snipes shouted while grappling with a siren.

Aiming once more, Bast pressed the trigger. The blast sent the siren overboard, a look of shock in her eyes as she glared at the open hole in her stomach.

Bast fired at another enemy, but a hollow click told him the weapon had to be reloaded. Flinging it aside, he summoned his whip, tossing sirens up in the air before his storm of darkness swallowed them entirely.

An eager grin cut across his face, a thirst for blood he couldn't satiate as he went on and on, helping the crew clear the deck with his explosions of night. His sharp fangs poked at his lower lip.

"Who's next?" he thundered with a laugh, but there were no sirens left.

The motionless crew stared at him in either shock or horror. Maybe both.

Bast panted from the effort, trying to steady himself. His

darkness retreated into his core, his common sense returning to him.

Sarking nightblood...

Removing his hat, Flint pressed it against his chest. "I'd heard stories, but this? It's beyond anything I could have imagined. Remind me to never piss ye off, Night Prince."

Bast chuckled wearily. "Something tells me I'll never have to."

"Well, I'm glad at least *I* kept a cool head, lad." Flint winked at him, then stepped aside to reveal a wounded siren near his feet.

Thank Danu. If not for the captain, they wouldn't have a lead.

Bast's whip of night wrapped around the siren's ankle, lifting the *akritana* in the air. The bald female screamed when her skin burned, but Bast controlled his power enough to avoid cutting through the bone.

The madness from before returned with a vice. Stepping closer, he assessed the gray-skinned, lanky little thing. "Why do you all look like Azinor?"

Hanging upside down, she glared at him with pure fury, pain cutting deep wrinkles across her face. "Poseidon! He's Poseidon risen from the trenches!"

"Oh, you stupid minion..."

"To the trenches with you, landrider! I won't talk." The siren spat at him, but Bast leaned his head to the side, escaping her spittle.

"You will, *akritana*." Bast grinned wickedly. "You will sing like a little bird."

CHAPTER 15

"Mer?" Belinda's voice echoed through the dark. "Are you okay?"

Mera blinked, waking to find herself floating amidst town. She remembered everything, though. The chase, the explosion, and most of all, the fact that she'd killed a siren using a power she didn't quite understand.

Centering herself, she swam to a standing position. "I'm fine," she assured, the worry in Belinda's face not going amiss.

"We should take you to a hospital. That thing you did—"

"We can't waste time. Azinor is out there and we have to stop him." Her friend opened her mouth to speak, but Mera was faster. "Besides, I feel fine," she lied.

The truth was, being hit by a train had to feel better than this, but Mera would be damned if she would let that stop her.

"You've always been a stubborn sturgeon, haven't you?" Letting out a sigh through her gills, Belinda shook her head. "We should at least talk to the commissioner and the king about what you did. Maybe they can help."

"They have enough on their plates. Did you get the enhancer?"

Her friend nodded, opening her palm to show a metallic pendant with an emerald in its middle. Relief washed through Mera.

"I reported to the commissioner everything that happened, except the whole," Belinda waved her arms around, "lightning-underwater-that-kills-sirens thing."

"Good. Let's go, then. We need to find the asshole who escaped."

"Mer, I won't stop you, but I think you should at least go to a doctor."

Arching a challenging brow, Mera crossed her arms. Belinda should know she wasn't a delicate flower. "Noted. Now, let's dash."

They went on to interrogate Belinda's informant network, trying to figure out Azinor's angle—or where his lackey might be. They weren't alone, of course. By the end of the day, almost the entire police force patrolled the streets, hunting for leads, but so far, they'd gotten nothing on their radars.

Body scanners had always controlled the flux of sirens passing through the tunnels, especially after Azinor began attacking the city a few months back, which meant that the two sirens had fabricated the bomb inside Atlantea.

If they'd built one bomb, they could build more. Also, who could have tipped them off about the location of the magic enhancer, if not someone from the Atlantean police force? Belinda hadn't shared the location of the enhancer with any civilian, but an officer with clearance could've easily had access to it.

Suspicion festered in Mera's chest while she observed the officers rushing around the precinct. Those walls had eyes, just like in the first case she'd worked with Bast. They had to thread carefully.

After an entire day of searching, Belinda let out a frustrated sigh. She scrolled through a blue screen that popped out of thin water, coming from her silver bracelet.

"It's pointless," she grumbled as she tapped closed the holo-display. "All we've got is the dickweed's name: Victor Redtail, but he's vanished. Probably left through the tunnels during the chaos after the bomb."

Mera floated inches above the precinct's floor, facing a large, glass wall. "You mean after I killed his accomplice," she muttered, observing the rainbow city that glinted below the moon orb.

"You shouldn't feel bad. You did what you had to do."

"I don't regret it." She honestly didn't. That criminal wanted the world to burn, just like Azinor. Deep down, Mera wished she'd killed Victor Redtail too, and if that made her as cruel as the queen, so be it. "Have you tried tracking Azinor's lackeys before? Bring the fight to him?"

"Oh, we really did, but they always lost us one way or another. My guess is the greasy walrus set up a base in the trenches. All the drones we sent there came out empty handed."

"Could he be using a cloaking device?"

Belinda shook her head. "The drones would have caught it."

"How about cloaking magic?"

"They're not designed to find *that*." She raised her shoulders. "Doesn't matter. Waterbreakers can't do cloaking magic."

Azinor could. Mera had seen it firsthand.

"Let's bomb the trenches, then." She nodded to herself. "Blow him into oblivion."

Belinda's eyes widened, and she stared at Mera as if she'd gone mad. "If we do, we might hit the lava pockets, not to mention the chasms. One wrong hit, and we could cause random eruptions and earthquakes for miles. Look, I want to catch the bastard as much as anyone else, but vaporizing Atlantea isn't the way."

She was right, of course.

"Then there's one thing left to do."

Her friend rolled her eyes. "No way. Look, you can help me hide the enhancer again. It will be a better use of your time."

"She said she would tell me where he's hiding if I came back. She'll give me a location, Bel. She has to."

"The queen is leading you on. Ariella Wavestorm is a master manipulator, and you should know better."

She had a point. Deceit, hate, and violence were Mother's specialties, but Mera didn't have much of a choice. She was their only path to Azinor, and gods help her, Mera would make her talk.

Even if she had to kill the bitch for a third time.

THE QUEEN FLOATED in the middle of her cell, watching Mera with cunning green eyes. "Last time you looked at me that way, you jammed icicles through my body, then beheaded me."

"It must have hurt."

"Tremendously."

"Fantastic." Mera watched her own slender hand and the thin membranes between her fingers. "When did you know I had the same powers he does?"

"I didn't, not until I was reborn. But you don't have the same powers, child. You're a different beast altogether."

"Am I? I can shoot lightning like a warlock, only underwater. Does that mean I'm a siren-witch, like *him*?"

"In a way, and yet, not at all." The queen didn't break eye contact. "You're his blood. It's only natural that you inherited some of his abilities, as you did mine."

Mera narrowed her eyes at her. "Then why did one of his lackeys call me 'Soulbreaker'?"

The queen's nostrils flared, her eyes widening for a second, but she quickly masked her shock. "You can never access the world beyond; what Poseidon calls the great unending space. You cannot raise the dead, but you hear the whispers, yes?"

When Mera nodded, the queen began to swim in circles inside her cell.

"Waterbreakers manipulate water. Soulbreakers manipulate..." She made a flourish with her hand, not needing to complete the thought.

"I can't manipulate souls." Mera snorted. "That's ridiculo—"

"You can't. Not yet, but you should be able to give or take from them. I heard that's precisely what happened this morning."

"How do you know?"

"We are *everywhere*."

Mera swallowed dry, which said something since she was underwater. "How can I suddenly do things I've never done before?"

"I suppose that when you faced your father, whatever blocked that side of you cracked."

Becoming silent for a moment, she connected the dots, or at least tried. "Soulbreaker or not, the question remains. Why am I hearing these voices?"

"The voices are your soul. It's speaking to you, for you are one and the same." She waved a hand as if any of that made sense. "Listen to what it has to say, let it guide you. Let it unlock the doors that guard your potential."

"How can the voices be mine if I can barely understand them? They speak another language!"

"The language of souls, child." The queen leaned forward, grabbing the bars. "*Hart et maki na?*"

"*Hersh tu falut,*" Mera instinctively countered, and her eyes widened. She'd just told Mother to go fuck herself in a language she'd never learned.

"See?" Ariella smirked. "All the same in the end."

Clearing her throat, she held both hands behind her back.

She couldn't lose focus; couldn't forget why she was there. Her questions would have to wait. "I came back as you requested. You need to keep your end of the bargain. So, tell me where Azinor is hiding."

"No. If I told you, you would go after him."

Mera's mouth pressed into a line, heat shooting up her head. Belinda was right; the bitch had been leading her on. "You promised that if I came by, you would tell me where—"

"I did, but I'm not exactly reliable, am I?" The queen frowned. "Frankly, I'm surprised you believed me."

"You asshole!" She boosted toward her, shaking the bars.

Startled, the queen swam back while Mera kept flinging herself against the cold silver, taken by an urge to squeeze the life out of the monster's frail neck.

She clawed at the water pointlessly. "Tell me where he is!"

"If you face him, you'll lose."

A knot clogged Mera's throat. "Don't pretend you care!"

"You must fight him with this." The queen tapped her temple, then lowered her bony hand to her chest. "And this. Your father will descend upon this nation with fury, so you must hurry. He doesn't like losing things he considers his."

"You mean he's coming for you? We're counting on that, *Mother*. You do realize your relationship is sick, right?"

The queen lowered her head. "That's what *she* said in the world beyond."

Confusion scrunched Mera's nose. "Who are you talking about?"

"There's no escaping your father." Ariella turned to her, regaining her composure. "Perhaps, joining him would be for your own good."

"My own good?" She chortled, the sound bitter and sharp. "Stop the mind games, they won't be of any use to you here. Where. Is. He?"

Her keen gaze studied Mera for a moment. "If I tell you, how do you intend on killing him?"

"Chopping him to bits should do the trick just fine."

A certain pity flashed in those cold green eyes. "Weakling, I thought you were smarter than that. Your friend shot him in the face, and still, he prevailed. Chopping him to bits will neutralize him for a while, not forever. Deep down, you know that."

The bitch was right, and it left a sour taste in Mera's mouth. "How do I kill him, then?"

"He cannot die."

"Everything dies!" Mera bellowed, the memory of Ruth's smile jumping to mind.

Her mom had been larger than life; the one, steady pillar in Mera's existence, and the queen killed her. Tears pricked her eyes, but she wouldn't shed them; wouldn't let Mother taste them.

The water above Mera's hand cooled off, shaping a sharp icicle. "You *will* tell me what I need to know."

A shimmer of pride shone in Ariella's irises. Opening her arms, she grinned. "Do your best."

"Little fry!" the professor shouted, coming out from a tunnel next to the elevator on the far left—an emergency exit, or entrance, in this case. He panted through his gills.

The icicle atop her hand dissipated before he could notice it. "What happened?"

"A frigate was attacked by a group of Poseidon's men. A ship with black sails, and a silver crest of a half-moon crossed with a curved dagger."

The Night Court's crest. Mera's heart dropped.

Bast!

"Are they all right?"

"We can't be certain. It seems the landriders defeated them, and according to our scouts, the frigate is heading to the Isles of Fog. We haven't made contact, since the lines between us and land can be tricky to cross. I figured you could rendezvous with your friends to start a conversation."

Knowing Bast would be there, she nodded. Mera turned to leave, but a shriek boomed from behind, sending her toppling forward. Bringing herself to a halt, she turned around and released her siren's shriek, fighting Mother's own.

Water rushed into the professor's gills instantly, and he puffed up his chest. When he opened his mouth, his scream broke both of theirs, making pebbles fall from the walls and ceiling.

"Enough!" He pulled out a phaser from his holster and aimed at the queen. "Go, Mera!"

Ariella stretched her arms between the bars, trying to reach out for her. "It's not safe!"

The sound of a mighty blast roared from outside, and the dungeons' rocky walls suddenly shook. Loud explosions rumbled in the far distance, one after the other, almost as if in synchrony. They went on like dominos, circling Atlantea.

Professor Currenter glared at Mera as the same realization dawned on him.

The dome!

"Stay here!" He zinged up the tunnel, rushing out of the dungeons.

"The hell I will!"

Just as Mera was about to follow, another boom roared outside, this time all too close. The place shook violently, and she watched in horror as the exit's walls groaned then collapsed, blocking the path with stony rubble.

The blast must have hit the palace, probably the courtyard.

"Professor!" Mera bellowed, but he wouldn't be able to listen. She could only hope he'd left before the tunnel collapsed.

"He's early," the queen muttered. "He wasn't supposed to..." Ariella's grin resembled a broken twig, a fake, nervous smile that oozed with madness and fear. "Regneerik is coming."

CHAPTER 16

MUFFLED BLASTS THUNDERED OUTSIDE. *Boom, boom, boom* everywhere, sprouting across Atlantea.

The floating orbs that illuminated the dark dungeons flickered when some of the attacks hit the palace, until suddenly, the rumbling stopped. Dim explosions still rang from a distance, but they sounded smaller, more scattered.

Mera pulled out her phaser. The whirring sound of her weapon loading echoed across the space.

The queen stared at her with a gut-wrenching sadness. It looked foreign in her bitter face, a face where hate and malice fit like a glove. "Run, Daughter." She pointed to the glass elevator shaft, which was somehow still standing. The only way in and out of the dungeons. "He might be weakened, but you will lose if you face him."

Mera wanted to go. She really did, but she'd never run from a fight before, and she wouldn't start now.

"We'll see about that," she countered, hating that she couldn't check on Belinda, Uncle Barrimond, and Professor Currenter.

She could only hope they were okay.

As if on cue, Belinda's voice came through the comm in her ear, her words broken by interference. "Mer... you copy?"

"Yes!" A relieved sigh escaped her gills. "I'm in the dungeons. Are you all right?"

Static came from the other side, stretching time itself as she waited.

"Fine. Intercepted... lackeys." A long pause followed, one in which Mera could only hear the sounds of blasts, waterbreaking, and orders to advance.

"Bel?"

"I'm here," she panted. "Lost... enhancer... somewhere."

Belinda had been heading to a secret location in Atlantea to hide the device. Losing it wasn't bad news, though. If they struggled to find it, so would Azinor.

Static sparkled once more. "Get out. He'll be coming for..."

Silence.

He'll be coming for the queen.

"I'll be fine." Mera swallowed, centering herself. "Did you hear from the professor or my uncle? The palace was under attack."

Belinda shouted orders to someone next to her, her voice cracked by interference. "Cursed the... Sending reinforcements."

Mera's attention shifted to the elevator shaft, the only way in or out of there. "All right. Stay safe."

With that, she ended the connection.

Leaning against the rocky walls, she tried to make sense of it all. Azinor's lackeys must be spreading hell throughout Atlantea. Their bombs had gone off everywhere around town, and if they'd disabled the dome, then the prick could waltz in anytime he wanted.

A deep, cold silence hung heavy across the space, making the water flowing through it thicker. Mera's grasp on her phaser tightened.

"You always expected me to love you," the queen blurted out of nowhere. "But love isn't something to be owed. It has to be earned."

"You love Azinor. After everything he did to you, you still..." Mera shook her head, a bitter laugh escaping her lips. "No, I won't start this again."

"I thought I loved him. I was wrong." She pointed to the back wall of her cell, toward the city they couldn't quite see from there. "I might have been hard on you, but I was preparing you to lead, child. To survive."

"Bullshit. You enjoyed making me suffer."

"I did. Still, you can't deny I succeeded in my task. After all, you killed me twice." She turned away as if in deep thought. "And yet, back at the beach, I had a glimpse of what might have been between you and me, had I not..."

Rage burned in Mera's veins, and she pointed at the bitch, holding down the urge to blow off her head with the phaser. "You're a bug. A vermin, *Mother*. Ruth was the fucking stars, and you took her from me." Anger coursed through her, making her body shake. "Bold of you to grow a consciousness now."

"Ruth—"

"Don't say her name!" Mera barked, fully aware of how badly she was losing it.

A loud rumble came from outside, followed by another. Mera raised her weapon and turned to the elevator shaft, waiting, since it was the only access point to the queen.

Everything went quiet. The next moment, a deafening boom filled her ears, and the back of Mother's cell crumbled. The force of the explosion sent the queen hurling against the bars, and Mera crashed against the hallway wall.

The large hole on the cell showed the city in the distance.

The queen shot Mera a panicked glare, right before Azinor rose from beyond the gap. Half of his gray-skinned face was missing, the other half under construction. His left eye dangled from its socket, and a big gap on his left cheek showed Mera the bones in his jaw, the red tendons fresh and new.

Crap! She'd expected the asshole to use the elevator shaft, not blow a hole in the dungeons' façade.

Grinning, or at least trying to, the monster raised his fist to show her a necklace with a dark-silver pendant shaped like a hexagon. It had an emerald encrusted in its middle.

Fuck! He'd found the enhancer.

Mera raised her gun, aiming through the cell's bars. "Drop it."

"Your friend vaporized my head, yet here I stand." His voice didn't come from his mouth—or whatever remained of it—but from the water around him. Like Azinor was and wasn't there; his presence a part of two different realms, if that made any sense. He nudged his halved chin toward her hands. "You cannot stop me with that pitiful weapon."

Mera pressed the trigger, hoping to prove him wrong. Scorching blue comets zinged at him, but they burst into nothing when they hit the magic shield around the prick.

Azinor merely stared at her through his drooping green eye, clearly unfazed. "Your friend lost the enhancer to help her fellows." He chuckled to himself. "She never noticed my presence. Oh, how easily I could have twisted her frail little neck... Rest assured, I'll savor her death when I'm fully formed."

"You won't touch a hair on Belinda's head!"

"Always making promises you can't keep." Giving Ariella his hand, he motioned for her to come closer. "I'd hoped our offspring would be smarter."

The queen stared at Mera, and maybe she was losing her mind, but she saw doubt in her bitter face.

It only lasted a second, though. A sneer filled with all the malice in the world swiftly captured Ariella's face, ever the hateful bitch that birthed her. "I've stopped expecting greatness from our child, my lord."

Her words stung. Mera hated admitting it, but they did.

Whispers suddenly washed over her ears, and though she couldn't understand what they said, she somehow knew what to do. The tingling of inky inscriptions bloomed on her skin, dancing under her bodysuit.

An invisible surge suddenly lunged from her core, piercing through Azinor's shield and slamming into him. The power trapped the dickwart where he was, and although he fought against her magic, he couldn't move.

Ariella stared in awe, a small grin hooking up her left cheek. She tapped her temple, then her heart.

Azinor's horrid, barely-there face twisted in anger, his focus on Mera. "The sheer audacity!"

The enhancer he held shone bright green. With a violent pulse, he broke free of her magic, sending her slamming against the stone wall near the elevator.

Mera's mind spun, her ears ringing. Blinking, she tried to center herself.

The asshole pointed a finger at her from inside the cell, his other hand wrapped around the queen's wrist. "You will suffer for this." His gaze lifted toward the surface. "I'll kill what empowers you."

With that, he dashed into the deep blue, taking Ariella with him. Mera boosted toward them, bellowing an angry cry, but she couldn't break through the cell's silver bars. So she zinged back, building a whirlpool of rushing water that rammed into the elevator's shaft.

Boosting up, she followed the elevator's stem, racing past halls and corridors. Rubble peppered the palace's rooms, but the damage wasn't as extensive as she'd imagined. She didn't take time to assess it, though—she was already breaking through the glass ceiling.

Hovering above the silver castle, she watched the city below her. To the left, she spotted the professor and the king giving out orders to officers. Mera let out a relieved breath through her gills.

Concentrating, she listened to the ocean, trying to track Azinor's presence. Alarms wailed everywhere while water-breakers and vehicles rushed around town. Giant buildings stood with missing chunks, as if a leviathan had gnawed at them. The shining orb above the city flickered, but it kept burning at a steady pace, even though cracks spread along its surface. In the distance, the dome flashed with blue light, blinking in and out of existence.

She would never find the prick amid the madness.

"Mera!" Belinda rushed closer, her gun in hand.

A group of officers followed after her, all in rough shape. A deep cut slashed the upper side of her friend's forehead, and a purpling bruise decorated her left cheek, but other than that, Belinda seemed fine.

"He has the queen," Mera grumbled. "And the enhancer."

Her friend paled. "I never saw him!"

"Well, he saw you." *And she was lucky to be alive.* "It was a rescue mission disguised as an attack."

Belinda gulped, turning to the damage throughout Atlantea. "If this wasn't a proper attack... we better be ready next time. We have to reconvene with the commissioner."

Mera nodded, trying to ignore the bitter taste of defeat. The image of Azinor, looking up to the surface suddenly flashed in her memory.

"I'll kill what empowers you."

A gasp escaped her, her heart beating loudly in her ears. Surely the bastard couldn't mean...

"Mer?"

"Bast," she croaked, panic rising inside her. "He's going after Bast."

CHAPTER 17

BAST'S GAZE didn't leave the siren. She sat with her wrists and ankles tied together, glaring at him with pure, undiluted hatred. Her beady yellow eyes had long since turned hazel, her fins and gills receded, and her dark-gray skin acquired a healthy rosy shade.

"You must despise looking human," he remarked with a grin. "Why do you resemble him in your original form? Is it magic?"

"Magic and technology, landrider." Her lips formed a bitter line. "Atlantea will soon be ours, and Tagrad will follow. Resistance is futile."

He didn't feel threatened, not one bit. Considering Azinor's strength, perhaps he should have. "We'll see about that."

"Prepare to land, lads!" Captain Flint called out from the bridge, and the crew began preparations.

Bast crouched, staring directly at the siren. "You're a resilient one, I'll give you that. But you see, I've lost my patience."

She raised her chin in contempt. "I'll die before telling you anything."

"No, you won't." Pushing his fingers against her temple, he closed his eyes.

It would have been better if she'd talked, since he couldn't see clearly into someone's mind, but this would have to do. Sure, he could blur her thoughts to make the *akritana* forget certain memories, maybe even input new ones if he was lucky, but getting a front row seat to what went on in her head would be difficult, if not impossible.

He soon caught glimpses of Azinor with half his face missing. The *shig* looked like a walking nightmare. Flashes of *akritanas* wearing moss-green suits came up, hundreds and hundreds of them. They gathered in caves, hiding, waiting in the dark with bright, feral eyes.

A force pushed him out of her head, and Bast nearly stumbled back. She was fighting him. The siren was the ruler of her own mind, which meant no matter how hard he fought her, she would win.

Tapping his knees, he stood. "I didn't want to do this, but you leave me no choice."

A string of darkness bloomed from his palm, wrapping around the woman's left ankle. Smoke billowed from the wound as the whip tightened, nearly reaching the bone. The siren's screams split the air, but the crew kept on with their duties, ignoring her.

"Speak," Bast ordered, his voice drowned by her loud wails.

"Stop!" she cried, tears drenching her cheeks.

He eased his darkness just a little. "Yes?"

With a gulp, she tried to steady her breaths. "He wants to take it all. Land and sea, they will be ours soon."

"And how does he intend to do that?"

"With blood and fury, landrider."

His whip tightened around her ankle, burning through the bone.

"Stop!" she bellowed again.

"Last chance."

"He will conquer Atlantea when he's stronger. He wants the princess' power. She's the only one who—" The siren gasped, eyes widening. She clawed at her throat while black veins spread under her skin.

"*Halle!*" Bast shot his magic against the spell taking over her —a fail-safe Azinor must have enchanted her with in case she was caught. "I need a healer!"

"We lost him in the attack, lad!" Flint rushed closer, assessing the woman. His eyes glowed a bright gold, so did the tattoos around his body. He pushed his power into her, but his shoulders soon dropped. "There's nothing we can do."

"*Fuchst ach!*" Bast grasped the siren by the lapel of her bodysuit. "Speak! Make him pay for what he did to you!"

Her skin turned purple, her eyes nearly bugging out of their sockets as she tried to breathe. "It ends," she wheezed, "in fire and lightning."

With one last exhale, the siren's form went limp. Her eyes rolled back in her skull, and her mouth gaped open, forever reaching for air.

"Fucking *shig!*" Bast let her go just as the ship anchored near a beach.

Rage took over him, and his wings flashed to life. Against Flint's protests, he flew up, drawing an arch in the air.

"We have to stay together!" the captain yelled. "Come back here!"

Bast landed on the beach with a loud thump, stirring the sand. Narrowing his eyes, he noticed a forest ahead, where humans dressed in rags that barely covered their privates watched him from behind the trees.

The natives of the isles. Humans who worshipped sirens as gods, or any supernatural creature for that matter.

They held wooden bows and arrows, but their arms shook in fear, stopping them from taking proper aim.

"Sebastian!" Flint yelled from above as a nightling carried him. "This is *my* mission and *my* territory!"

The captain nearly toppled forward when his nightling hit the sand. The rest of the crew dropped behind Bast like ripe fruit.

The fae's wings quickly disappeared, and they clutched their hands behind their backs, waiting for Flint's orders. Mr. Snipes patted his coat, and thanked the nightling who'd carried him with a kind smile.

Flint fixed his hat stubbornly, then stomped toward Bast. "I don't care that yer royalty. I don't care ye desperate for yer lass. You will do as you're told, aye?"

"I'm sorry," Bast admitted quietly, knowing his temper had taken the best of him. "I just... I need to contact her. I'm tired of running around in circles."

He lifted one finger too close to Bast's nose. "Next time, do as I say." With a grumble, the captain pulled down the hem of his shirt, then nodded. "Go on. I'll start the usual proceedings."

He turned around and waved at the natives with a grin.

"*Habakima!*" the humans called out, bright smiles taking over their faces.

Flint opened his arms, and the natives dropped their makeshift weapons, coming out of the forest to greet him.

Ignoring the crew, the natives, and the two warlocks behind him, Bast looked up to the bright summer sky.

The deep blue was devoid of any clouds, which must be a rarity in isles that were covered in fog during most of the year. He then turned to the vast ocean and closed his eyes, feeling the warmth of the sun on his skin.

It took him a while to catch Mera's presence. It pulsed on the other side of their bond, but he couldn't reach her. She was still too far away.

Halle.

He would have to go for a swim, wouldn't he?

"Lad, open yer eyes," Flint's voice called out from behind him.

Bast followed his command, and immediately stepped back. Bald, grey heads peeked out of the water, popping out of the surface like pixie blooms.

The sirens stomped toward the beach with bloodthirsty grins. There were too many of them—forty at least—against the remaining crew of the Marauder, not more than fifteen souls.

They wore the usual moss-green bodysuits, most of them carrying rusty swords. Yet, a few of them held bulky weapons similar to the guns used during the first attack, only these bigger beasts clearly packed more power.

Rushing back, Bast acquired a battle stance alongside Flint and the crew.

The island natives yelled in the background, standing back with their feeble makeshift weapons, lost on what to do. All too quickly, however, they decided to flee toward the forest.

A wise choice, really.

Without hesitation, the sirens took aim and fired, but Bast raised a magic shield around the crew just in time. His darkness popped up in small portals that swallowed the thick, blue blasts before vanishing.

"I won't be able to hold them off for long," he grumbled.

Flint cracked his neck left to right, his eyes shining a bright yellow, the same color of the tattoos across his body. "Then we better charge."

He ran forward, letting out a battle cry. The nightlings and Mr. Snipes followed, while Bast pulled two whips of darkness that bloomed around his wrists, charging after them.

The sirens rushed forward and shot frantically, but most of the crew's magic shields were enough to protect them. Just as they clashed against the *shigs*, Bast winnowed, appearing next to the woman who led the front.

It took him a second to snap her neck. He then winnowed

away just as a male close by pulled his gun's trigger. A blue sphere shot from the muzzle, hitting another *akritana* in the head. Bast reappeared behind the shooter in an eye-blink. The *baku* turned to him in horror, gawking as a whip of darkness wrapped around his neck and squeezed, chopping off his head.

A heavy exhaustion weighed on Bast, and he drew a sharp breath while tiny blue comets slammed against his magic shield. He shouldn't winnow so much, since using that sort of magic depleted his energies. Also, he hadn't fully recovered from the previous battle.

Not far from him, Flint's golden lightning shot forward, hitting three sirens at once. Mr. Snipes dodged an attack from the left, only to slam his sword through an *akritana*'s torso.

One blue blast hit a nightling near Bast in the stomach, and she fell limp on the sand. Another nightling shoved his sword into an *akritana*'s chest, but forgot to keep up his magic shield. His body swelled and blew into a thousand pieces, as did the nightling next to him.

"Shields up!" Bast bellowed, even though his brothers of night might not be strong enough to fight and keep their shields at the same time.

A blue sphere zinged far too close to his head, and his nostrils flared. Bast's whip yanked the gun from the siren's grip with ease, delivering it to himself.

"Night Prince!" Mr. Snipes called out, and Bast turned left to see he also carried one of the siren's strange guns.

The warlock fired at Bast's enemy, and Bast covered his flank in return, neutralizing two *akritanas* with one blast.

He stared at the weapon. He didn't usually approve of guns, but *halle*, he approved that one.

On they went, shooting non-stop, but there were too many sirens. More rose from the water, accompanied by something... Blinking, he wondered if he'd lost his *sarking* mind.

Shaped like a siren, the *thing* was made of cogs and wheels that whirred madly underneath silver plates; panels that formed its skin. Its round, neon-red eyes shone without any sign of a soul within it. The machine walked in an unnatural manner, its movements jerky and heavy.

Mr. Snipes frowned, nearly dropping his gun. "What's *that?*"

When the thing stepped on dry sand, it turned toward them with a metallic, shrill sound. Its jaw snapped open, and its chest shone a bright, ruby-red that beamed from the back of its throat.

"Take cover!" Bast bellowed, just as the thing vomited red light.

He jumped in front of the blast and raised a large shield. The impact slammed against his power; against Bast himself, pushing him back. Every bone in his body thrummed, a merciless pain squeezing him from the inside out. He fell to his knees in the sand, panting. Sweat beaded on his forehead as the remaining nightlings, Flint, and Mr. Snipes gathered behind his shield.

The thing didn't stop spewing scorching light at them.

"Hecate's hells," Flint grumbled under his breath. "We can't beat them."

When the machine snapped its mouth shut, it emitted a sound similar to when the guns reloaded. However, the remaining sirens didn't give them any time to recover. They shot at Bast's shield while marching closer.

Clenching his teeth, he forced himself to hold the shield, but if that thing fired again, specially from up close…

"*Bast!*"

He lost a breath as Mera's voice flowed through their bond.

Within seconds, Blue blasts came from behind their assailants, shooting them down one by one. Their enemies turned around, firing back at the group that attacked them.

The newcomers were also sirens, but they wore black body-suits with silver details similar to Flint's coat.

Leading them was none other than Mera, wearing an onyx bodysuit that fit her curves perfectly. She had a silver belt wrapped around her waist, and a weapon in her hand. Her russet hair fluttered like a flag as she rushed out of the water.

His *hart* fired at their enemies, and when they fired back, patches of ice bloomed out of thin air, shielding her from the attacks just like his darkness did.

A blonde siren with hair trapped in a low ponytail covered her flank, shooting at Azinor's soldiers without mercy. She never missed her targets.

"Attack!" Flint shouted, dashing forward. The remaining nightlings and Mr. Snipes followed him.

"Mera!" Bast wanted to run to her, but he was so spent that all he managed was to crouch on the sand. Taking deep breaths, he focused, pulling from the little magic left in his body.

How could he be so weakened?

Bast had gone through harder fights in his life. He should have recovered by now... or perhaps, he was being too hard on himself.

The machine standing ahead glanced at him without any emotion. It stepped closer, its metallic jaw opening. A red glow beamed from the back of its throat, drenching Bast in blazing light.

This was it. This was how he met his end.

At least he'd seen Mera one last time.

"No!" she bellowed.

An ice spear pierced into the gaps between the thing's metallic plates, jamming the whirs and cogs inside it. Soon after, a blue blast hit its head, burning a hole through its skull. The machine's remaining red eye flickered, but the engines in its head still whirred. It bent over, ready to spew a red beam on Bast, when another spear broke through its torso.

Eyes blinking out, the machine fell limp on the spears.

Bast wiped sweat off his forehead, a smile blooming on his

lips when he spotted Mera. His *hart* watched him with relief, love, and then panic as two strong arms caught him in a chokehold.

His whips of darkness lashed at his assailant, but the siren was powerful. He blocked his attacks with icy water similar to Mera's.

Kura!

Bast tried winnowing, but he was too weak, and then a cold blade pressed against his neck. "Poseidon sends his regards," the *akritana* trapping him whispered in his ear.

Deafening claps took over the air, as if a thousand thunders were cracking at once. Blue lightning rose around the beach, splitting the sky in a wide, neon-blue web that buzzed loudly. And the source was...

Mera.

His *hart* stared at Bast's attacker with a world of fury, her lips a line and her nostrils flared. Her hair waved wildly around her. She'd never looked more like Ariella Wavestorm than she did in that moment, but Bast could never tell her that, not without breaking her heart.

Her lightning plunged into their enemies' bodies, making them thrash violently. When it crashed against his assailant's forehead, Bast managed to elbow the *suket* and pull himself away, falling with his back on the sand.

"*Fuchst ach,*" he mumbled as the lightning lifted the siren in the air, along with every single one of Azinor's lackeys.

Their bodies convulsed so harshly that foam formed at the edges of their mouths, their skin began turning purple, and their faces puffed.

"Kitten, don't!" Bast shouted, stretching his arm toward her. "We have to interrogate them!"

But she didn't listen. Right then, Mera was wrath and pain, and he couldn't get to her, not even through their bond.

His *hart's* power beamed like a small sun. Wincing, Bast

closed his eyes, and when the bright burst dimmed along with the rumbling thunder, he surveyed the beach.

"*Sakala mi...*"

The charred remains of Azinor's lackeys dropped onto the sand with hollow thuds, falling everywhere like broken marionettes.

Dead. Every single one of them.

Mera wobbled on her feet, the effort clearly taking its toll. She was losing consciousness, Bast felt it through their link.

Ignoring the bodies strewn between them, he rushed toward her, his muscles and bones heavy and aching. He caught her in his arms right before she collapsed.

He always would.

"*Min hart!*" He held her close, relief and fear making for a strange mix inside him. He tried to shake her awake, but Mera was too weak to remain conscious. Cupping her left cheek, he stamped a kiss on her forehead. "Wake up."

She didn't.

The blonde *akritana* stepped closer, panic clear in her wide, hazel eyes as she stared at Mera.

"Whatever is inside her, it's getting stronger."

CHAPTER 18

MERA'S back gently thudded against a straight surface as soft currents coursed around her. Even drenched in darkness, she could feel the water rushing into her gills, her bones heavy as iron. She was definitely underwater, but she recalled being at a beach not a moment ago.

Prying her eyes open, she stared at Bast. He watched her with a roguish grin, the same one that always made her heart skip a beat.

He couldn't be real, of course. She must have been hallucinating.

Mera studied him while her brain tried to punch out of her skull. For a figment of her imagination, he looked so real...

"I'm dead, aren't I?" she groaned.

"You're fine." His voice came out slightly mechanical, as if he were speaking through an intercom.

Only then did Mera realize that his hair didn't float around him, neither did his clothes. In fact, for someone underwater, Bast seemed perfectly dry.

He pulled her up so that she floated straight. A thin membrane buzzed between his palm and hers, a layer that coursed atop his entire body like a bubble, or perhaps, a magic shield. It followed his movements perfectly.

They floated in the middle of her room in the palace, and Mera stamped a hand on her forehead, still unsure whether she was dreaming.

Giving her an excited grin, Bast pointed to his own face. "It's incredible, isn't it? This 'bubble' protects my entire body. Atlantean devices, kitten!" He waved to the space around them as if it were the entire city. "I hate technology, but even I have to admit this is spectacular."

"You're really here?" she stated the obvious before wrapping her arms around him, hugging Bast with the feeble remainder of strength she had left.

It wasn't enough. She wasn't touching him, only the bubble around him. She couldn't kiss her *hart* senseless; not there.

Not yet.

He hugged her back, burrowing his face in the curve of her neck. The bubble felt cold against her skin. "I'm here, Princess."

"Don't call me that." Mera swam back, an invisible iron poker sticking through her chest.

Bast waded closer. "Your uncle and his mate have kept me in the loop. They asked me to convince you to take the throne." Cupping her cheek, he watched her with soothing, blue eyes. "Clearly, they've forgotten how stubborn you are."

Mera leaned against his palm, hating that she couldn't feel the warmth of his touch. "I don't want the throne."

"Corvus didn't either, but he's turned out to be a good king." A certain sadness fell upon his face. "Also, King Wavestorm has no heirs. You're bound to take the throne eventually."

"My uncle still has many years ahead of him, okay?" She pointed at the bubble surrounding him, eager to change the subject. "How does this work?"

Her *hart* saw right through her gimmicks—his certainty flowed through their bond—but he played along. "It's a malleable suit that filters the oxygen in the water and feeds it to me. According to Harold, it controls the pressure around my body as well, since we're quite deep underwater."

Harold.

So he'd met the professor already.

Mera could practically see Bast refusing to leave her side, his canines sharp and his eyes beady black, which must have forced her friends to find a way to bring him with them.

"Your people's technology defies imagination." He scratched the back of his neck, even if he couldn't complete the motion. "I haven't seen much of Atlantea, but I already know it puts Clifftown to shame."

Catching the worry in his tone, she turned around, facing the rainbow city and the blinking dome in the distance. "If Azinor ever conquers Atlantea, we'll be in serious trouble."

Bast swam closer, soon halting next to her. "From what your friend Belinda told me, he nearly did. And now, he has everything he needs to finish the job."

She watched her own hands, not knowing what to think as flashes of lightning blinked in her memory. Closing her eyes, she ignored them, trying to burrow what she'd done at the beach in a place deep within herself.

It didn't work.

"It was self-defense," Mera muttered, even if she didn't believe her own words. "They were going to kill you."

Bast wrapped his arms around her waist, resting his chin on her shoulder. "I know."

"The queen told me she fuels Azinor's power because she's his soulmate." A pit settled in her stomach. "Do you think something like that happened at the beach? With us?"

He seemed to consider it. "I did feel awfully weak. But if that is true, why has it never happened before?"

"I don't know." She turned around, facing him as she wrapped both arms over his shoulders. "Whatever it was, it won't happen again. If boosting my magic means siphoning yours, I—"

"It's fine, kitten. You didn't know." His lips placed a kiss on her forehead, but she only felt the bubble's cold membrane. "You saved us. It's all that matters."

"*Soulbreaker*," the queen's voice echoed in her memory, and a shiver ran down her spine.

Mera would never, ever, use Bast to propel her powers again, no matter the cost. Her *hart* wasn't a thing to be used, he was her equal. Her partner. Her everything.

They stayed there, in silence, until she inhaled a batch of water through her gills. "So, what's the plan?"

"Your uncle wants to speak to us. He's waiting in the gardens."

She frowned. "You know the gardens?"

"You were out for a while." Bast floated out of the way, showing her the room's arched exit. "Shall we?"

Mera boosted forward, but before she could bring him along, he quickly caught up, breaking water right next to her.

"How are you doing this?"

Bast raised his hand to show her a swirling cloud of darkness floating inches from his palm. It shaped a whirlpool. "The magic works like a propeller. It's my own way to waterbreak, I suppose." He nodded downwards, and the same clouds swirled from the pads of his feet.

"Full of surprises, aren't you?"

He winked at her. "Always."

A warm sensation swelled Mera's chest. She was so happy to see him, so happy he was there. She never imagined she could burst from joy within the corridors and halls that housed her misery for so many years, and yet, there she was.

Uncle Barrimond waited for them in one of the palace's outer coral gardens. Stone boulders littered the space, crushing the colorful display. During the attack, big, silver shards had detached from the castle's front and pierced through the ground like arrows, revealing patches of dark stone on the façade.

Her uncle waved at them just as an automaton walked into view, heading toward a big stone on the right.

"Take cover!" Bast shouted, yanking Mera back so that he stood between her and the machine. Clouds of night and stars bloomed from his fisted hands, making the water around his magic boil.

"No, Detective Dhay!" the king cried out, putting himself in the way. "Don't shoot. He's one of ours."

Bast growled deep in his chest, refusing to move an inch.

Settling a hand on his shoulder, Mera pulled him back to face her. "It's just a machine. It does what it's programmed to do."

"Indeed." The king motioned for the automaton to approach. "The one who faced you at the beach has already been dismantled. This one is named Beta Three."

The automaton's steps were heavy against the stony ground as he faced Mera, his round, neon-blue eyes blinking. "It's a pleasure to meet you, Princess."

Beta Three moved more fluidly than other automatons, which didn't mean much given the machines walked slowly and kind of funny. Unlike his peers, his jaw opened and closed in synchrony with the words when he spoke. The silver plates on his body looked sleek, tighter around his form, leaving only small gaps that revealed the cogs and wheels that made him function.

"Don't call me Princess, please," she begged. "I'm a detective, just like Bast."

The automaton turned to the king, as if waiting for an explanation or further instructions. Maybe both.

"She'll come around, Beta Three. Give her time." Swimming closer, her uncle trapped Mera in a hug so tight that her gills barely had any room to filter the water. "I'm glad you're feeling better, dear."

She returned the hug, her fingers digging on his back. "And I'm glad you're safe."

After a long moment, he let her go and faced Bast. "Tell me, Detective Dhay. How does it feel to be the first of your kind to enter Atlantea in the last two thousand years?"

Still eyeing Beta Three with suspicion, Bast crossed his arms. "It's an honor, King Wavestorm."

"Good." He tapped Bast's back with a hollow sound, and the membrane around her *hart* wavered slightly. "Let it be the beginning of a great change."

As if on cue, the domed shield that protected Atlantea stopped flickering in the distance. Little dots flashed randomly, a sign that bigger fish were slamming against the surface.

"Ah! I see Harold and Belinda's mission was a success." Her uncle smiled, but noticing Mera's confusion, he elaborated. "They restored the shield by using the secondary beacons, and placed them in secret locations. They're also planting decoys."

She nodded. "So Azinor won't break through so easily next time."

"Which doesn't mean he won't. With his lackeys still around town, it's only a matter of time." He turned to the automaton. "And that is why we're here. Beta Three is a prototype we're testing to aid law enforcement. He's the first of his kind, and his existence is a secret few are aware of. He's better than his peers. Faster, too. Not to mention, his matrix is incredibly more complex, which means he can form his own thoughts based on the experiences he faces."

Mera frowned. "Meaning, he can think on his own?"

"Yes, he can," Beta Three answered for the king, his voice a steady, mechanical monotone that rung rather soothingly.

"I don't like this." Bast let out a displeased gruff. "Machines shouldn't behave like living beings, and they shouldn't make decisions of their own. They shouldn't... feel."

"I cannot feel, Detective, only rationalize." Beta Three cocked his head at him, staring at Bast through soulless blue eyes. "That means my decisions are more efficient than those of a carbon-based creature, such as yourself."

Mera laughed, but when Bast sent her an annoyed glance, she cleared her throat. "Beta Three, that was uncalled for."

"My apologies. I did not mean to offend. I shall add the occurrence to my log to prevent it from happening." He cocked his head to the side again. "According to my records, faeries do not approve of technology. Is that why you do not approve of me, Detective Dhay?"

Bast never broke eye contact with him. "Among other reasons."

"Well, I can assure you I—"

Uncle Barrimond raised his hand, and Beta Three immediately became silent. "Poseidon will come for sea *and* land sooner than we expected. As we've seen, there's little we can do to stop him on our own. We must unite if we're to defeat him, which means extreme measures. This is why our prime automaton is here."

His intentions suddenly dawned on her. "You want us to take Beta Three to Tagrad."

"The pinnacle of our technology in exchange for help. Besides, Poseidon shouldn't get his hands on Beta Three. If you broker a deal with Tagrad—"

"Me?"

He gave her a knowing grin. "You're our best hope. An Atlantean princess who experienced life on both worlds."

"We did *not* agree to this," Bast grumbled. "I'll take Mera back, but let's keep her out of anything related to the council. Making those thick-minded *shigs* agree to an alliance will be nearly impossible." Sighing wearily, he eyed the automaton. "I suppose this *thing* might do the trick, if it keeps its mouth shut."

"I have been trained extensively in the art of diplomacy," Beta Three countered. "I can assure you that I'm prepared for the task."

"Yeah, we've seen your diplomatic skills," Mera chuckled. "Sometimes less is better, Beta Three."

Maybe Mera's mind was playing tricks on her, but she could swear the automaton seemed a little disappointed.

"I'll tell Flint to prepare the ship." Bast kissed her forehead, even if his lips couldn't touch her. "I'll meet you in the isles."

"You forget that I'll be shot to death if I return to Tagrad. The council, and everyone else, knows I'm a siren now." Mera crossed her arms. "Or did they miss the fact that I held down a tidal wave all on my own?"

He watched her for a moment, as if debating whether to tell her the truth. "They do know, but you won't be shot. They want you to stand trial. Rest assured that I won't let it happen."

"I should stay here with my family," she countered. "Especially since Azinor is coming back."

Bast exchanged one weary glance with the king. "If the *suket* conquers Atlantea, he *will* capture you. That's a risk we're not willing to take. Besides, you must come along, especially if we're to bring that thing to land." Nodding to Beta Three, he curled his own lips. "I already want to dismantle it to pieces, and we haven't even started the journey."

Before she could argue, he blinked out of existence. One moment he was there, the next he was gone.

"Bast! Gods damn it!"

"Is that what they call winnowing?" her uncle muttered. "Remarkable! You have a dashing soulmate, my dear. Stubborn, surely, but dashing nonetheless."

"Speaking of soulmates," Mera raised one eyebrow at him, "you and the professor are an item."

The king stared at her in shock, then fidgeted with his long fingers. "We weren't sure how to tell you. Finding happiness after we lost you felt wrong."

"I'm glad you have each other." Taking his hands, she smiled. "You have nothing to feel sorry about."

Gratitude and worry warred in his eyes. "Can you promise me you'll be safe? The council will listen, won't they?"

"With Bast in the room?" She chortled. "Even Azinor should be afraid."

"The shield is up!" Belinda's voice came from behind them as she and the professor arrived at the garden, but when she spotted the automaton, her eyes narrowed and her smile vanished. "Beta Three."

Bowing his head in a greeting, he placed a metallic hand over his chest. "Officer Tiderider. Commissioner."

Mera frowned. "You know each other?"

"Sort of." Breaking water, Belinda halted next to her. "I've been helping to test Beta Three's protocols. He's not exactly smooth."

"Yeah, I've noticed."

"Trust me, you haven't." She crossed her arms, sending the automaton a hateful glare. "He can be such a blobfish's ass."

"I see you resent me for pointing out your unhealthy habit of drinking fermented seaweed." Blinking innocently, he turned to Mera. "I must clarify that this is akin to what landriders call 'drinking alcohol.'"

As if she needed a translation.

"It was after work!" Belinda cried out, raising her arms. "Everyone goes to a bar after work, you dumb pile of rust! You're so annoying, Beta Three."

Mera couldn't hold back her laughter as her friend swam forward and began arguing with the automaton.

The professor approached her, watching the two of them

with mirth. "We still have to work on some of his configurations, but Beta Three should do well. Hopefully."

Mera laughed when Belinda nearly slapped the automaton's metallic face—a bad idea for her hand. "You're sending Beta Three with us so you can get rid of him, aren't you?"

Winking at her, he faked outrage. "Why, I would *never*."

Ahead, Belinda created a whirlpool around the automaton. It lifted him from the ground, turning him upside down, before slamming him head first against the harsh surface with a loud bang.

Before Mera could worry, Beta Three slowly stood on his feet, not a scratch on him.

Those things were resilient.

Dangerous.

Turning to Belinda, he cocked his head as if she hadn't just attacked him. "All that seaweed drinking is not improving your behavior, Officer."

Mera rubbed the bridge of her nose. Either Beta Three would help break truce between land and sea, or he would start a new war altogether.

Could go either way.

CHAPTER 19

THE MARAUDER WAS PAINTED ENTIRELY black, except for the silver crest of the Night Court adorning the sails. The ship was sleek for a vessel of its size. Fast, too. Captain Flint's wind magic helped, of course. Added to Mera's waterbreaking, they should make it to Tagrad within a couple of days.

The captain was a strange warlock who seemed to be out of his mind sometimes, but Mera liked him. After spending a day aboard the Marauder, she'd gotten used to his quirks. Like when he randomly broke into song, booming a sea shanty from the top of his lungs, or when he called her a princess-detective, despite Mera's protests, because according to him, *"It seems you are both, my dear, and perhaps, none at all."*

Mera watched him from the quarterdeck of the Marauder, her hands drawing small circles in the air. Water thrashed down below in synchrony with her magic, working like invisible engines that sped up the boat.

Meanwhile, Captain Flint steered the ship from the bridge as if he didn't have a worry in the world, whistling a song while his second-in-command, Mr. Snipes, worked around the deck.

She counted ten nightlings joining him. She'd expected a

bigger crew for a ship that size, but two attacks by Azinor's followers had clearly taken their toll.

Not far from Mr. Snipes, Bast grabbed some ropes, helping him and the rest of the crew. Even though the night Sidhe behaved with deference around their prince, they seemed eager to please their captain and Mr. Snipes. It was clear who led the crew, status be damned.

Not that Bast seemed to mind.

Her thoughtful, wonderful *hart* had brought her a fresh change of clothes—underpants, a white shirt, jeans, and shoes, plus a black leather jacket similar to her old one. Wearing human clothes again felt slightly odd, but she'd appreciated the gesture.

The wind picked up from above, puffing the sails. When Mera turned to the captain, she noticed that the black runes atop Flint's hands glowed a golden color for a moment before dimming down, yet his magic kept working.

She glanced at her own hands, wondering if her runes worked the same way, even if she couldn't see them. They still coursed underneath her skin, unseen, unfelt, but there; always there.

When she'd asked Flint and Mr. Snipes about them, worry and pity mixed on their faces. *"You were born with your runes, they weren't poked into ye. Yer no witch, lass,"* Captain Flint had explained. *"Yer something else."*

Though what, he couldn't tell.

Her hair flowed wildly with the wind, and she spat out a russet thread that went into her mouth. Mera kept waterbreaking, knowing she would feel exhausted when they reached Lunor Insul, but gaining the extra time would be worth it.

Beta Three stood next to her like a watch tower. His neon, unblinking eyes stared at the horizon while the sun began lowering in the sky. The automaton hadn't moved or spoken much today, which was abnormal for him.

"You're awfully quiet."

"I apologize." He didn't turn to her, he simply kept staring at the landscape before them. "I suppose I enjoy watching the ocean. I have never seen it from this perspective before."

"Are you supposed to enjoy things?"

For a moment, he seemed to think about it. "I do not know."

Mera chuckled, facing the horizon. "I think you do. I mean, you clearly enjoy annoying Belinda."

"Do I? I have freedom to interpret data and to react to it as I see fit; within my programmed parameters, of course. Perhaps I should revise them."

"As long as you're not left alone with her, you'll be fine." Mera frowned, trying to understand the concepts that sounded familiar, yet incredibly strange. "What if someone tried to reprogram your parameters?"

Like Azinor had done to the automaton that attacked them at the beach.

Beta Three cocked his head to the side, his unblinking stare still locked on the horizon. "The commissioner installed a fail-safe to avoid it. If someone tries to tamper with my systems, my plasma core will explode. I advise you to keep a fair distance if that happens. The explosion would wipe out any lifeforms within miles."

He'd said it so casually, as if said fail-safe didn't mean his death—if that even applied to someone like Beta Three.

Mera cleared her throat. "Did he install it on every automaton?"

"No. They do not have the same processors. Implanting fail-safes in them would be risky. The machines could blow up randomly and hurt civilians." The engines near his neck whirred when he turned toward her. "Hurting the innocent is *not* our purpose."

But it could be, if Azinor ever got his hands on them. "How many automatons exist in Atlantea?"

"Like me? None. The older models, however…" he seemed to consider it, "twenty-one thousand, eight hundred and fifty-five."

A certain dread spread in Mera's gut. "That's a lot of automatons."

Beta Three admired the sky as warm shades of orange and pink began overtaking the horizon. "I suppose."

A thousand thoughts rushed through her mind, but her hands kept moving in slow circles. "Since you're an autonomous machine, wouldn't the professor need your permission to install the fail-safe?"

"As commissioner, his access overrides my will. He was kind enough to ask, however, and I gladly obliged." He went silent for a quick moment. "May I ask you a question?"

"Shoot."

His head turned, eyes blinking. "Why would I shoot you? Your safety is my priority."

"No." Mera laughed. "I meant you can ask me."

"Ah." He cocked his head to the side, as if he was still trying to understand the expression. "From my observations, water-breakers tend to be fond of their biological family. Yet this is not the case with you when it comes to your mother."

"That's not a question. Also, how do you know about that?"

He tapped his temple with his finger, making a metallic clang. "I have access to all intelligence files. Also, photographic memory, so I register everything you tell me."

"I see," Mera grumbled, focusing on her waterbreaking. "Ariella Wavestorm mistreated me for years, and my father is a lunatic who wants the world to burn. Not exactly the best role models. Guess I won the lottery, haven't I?"

"Quite the opposite. I dare say you're extremely unfortunate."

Laughing, she shook her head. "Remind me to teach you about irony."

"Certainly." He went quiet for a short moment. "You do not

care about your biological parents, but you worry about the king and the commissioner. Officer Tiderider, too." Before she could ask how he knew, he added, "I've been monitoring your vital signs."

"Rude." She briefly glared at him, but shrugged it off. She couldn't expect anything different from a machine. "They're my family. Blood family in the case of my uncle, and chosen family with Bel and the professor."

"You chose them like you chose Ruth Maurea?"

Mera only had herself to blame, since she'd told him about Ruth the previous day. Smiling to herself, she watched the ocean. "I'm not sure if I chose her, or if she chose me."

"Interesting." He seemed to ponder a thousand variables at once. "You must miss them. Perhaps I can help."

A metallic whirring came from behind the plates in his chest, until they opened to reveal a blue, holo-screen inside him. It stayed blank for a moment or two before the professor and Belinda popped on the display.

"Hey, Mer! Everything okay?" Her friend waved at her. "It's ridiculous that I'm not there. I'm your security detail, for dolphin's sake."

Professor Currenter rubbed the bridge of his nose, letting out a weary sigh through his gills. "As I've stated tirelessly, you would turn to dust the moment they crossed the forbidden zone."

Belinda simply rolled her eyes.

"Everything is fine," Mera chuckled. "Just wanted to check on you."

"All good here," Belinda offered. "Actually, *too* good."

"Suspicious to the end, dear." He shook his head. "I say it's a much-needed reprieve. By the way, we might lose contact once you enter the forbidden zone. Beta Three's systems should take a moment to reroute until we're able to communicate again."

"I sensed no interference," the automaton countered, his head turning to Mera in a curious manner.

"Yeah. We crossed it three hours ago."

Mera remembered how the captain had stared at her in a panic as they did, waiting for her to crumble into dust. He and Mr. Snipes blinked in awe once she remained in one piece. Flint even double-checked his charts, but the figures didn't lie. They *had* pierced into the spell that dissolved sirens to the bone without a shadow of a doubt—well, all sirens except Mera, the dead queen, and Azinor.

"Odd," the professor frowned. "I suppose our technology is better than I'd anticipated."

Belinda turned to the side, watching something, or someone, with a furrowed brow. "All right, Mer, we have to go. Watch out for yourself, okay?"

"You too."

With that they blinked away. Beta Three's plates closed with a shy clang, and he focused on the horizon.

Mera's hands started moving in circles again, and the sea reacted to her waterbreaking, propelling them.

"Thanks for that, Beta Three."

He gave her the smallest of nods, his attention locked on the sunset.

Orange and pink hues drenched them, deepening while the sun nearly touched the line of water in the distance. Soon enough, strong arms wrapped around Mera's waist, and a squared chin rested on the top of her head.

"Flint said we're good for the day." Bast's skin was warm and smooth to the touch, the muscles in his forearms perfectly corded. "You can rest now, kitten."

Bast didn't have to say that twice.

Ceasing her waterbreaking, she let the back of her head lean against his strong chest. "Are we sure that we crossed the protection zone? Absolutely, positively sure?"

"Flint has been doing these routes for decades. I doubt he would be wrong. Why?"

Mera's gaze searched the horizon, an uneasy sensation settling in her stomach as she intertwined her hands with his. "I'm not sure."

CHAPTER 20

A FLEET of pitch-black nightbringers stood between the mainland and Lunor Insul in a clear preparation for war. Mera shrunk next to Bast, shivers going down her spine as she observed the iron beasts in the far distance.

His strong arm wrapped around her, bringing her to him. "They can't harm you, kitten. They're too far away."

Sure, the ships weren't in the Marauder's route, which meant they weren't an immediate threat, but they might become a major headache later. Ponting to the vessels, she frowned. "The fact they're here can't be good news. We have to stay low."

As soon as the Marauder docked in the Night island's port, Bast hurried out of the ship, claiming they had to visit Corvus. Mera couldn't agree more, but her *hart* wanted to winnow with her, and she couldn't leave Beta Three behind with a crew of Sidhe and two warlocks who glared at him as if he was an abomination.

"I can't predict what winnowing might do to the thing," Bast said pointedly, the message clear.

Better not risk it. Especially considering Beta Three's plasma core.

So they threw a blanket over the automaton, took a magic carriage to the palace, then went on foot.

Bast led the way through the mighty halls of the Night Court palace, and Mera quickly followed. Beta Three tried to catch up, but he was too slow—he hadn't been built for running.

"Walking on land is more difficult than anticipated," he stated, staring at his metallic feet while he took slow, uneasy steps. "My systems will need a moment to catch up."

"Can't you fly?" Bast grumbled ahead.

"I can propel myself underwater, not into air." He gripped the edges of the gray blanket that covered him. "Not yet, at least."

"Give him time, Bast. He weighs less underwater."

"Correct. Do go on," the automaton urged. "I will be fine."

"You heard the thing." Bast sped up, nearly jumping up the stairs that led to the throne room.

They soon reached a big, heavy door with silver engravings depicting the history of Lunor Insul. The wood creaked loudly when Bast pushed it open. Their boots thumped against the marbled floor, while Beta Three's heavy steps rang faintly from the base of the staircase.

Swiftly jumping from his ivory throne, Corvus rushed toward them, a certain relief shining in his cat-like eyes. He went to hug his brother, but stopped at the last minute, as if he'd caught himself off-guard. Instead, he bowed his head politely at him, then at Mera. "I'm glad to see you're in good shape, Detective. How was your vacation back home?"

"Definitely not a vacation, dickwart."

"Ah! I've missed your colorful vocabulary."

"And I your shenanigans." Waving a hand dismissively, she hid the grin that wanted to take over her lips. "Look, we have a problem. Azinor is attacking my people. If he seizes power over Atlantea, Tagrad won't stand a chance."

He frowned. "Why?"

"Their technology, *broer*," Bast muttered. "It's beyond anything you can imagine."

"I see." Worry filled Corvus' gaze. "First things first, however. I spoke to the council yesterday. Tagrad is ready for war, but the councilors still demand Mera's trial. News of her return will soon reach them, though fear not, we'll stick to my plan."

"What plan?" she prodded.

"Lunor Insul will provide sanctuary to you. If the council opposes, they're free to go to war with us."

She turned to the landscape beyond the throne room's marbled arches, narrowing her eyes at the fleet of nightbringers placed between the mainland and Lunor Insul. "They're here for me?"

"Of course not, Detective. They're for Poseidon, in case he decides to show his ugly face." He raised his shoulders. "Things could always change, of course, but that's future Corvus' problem."

"I can't let you risk—"

"Thank you, *broer*." Jolting forward, Bast trapped the Night King in a hug. "Thank you."

Corvus hugged him back awkwardly, like he couldn't remember how hugs worked.

Unable to believe they were going ahead with it, Mera blinked. "I appreciate what you're doing, but I can't let you risk your entire island for me."

Stepping back, Corvus frowned at Bast. "Why is your *hart* speaking as if she has any say in this?"

He shrugged, giving her a naughty grin. "No idea."

Unnerving, silly nightlings!

"Worry not. There's a method to our madness, Detective. See —WHAT IS THAT THING?!" Corvus pointed to Beta Three, who'd just stepped in the throne room. Somehow, along the way, he'd lost his blanket.

Raising her palms, she silently assured the Night King that there was no danger. "This is an Atlantean robot. An automaton, actually. We brought him to convince the council to join forces with Atlantea."

Corvus' yellow eyes nearly bugged out of their sockets as he assessed the machine. "Danu in the prairies. Is this *thing* alive?"

Beta Three approached them, the cogs in his kneecaps whirring loudly. "I'm afraid a yes or no answer wouldn't suffice."

Jumping back, the Night King squealed in a surprisingly high pitch. "Aagh! It speaks! What sorcery is this?"

Before Mera could tell him there was no magic involved, a wailing bell resounded around the entire island; an alarm similar to the one from when she'd stopped the tsunami.

Corvus and Bast stared at each other, then hurried past the open arches of the throne room, stepping onto the thin balcony that surrounded the domed space.

"Citizens of Tir Na Nog, this is an important announcement."

The voice boomed throughout the sky and Mera instantly recognized it. Colin Asherath, the councilor of the fae borough. She'd heard the same voice while holding down the giant wave.

"As our nation prepares for war, we thank you for your sacrifices and your service. It is because of you that Tagrad is ready to face its greatest enemy."

Loud huzzas came from down below, echoing across the entire island.

"Sadly, we must report that at eight-hundred hours yesterday, the spell that protected Tagrad from sirens was destroyed. The protection zone is gone." Gasps echoed throughout the castle—no, throughout all of Lunor Insul. "Please avoid panic. Your local leaders will be handing out further information. Stay put, and follow their commands. Our fleet is ready. We *will* triumph."

With that, he silenced.

"*That's* why the nightbringers are here," Corvus muttered, anger slowly replacing his shock. "We're on a fucking island and they didn't bother to tell us the protection zone went down. We're an easy target!"

He hurried toward the ivory throne inside, climbing up the steps to the dais. When he pressed a panel on the seating's left side, the carvings opened into a smooth, marbled surface. Setting his hand on top of it, Corvus closed his eyes, muttering words Mera couldn't understand.

A cloud of night and stars bloomed around him nonstop, but something inside the throne sucked his power the way a vacuum swiper would clean a dirty floor. Corvus' muscles clenched, his teeth grinding, until all the darkness puffing from him was gone. The Night King then forced himself up, but toppled backwards instead, falling off the throne's stand.

Bast winnowed at the last minute, catching his brother before he hit the floor. "*Kura*, Corvus!"

"Is he okay?" Mera asked.

A pulse suddenly ripped from the castle, making the walls shake with a loud roar. It spread throughout the entire island, rumbling loudly before it reached the water. The buzz of magic thrummed in the air as a dome went up around Lunor Insul, enclosing it from one moment to the next. The magic flashed purple whenever sunlight hit it at the right angle.

The barrier was awfully similar to Atlantea's. *Magic and technology.* Same result in the end.

"This should buy us some time," Corvus croaked.

"Shut up, you *baku*. You should have done this with a healer in here."

A weak chuckle thrummed in his chest. "I should have."

"Hang on." Bast set a hand on Corvus' forehead, the darkness flowing out of him and into his brother, but Mera's *hart* wasn't a healer. There was no telling if that would work, and even if it did, he would be left as weak as Corvus. Maybe even worse.

Worth trying, though.

Stepping closer, she pressed both hands on Corvus' chest. Blue wisps glimmered from her palms before venturing inside him, except Mera wasn't a healer, either. The magic flowed from her the way water flowed downriver. She couldn't explain why or how; it just did. Soon enough, however, the voices inside her whispered, wanting to pull energy from Corvus instead of giving it.

"No," she snapped, and surprisingly, they silenced.

It took her and Bast a while to help him, but eventually, Corvus felt strong enough to stand.

"Much obliged, Detectives." Right as he settled on his own feet, the phone she'd once given him rang from his pocket.

The Night King looked at the screen and growled. "It's Colin." Excusing himself, he walked toward the staircase, heading to another room, but not before barking at the councilor. "Fuck you, fuck your ancestors, and fuck your council! Lunor Insul is surrounded by water, you *suket*! We're the most vulnerable, and you..." His voice dimmed, until it vanished completely.

Mera stayed sitting next to Bast, who hunched over his knees, both of them not ready to stand. Both somewhat defeated.

"How did he reach the magic core that fueled the protection zone?" she muttered, watching the arches that broke through the throne room's walls, studying the horizon. "It's in the mainland."

"Well, he has visited before." Bast rubbed his brow with the balls of his hands. "*Halle.* Now any of his sirens can waltz into Tagrad."

Lunor Insul might be safe for now, but the rest of the country didn't have a shield, not anymore.

A cold, numbing sensation squeezed Mera's heart. Every time she expected Azinor to act one way, he did something completely different. She couldn't predict his next move; couldn't catch up to the prick.

"Sometimes, I feel like he's already won, Bast. Like he beat us, and we haven't even noticed."

CHAPTER 21

"I'm going there right now," Belinda snarled from the blue screen inside Beta Three's chest. "That bastard is up to something."

"It could be a diversion," Mera countered, but if that was the case, what could be the prick's end goal?

Azinor couldn't take Tagrad without conquering Atlantea first, or so she'd thought. Now the protection zone was gone, and Tagrad was left exposed.

Uncle Barrimond snatched the device they used to communicate from Belinda's hands. "Belinda will go with a convoy of our best officers. Beta Three is authorized to attack anyone who threatens their lives once they arrive."

The situation was escalating quickly.

"He won't have to, Uncle. Lunor Insul is providing sanctuary to waterbreakers, but the political situation on our end is complicated. Sending more of our people right now—"

"You can't stop this, dear."

Mera clicked her tongue, searching for arguments. "You need Bel, and any officer you can spare, to hold the fort in Atlantea."

"Giving you a few officers will hardly cripple us." It was Professor Currenter who spoke, taking the device. His face nearly filled the screen. "Our soldiers are ready, and so are the automatons. Besides, Belinda managed to shoot Poseidon in the head. She's the best choice to protect you. We have everything under control on our end, rest assured."

"I don't need protection," Mera countered begrudgingly. "I can take care of myself. Also, I have Bast."

Belinda snatched the device again, her brow raised. "Oh, you mean the nightling who got his tail handed to him at the isles?"

"Officer Tiderider might have a point," Beta Three noted in his usual, droning monotone, looking down at Mera from above his open chest.

"You should learn how to read a room," she grumbled. Shaking her head, Mera glanced at Belinda. "I think this is reckless at best, and foolish at worst."

"I'm coming over and that's that, Mer. We're taking a few cars at full speed, so expect us within a day."

"Do you have the map?" The professor's voice came from the left, though Mera couldn't see him anymore. "You must check in with me every hour, understand?"

Belinda nodded.

Sighing in defeat, Mera knew there was nothing she could say or do to stop her friend. "Once you approach the shore, send a transmission to Beta Three. Bast will winnow you inside the barrier."

"Will do. Be there soon."

"Oh, joy," Beta Three replied, a certain irony coming through his metallic voice.

"Watch it, pile of rust." With that, she blinked away.

～

MERA SET A SMALL, squared projector atop the wine cupboard in the throne room, then connected it to Corvus' phone, turning it on. A blank screen popped out of thin air, the image wavering and unstable while a tiny drone jumped from the top of the projector, following from above her.

Tagradian technology wasn't as smooth as her people's, but it would have to do.

"Are you ready?" she asked Corvus and Bast, who stood ahead, facing the screen.

"Born ready," her *hart* countered.

Corvus simply served himself a glass of red wine and nodded in agreement.

She turned to Beta Three, who watched a white marbled statue they'd placed on the left side of the room, near the arches that showed a cloudy sky outside.

The statue depicted an Autumn fae atop a squared stand. She stood on the tip of her toes, her draconian wings nearly twice her size. Long, curly hair seemed to flutter gently behind her, even if the statue didn't move. The level of detail was astonishing; Mera could even spot the folds on the slender female's dress, and the dimples in her smiling cheeks. The woman forever watched a marbled butterfly on her index finger.

"How about you, Beta Three?" Mera asked.

"I'm fine. Such beautiful artwork..."

"I have tons more like it," Corvus added mindlessly, taking a sip of his wine. "The artist is a good friend, you see. She likes *giving me* things." A wicked grin spread on his lips.

"Too much information," Mera snapped just as the image of four councilors popped to life, each on a separate little square inside the holo-screen.

The picture blinked and wavered. Sometimes the colors intensified, others they vanished altogether.

Bast stepped closer with his hands behind his back. "Where's Colin?"

"He won't be attending," the werewolf councilor, a man named Harry Trotter if Mera wasn't mistaken, answered with disdain. "He has bigger priorities, it seems. But he's given me written confirmation that he'll agree with the majority's vote, so we may proceed."

"Busy, you say?" Corvus chortled in the back. "Ashamed is more like it, considering the trick this council pulled on us. How the tables turn. Now, Lunor Insul is safe and you're not."

An annoyed gruff rumbled in the wolfman's chest, but he didn't counter.

"Detective Maurea." Councilor Adams watched her with relief. His hair was slightly disheveled, his eyes glassy. He'd lost weight, too. "I'm glad you're safe."

"So am I," she countered politely. "The people of Atlantea rescued me from Azinor."

"Or so you say, *siren*." The witch councilor from Evanora scoffed, a female with curly blond hair and pouty lips.

If Mera's memory didn't fail her, the witch's name was Mia Hammond, and she'd been re-elected twice in a row.

Bast crossed his arms, a cold fury beaming from him. "You will show Detective Maurea respect. She dedicated her life to this country and—"

"She broke the law," Mia Hammond cut him off, her hazel eyes oozing with hate. "She must atone for her crimes."

"Her crimes? You're clueless if you think—"

"Good luck with that, *slatch*." Corvus raised a glass to the four squared images. "The detective is under Lunor Insul's protection. You do remember us, yes? We're a little island that's incredibly vulnerable without the protection zone, in case you forgot. You didn't inform us for a whole day that the spell was gone, but do tell me again how my people are an important part of Tagrad, you *shigs*." He took a long gulp. "Thank Danu we watch out for our own."

"I was against that choice, by the way," Councilor Adams added, looking less than pleased with his peers.

"We, *as a group*, did not want to create panic." Harry Trotter's tone was cold and devoid of any emotion. "Surely you understand that decision. We kept the rest of Tagrad in the dark just like you, and at this point, I should remind you that you have a magic barrier, while we do not."

"Not my *sarking* problem, *malachai*," he snarled. "Especially after your little stunt. You can all burn as far as I'm concerned."

"Corvus," Mera chided. "Azinor is already three steps ahead. We cannot win if we fight amongst ourselves."

"I must remind the Night King that Lunor Insul is under Tir Na Nog's jurisdiction," the vampire councilor added shily, a woman with pearly skin and red hair whose name Mera couldn't remember. "His compliance is not simply desirable; it's determined by law."

Corvus looked to the sides as if searching for someone. "I don't see Colin forcing me to comply. Do you?"

"Night King, please," Councilor Adams asked wearily. "We can discuss proper atonement later."

That seemed to appease him. Shrugging, Corvus took another sip of his wine.

"The war will soon be upon us, and we must be ready." Mera stepped forward, facing the holo-screen. The little drone hovered from above, filming her. She pointed to the automaton standing behind them, who still observed the statue with a certain sadness. "Councilors, this is Beta Three. He's a machine from Atlantea."

Taking his cue, Beta Three approached, his steps heavy on the marble. When he reached Mera's side, he bowed his head slightly. "It is a delight to meet you, Councilors."

They gasped in shock.

"I thought it was just an ugly statue!" Harry Trotter

exclaimed, his eyes shining a bright gold as his canines sharpened—a wolf's response to a threat, even if from afar.

A wrinkled frown captured Mia Hammond's forehead. "What sort of abomination is this?"

"Is it alive?" the vampire councilor asked. Unlike her peers, she stared at Beta Three with more curiosity than shock. So did Councilor Adams.

Cocking his head to the side, Beta Three seemed to consider his answer. "It depends on your definition of alive, Councilor."

"This is Atlantea's prime creation." Mera nodded to the automaton in a go ahead.

He bowed slightly, then turned to the statue. When Beta Three opened his mouth, blue plasma burst from the back of his throat. It smashed against the marbled woman, disintegrating her with a loud boom. A cloud of dust rose in the air, and when it settled, only the statue's ankles remained.

"Dear God," Councilor Adams mumbled.

"Twenty-one thousand. That's how many automatons Atlantea possesses right now," Mera explained. "My people could have attacked Tagrad without losing one single siren. They could have conquered us a long time ago, and yet, they didn't. King Wavestorm is a kind and fair ruler, and he needs our help."

"*Your* people are safe. Poseidon cannot attack on two fronts," the witch scoffed. "He destroyed the protection zone for a reason. He plans on attacking us, not them."

"And yet, he's doing both." Bast stepped forward, approaching Mera. "By the way, how did he do it? I'd always assumed the protection zone was indestructible."

The councilors exchanged a weary glance, and the witch shifted nervously in her seat. "He attacked the protection pillars with powerful warlock magic, somehow escaping before the whole complex exploded."

"The watch guards were killed," Councilor Adams added with a world of grief. "All fifty of them."

"Don't you see? Azinor infiltrated both realms. He can come and go as he pleases." Mera pointed at Beta Three. "If he conquers Atlantea, he'll have twenty-one-thousand automatons at his disposal, plus phasers and technology beyond your wildest dreams. It's a risk we cannot take. We must unite with my people—"

"We?" Harry Trotter cleared his throat. "*We* will not be strong armed. An emergency assembly will be held in the mainland, where *we* will decide the next steps. Including your fate, Ms. Maurea."

Miss, not detective. Her fists balled.

Mera was safe in Lunor Insul. Colin Asherath wouldn't dare go against Corvus—few ever would—but the moment she stepped on the mainland, she would be arrested. It was why the councilor insisted on it.

"You have lost your *sarking* minds," Bast sneered, stepping closer to the wine cabinet. "The assembly will be held in Lunor Insul, where Mera has sanctuary. If you need to vote on something so simple, do it quickly. Time is of the essence." Slamming his palm on the projector, he turned it off. The holo-screen blinked away.

Before Mera could say anything, the device beeped, and Councilor Adams' square blinked back on, floating in the air.

"The meeting went better than I'd expected, albeit still disastrous." He chuckled to himself. "I'll convince the council. You have my word the meeting will take place in Lunor Insul."

"I take issue with your word," Bast retorted. "It doesn't mean much these days."

"Bast, he's trying." Mera bowed her head to Councilor Adams. "Thank you, Peter. I wish your colleagues understood what's at stake as well as you do."

"They will, which brings me to my next point. I can easily

sway Erinna from Kazania to vote against Mera's trial, but Trotter and Hammond are another story. They want blood." Lowering his head, he fumbled with his fingers. "Sebastian, you have to win Colin over. We will need his vote to sway things our way."

"Colin hates me." Bast scoffed. "That thick-headed *malachai* will never—"

"You and Corvus are definitely on his blacklist. That needs to change if we're to bring him to our side, understand?"

"But—"

"We don't have another choice." His screen vanished.

Corvus' jaw hung open, his eyes wide. Slowly setting his wine glass on the counter, he muttered quietly. "There has to be another way."

"There isn't." Bast stared at Mera, horror stamped in his clear, blue eyes. "Kitten, we're fucked."

CHAPTER 22

"*Fuchst ach!*" Bast cursed at the sky as he stepped out into the garden.

He wished he could erase every politician from existence. The *shigs* demanded respect and decorum, yet did nothing to deserve it.

Wastes of air, all of them!

He'd spent over an hour with Corvus, trying to find a way to approach Colin, but every scenario they played out, every argument they used, it always ended with Bast ready to squeeze the *suket*'s neck.

Now, Mera watched him from the outdoor porch that led to the garden. She'd woven her hair into a low braid today. The look suited her, but then again, she always looked breathtaking.

"It's not that bad," she offered, clearly trying to be supportive.

Bast shoved both hands in his pockets, studying his feet as he tried to find a way to reason with Colin Pompous *Baku* Asherath. "You're right. It's a fucking disaster."

He had to ensure the *shig* would vote against Mera's trial, which seemed impossible considering a trial had been Colin's idea in the first place. Sure, he'd suggested it to avoid Mera's banishment, a small 'thank you' for holding down the wave and saving half of Tir Na Nog. But now, the councilor probably considered his debt paid.

Knowing Colin, Bast would get one chance—and even that was a big *if*, especially since the *suket* refused to take his calls. Things might have been easier if the councilor didn't have two chips on his shoulder with Corvus' and Bast's names engraved on them. How he wished he could solve this with his fists...

Not knowing what to do, he decided to call Fallon through their mind link. His captain, and closest friend, was much better at handling situations like this. He also happened to be Colin's cousin.

Last they'd spoken, Fallon was busy helping Tir Na Nog get back on its feet, along with Colin, though Bast doubted the councilor put in any of the effort. The *baku* wasn't the type, but he would surely take the credit.

"Hei, Bast," his captain answered through their link. *"I heard Mera is safe, and that Corvus sort of declared independence from Tagrad."*

He chuckled. *"Somewhat."*

"About time, if you ask me." Fallon's tone rang faint and muffled thanks to the distance. *"So, what can I do for you?"*

"I need help." Rubbing his forehead, Bast let out a weary sigh before telling him the whole story.

Once he was done, Fallon whistled. *"Kura. I expected more from my cousin, but then again, he has always been a little shig. Look, Colin might be a coward, but he's not without honor... mostly."* His focus dimmed as he addressed someone next to him. "Thanks, love," he replied out loud.

Care and warmth emanated from Fallon when he addressed whoever stood next to him, but Bast didn't think much of it. If his captain had a new affair, he would tell him the next time they went out for an ale.

"Colin hates being wrong," Fallon continued, "Problem is, you and Corvus disprove him all the time. You actually revel in it."

"Then he should try making sense for once," Bast grumbled.

"I agree, but you need Colin more than he needs you. If I know my cousin, he's well aware of that."

"He's a foolish suket!" Bast threw his hands up in the air. "If Tagrad doesn't unite with Atlantea, Azinor will destroy us all. I have no time to pet his fucking ego!"

"Neither of us do, but the councilors are the Tagradian authority, and you defy them constantly. You went to Atlantea to rescue Mera against their orders, remember? That's treason." Before Bast gave him a snarky reply, Fallon added, "It was the right thing to do, but you both defied the council. Now you need to atone for that."

"I'm not taking her to the mainland. I can't, Fallon."

"I wouldn't do that either, but you have to realize you're asking a lot of them."

"Me?" he barked. "Asking for a lot?"

"They hold the power, Bast. You're the one who has to walk on eggshells, not them. Halle, I know you can be charming when you want to, so put that to use. Calm your nightblood, and you should be fine. Stella says hi, by the way."

He gasped. "Stella? She was supposed to be safe in a healing convention in Evanora."

"She was, but she came here to help me."

Bast narrowed his eyes at nowhere in particular. "Funny, she didn't tell me."

"You had a lot on your plate. When all of this is over, let's go for an ale, shall we?"

Bast knew where this was going. "Fallon, she's my sister."

"I know." A moment of silence followed. "You've always trusted me with your life. Do you trust me on this, too?"

Risking his own life was much easier than risking Stella's happiness. If Fallon hurt her, Bast would pull his heart from his chest, friendship be damned. However, his captain and

Stella were adults, and he couldn't worry about them, especially now.

"We'll see about that," he grumbled before shutting down their link.

"Who did you call?" Mera asked from behind, startling him. A soothing smile filled with understanding decorated her lips.

Pulling her into his arms, Bast inhaled the sweet scent at the curve of her neck. "Fallon," he said quietly.

"Did he give you any insights?"

"Barely."

She hugged him tighter. "If it comes to it, I'll have to go to the capitol."

"No." He stepped back. "Absolutely not."

"Bast!" Corvus called from a balcony on the third floor, pointing to his phone. "Colin is inside the line!"

Mera chuckled, since Corvus had used the wrong expression, but she didn't correct him. Wrapping one arm around her waist, Bast winnowed them into the Night King's office.

Bookshelves packed with ancient tomes lined the walls. His brother stood by a table in front of a big, arched window. There was a silver screen on top of the wooden surface, and Corvus connected his phone to it—remarkable he even knew how. Then again, he only needed to link both devices with a cable. Hardly flying machine science, really.

Walking around the table, Bast soon faced an enraged Colin on the other side of the screen.

"Will you please stop wasting my time, Sebastian?" the councilor huffed. "Telling your brother to embargo imports to Tir Na Nog until we've talked is not exactly legal, is it?"

"He did what?" Frowning, Bast turned to Corvus. "Brilliant idea, really."

"Thank you." His chin lifted with pride. "I thought so, too."

A vein popped in Colin's forehead. "This conversation is over! Tir Na Nog's guard will be striking Lunor Insul soon."

Corvus bared his teeth at him. "I dare you to go ahead with this, you *suket*!"

"No dare needed, *malachai*!"

"Both of you, stop." Closing his arms, Bast stared at the screen. He couldn't believe what he was about to say next. "Colin, I'm sorry. You have enough on your plate and we pushed you too far. I understand why you weren't taking our calls, but we had to get your attention somehow. That's why Corvus embargoed the imports."

His brother's jaw dropped. Poking Bast's shoulder, he whispered, "What are you doing?"

Bast ignored him, his focus fully on the *baku* on the other side of the screen. "We will lift the embargo. I'm terribly sorry for the inconvenience."

Colin blinked, as if he couldn't believe what he'd just heard.

"I know rebuilding the borough is your number one priority," Bast continued carefully, "and you've done a remarkable job considering you're also preparing for a war."

The councilor narrowed his eyes at him, one eyebrow raised —probably trying to figure out Bast's angle. "Thank you."

"We must stop Azinor to save not only Tir Na Nog, but the entire country." Bast watched his *hart*, who stood ahead with encouragement beaming from her green eyes. "Mera and her people are vital in the fight against the *malachai*. She stopped his *ekrunami* on her own. A fucking *ekrunami*, Colin."

The councilor shifted uncomfortably in his seat. "Harry and Mia mentioned something about an automaton?" Bast nodded, and Colin seemed to ponder for a while. "I'll attend the meeting and urge for an alliance with Atlantea. Happy?"

How Bast managed to keep his tone calm was beyond himself. Taking a deep breath, he figured he'd had one victory, so maybe, he could snag another. "Mera is the link between land and sea. She cannot be kept in a prison when things go down, do you understand?"

"I won't go against Harry and Mia to protect your girlfriend, Sebastian. Besides, Lunor Insul isn't safe ground for an assembly." With the statement, he sent Corvus a suspicious glance. "She will have to come to the mainland and face trial. There's no other choice."

Bast rubbed the bridge of his nose. "Lunor Insul is the safest place for an assembly, as long as the magical shield around it is running. Let us all convey here before deciding to send her to trial. I give you my word Corvus will behave."

The councilor shook his head. "Not good enough."

"Fine," he grumbled. "Convince the councilors to come here, and I'll be in your debt. You know what that means."

"I won't accept bribery, Sebastian."

"Consider it a gift, then."

Colin's eyes still narrowed at the Night King with suspicion. If the *shig* answered to reason, he would have agreed—Mera was their best chance at defeating Azinor—but the councilor had a knack for missing the obvious. "I can't make any promises."

With that, he ended the call.

SILVER WISPS FLOATED near the ceiling, drenching Bast's bedroom in a soft afterlight. Marbled walls and floor surrounded the vast space, contrasting with the purple sheets of his king-sized bed; a bed that felt too big for him. So did the entire room. His quarters in the palace had always felt wrong, like a shoe that didn't quite fit.

Bast sat hunched on the mattress, looking out the arched windows that led to an outside balcony. The moon's reflection graced the ocean, casting a silver triangle on the dark surface.

The sea was calm tonight, but it wouldn't stay calm forever.

"We won't go to the mainland, no matter what," he assured without looking away from the landscape. "Agreed?"

Stepping closer, Mera sat next to him, wearing nothing but a thin, nearly see-through blue nightgown. Bast couldn't help but lose his train of thought for a moment, his attention falling to her chest.

"Is that new?"

She nodded.

Clearing his throat, he turned to the view ahead, forcing himself to ignore the magnificent sight next to him. He had to, otherwise he wouldn't think straight. "We're not going to the mainland," he insisted.

The tip of her nose nudged his cheek, and Bast forgot his own name for a second. "It's not up to you, *min hart.*"

As her soulmate, it was *partly* up to him, and he didn't care if she agreed or not. He knew he was being unreasonable, that Mera was her own woman, but he couldn't let her go.

They still hadn't heard from Colin, or Councilor Adams. It couldn't be a good sign.

"If facing trial means an alliance with Atlantea, then I'll gladly do it." She gave him a soft peck on his lips. "Can we focus on more pleasant things? I missed you. And we've been worrying ourselves sick the entire day."

He took her hand, his heart breaking. "Mera—"

"No, I'm not hearing it."

There it was, that familiar resolution in her eyes, that unwillingness to bend he so loved.

His stubborn *akritana…*

She kissed him again, but this time, her tongue danced with his, stealing his breath. Bast's fingers twirled around her russet hair, bringing her even closer.

She didn't stop kissing him as she slid over his legs and straddled his lap. Giving him a wicked grin, she began unbuckling his belt. "Be with me," she breathed against his lips.

"Evil siren," Bast grumbled, his hands running atop every

inch of her warm body. Already, his length hardened, pulsing for her. "I know what you're doing, kitten."

Distracting him... and saying goodbye.

"Then let me." She pulled the belt from his waistband, throwing it aside.

"They won't take you. I won't allow it." He nibbled at her lower lip. "Mera, you're everything to me."

"And you're my life." With a sweet smile, she unzipped his pants. "But you have to let me go."

Brushing his thumb on her lips, he tried hard to focus. "Would you do the same if you were in my place?"

She didn't answer. Instead, she freed his hard shaft from his pants, but she didn't remove her clothes; didn't give Bast time to remove his either. Lifting her hips slightly, she lowered onto him.

"Ah, Mera!" Bast clawed at her back as he felt her warm, wet flesh swallowing him.

Closing her eyes, she hissed through her teeth while lowering down to his lap. Bast feared he might be hurting her, but she was ready for him, that much was obvious. When she smiled, he realized she'd hissed in pleasure, not pain.

Kissing the curve of her neck, he wrapped his arms around her as she began rocking atop him.

She picked up the pace quickly, moving faster and faster, a certain desperation in the way she made love to him. An aching need to protect her from anything and anyone grew along the desire inside Bast.

"Kitten." He kissed her collarbone, then pulled down her night gown, exposing one perfect, full breast. Licking and kissing her nipple as he kneaded her other tit, he lost his train of thought.

"Hmm," she moaned, caressing the nape of his neck as she rode him; relentless, unstoppable.

When she increased the pace again, he nearly lost his damn

mind. Danu, how he loved her. Bast would give her anything she wanted, anything and everything. *Halle*, he would give her the entire world, and burn it all down on her command. But he couldn't lose her.

He would go mad if he did.

His tongue continued licking and kissing her breast while she rocked violently against him. Mera pulled his long hair, making him let go of her breast with a loud pop.

Bast stared at her, reveling in the delirium that consumed those green eyes he so loved. He bit her lower lip softly, his rushed breaths matching hers. "I love you, Mera," he croaked, struggling to hold off his release.

She drowned him in a long kiss, then pressed her forehead against his, all while riding him without mercy.

"You're my life, and my life is yours." She winced, her gaze slightly dazed. "Ah, Bast, I'm..." She moaned loudly, the sound akin to a song; a perfect, incredible melody she always sang before peaking.

Mera never broke eye contact with him as delirium consumed her completely. Her warm body shivered while she drenched his shaft with her release. Seeing her come so hard was too much, too soon, and it only fueled Bast's own demise.

"*Kura, min hart!*" he growled before following her, filling her womb with the thick streams of his undoing.

Panting, he stared at Mera as he rode the wave of his bliss. Her warm flesh enclosed his, their heartbeats synchronized, and Bast knew then that he could never let her go. He would kill the entire council if he had to, and he wouldn't give two shits about it, even if Mera hated him. Even if she stopped loving him.

At least she would be free.

"We have right now." Cupping his cheeks, she kissed him softly. "That has to be enough."

"No." Bast swallowed, catching his breath. "I want forever, kitten."

CHAPTER 23

THE FOLLOWING DAY, Mera waited in the gardens, eager for Belinda's arrival. The council still hadn't decided where they would hold the assembly, though they should have. Azinor loomed in the distance, a snake ready to lunge. The dickheads really should check their priorities.

The lack of contact, however, meant that Corvus didn't have to tell them about giving sanctuary not only to Mera, but to a dozen sirens. A double edged-sword, she supposed.

A portal of night and stars suddenly opened in the middle of the green lawn, and out came Bast, carrying Belinda. Her friend bent over immediately, nearly falling on her knees, before spewing the contents of her stomach on the ground.

Two nightlings whose presence Mera had completely ignored rushed closer. If their navy uniforms were any indication, they worked as servants in the palace. With a wave of their hands, they sent purple and yellow clouds of magic toward the spot, making the mess disappear from one moment to the next.

They bowed their heads at Mera and Bast then stepped away, but they didn't get far.

"Wait," he ordered before turning to her. "If your friend needs something for the nausea, we have—"

"I'm fine." Still bent over, Belinda coughed. "Go get the rest of my people."

With a nod, Bast motioned for the nightlings to follow him, then winnowed out of view, taking them along.

Of course. Her *hart* would need the servants to clean up the palace's east wing, which was where he and Corvus were taking the twelve officers from Belinda's convoy. Twelve sirens who'd never winnowed before in their lives.

Yeah, it wasn't going to be pretty.

Belinda's people had approached from the western side of Lunor Insul, making sure to stay off the nightbringers' radars. While Bast and Corvus winnowed the officers through the magic barrier, the convoy's cars would self-drive to the eastern side of the island, always remaining undetected and underwater.

"Mother of waterdragons." Wiping the edge of her mouth with the back of her arm, Belinda forced herself to stand. "I am never doing that again."

"You did better than expected." Mera trapped her in a hug. "Glad to have you here."

Belinda hugged her back with shaky hands. "I would say likewise, but everything is so strange on land." She curled a lock of Mera's hair around her index finger. "Even our hair feels different, for dolphin's sake."

Stepping away, Belinda glanced down at her own body as if to make her point. Her black bodysuit with silver embellishments remained the same, but her pink hide had begun acquiring a soft shade of peach. Her purple irises turned hazel, and her hair shifted into a lighter shade of yellow. Within moments, she looked as human as Mera.

Her friend swayed on her legs, probably getting accustomed to her heavier weight.

"You'll get used to it," Mera assured.

"Being on land isn't completely new to me. We occasionally patrolled the Isles of Fog to ensure no one was being a prick to the natives. I mean, it's why the bodysuits are mandatory—to help us adapt to the shift, among other things, like increasing speed and diminishing friction underwater. Still..." Belinda gawked at her membrane-less fingers, her mouth open. "So monumentally weird."

"Well, I'm glad you made it to Lunor Insul safely."

Her friend's lips formed a line. "Not exactly. Poseidon has scout patrols. We knew he was recruiting people from the outer rims, but..." She shook her head. "They tried to catch us. We lost two officers fighting those crabapples."

Mera's chest fell, her friend's loss achingly familiar. "I'm really sorry."

"The price we pay, right?"

Julian's face suddenly popped into her mind, but Mera pushed the memory away. She could only hope that he was safe in Clifftown, with Emma, and far away from the storm that was brewing.

Tir Na Nog was closest to Atlantea. If Azinor attacked, surely he had to start with the fae borough and not the others, as he'd done when he created the tsunami. Or so she thought. Mera couldn't predict his next move, couldn't guess what might be on his mind. She hated the powerlessness, hated the rage it spawned, but above all, she hated *him*.

"Did Azinor's lackeys follow you?"

Belinda shook her head. "We neutralized the entire party, so the dickweed won't be hearing about us." Glancing around the garden, her gaze suddenly went up the palace's giant façade, taking in every carved detail. "Wow. It looks like a giant water-dragon curling around the top of the mountain, doesn't it?"

Mera nodded with a smile.

Once Belinda finished surveying the space around them, she

shook a knowing finger at her. "You failed to mention your partner was stinking rich."

"This isn't his place, technically. Bast's brother is the Night King. The castle belongs to him."

"The sour mackerel with spiky short hair?" Her friend stuck out her tongue as if she'd tasted something rotten. "He plucked us from the water like coral roses without saying a word or acknowledging our presence. Not even a *'Hi, prepare yourself to puke'*. Pretentious idiot."

"Corvus can be difficult sometimes, but he's not a snob." Thinking twice about it, she cringed. "Okay, he can be a major dick when he wants to, but as king, he has a lot on his shoulders."

"We all do." Belinda's gaze fell to her feet. "Mer, back when we were thirteen; when you killed the queen and created a giant whirlpool around the arena..." The question dwindled with doubt.

"Go on."

Her friend inhaled deeply, the motion clunky and uneven. "I figured everything you'd gone through with her had culminated in that maelstrom. A world of hurt, released at once. But now you stop tidal waves, and you kill people in a flash by using a type of magic that's beyond forbidden."

Lowering her chin, Mera stared at the grass. "I can't understand why or how I do the things I do. It's because of Azinor, of course, but at the same time... I don't know."

"Maybe your powers are like his." Her friend shrugged, trading a knowing glance with her. "Maybe they're more."

Soulbreaker...

Mera bit her bottom lip, nails digging into her own palms. She didn't want to think about it, not now. Besides, they had more pressing matters to discuss.

"Look, there's a high chance I'll be arrested soon, but an

alliance with Atlantea might still be on the table. I need you to coordinate the war efforts with—"

"Wait. What?"

"The Tagradian council wants me to go on trial for lying about my nature for so long. We have to make sure—"

"With Poseidon looming on their backs? Are they daft?"

"Bel, please."

"No! Let them try and arrest you." She tapped the phaser attached to her belt. "You're the Atlantean Princess. You're not going to jail, and that isn't up for discussion."

Before Mera could try to dissuade her, two portals of night and stars blinked into the garden. Corvus and Bast stepped out of them almost simultaneously, both looking exhausted—the toll of winnowing non-stop.

"The convoy is settling in the east wing." Her *hart* stepped closer and wrapped one heavy arm over Mera's shoulders. He kissed her temple, his exhaustion weighing in on her, flowing through their bond.

She took it in, giving a bit of her energy to replenish his. Anything to make him feel better.

Corvus narrowed his eyes at Belinda. "Why aren't you in the east wing along with the rest of your fishlings, *akritana?*"

"My *fishlings?*"

"I asked Bast to bring her here," Mera answered. "Corvus, this is my oldest friend, Belinda Tiderider."

He didn't bother to greet her. "What does your oldest friend bring to the table, then?" Raising his chin, he arched one eyebrow. "Her pretty semblance?"

"My semblance doesn't matter." Belinda crossed her arms, unfazed by Corvus' attempt to annoy her. "I'm here to protect the princess."

"You think the detective needs protection?" He laughed loudly. "Did you hear that, *broer?*"

Bast rolled his eyes, letting out an exhausted sigh. "Corvus, will you behave? Officer Tiderider is our guest and—"

He raised his palm at Bast, his focus turning to Belinda. "No, please tell me, *akritana*. How can you do a better job than the detective herself, or my brother, who so happens to be a *sarking* Night Prince? A better job than the mighty Night King?" He waved at himself, head to bottom.

"Corvus," Mera snapped. "You better start playing nice."

"No need to defend me, Mer. I eat pricks like him for breakfast." Belinda stepped closer, and by the look in her hazel eyes, it seemed that Corvus was awfully close to being murdered. "Want to see what I can do, landrider? Attack her. You won't touch a thread of her hair before you're on the ground."

A wide grin spread on Corvus's face while he assessed Belinda from top to bottom, his eyes taking in every bit of her. Licking his lips, he chuckled low in his chest. "An invitation simply too good to be denied, little *starfish*."

"*Broer*, I swear—"

"The grownups are talking, Sebastian." Without looking away from Belinda, he raised his hand as if to touch Mera's hair.

With one quick move, Belinda grabbed his wrist and flipped him over her shoulder. Corvus' back slammed against the grass, and before he could take a breath, Belinda had her knee on his throat.

"You blocked my winnowing," he croaked, trying to raise his head, but her knee pressed harder against his windpipe. "I'm weakened after... winnowing your *fishlings*. Not... fair play!"

Belinda smirked. "Life isn't fair, landrider."

On the right, Beta Three's heavy steps thumped loudly as he walked into the garden. "Pardon my delay. One can get lost within—" He stopped, staring at Belinda and Corvus. His eyes suddenly turned red, which meant he'd engaged battle mode. "Officer in danger!"

Beta Three rushed toward them surprisingly fast, the ground

shaking with each step. His mouth opened, and a red glow beamed from the back of his throat.

"Beta Three, disengage!" Belinda shouted. "I'm fine!"

He froze midway, his eyes turning blue again. "Are you certain?" the automaton asked in his usual, polite monotone.

"Yes!"

"What in all the realms?" Corvus croaked, pushing her away and jumping to his feet. "That thing was going to kill me!"

Belinda stared at Beta Three with a frown. "Thank you. I didn't think you cared about me."

Truth be told, Mera couldn't believe what had happened either, especially considering how her friend and Beta Three fought constantly.

"I cannot care, Officer. However, someone once told me that we choose our own family. I suppose I chose you and the detective. If that's fine with you, of course."

Belinda glanced at Mera, a surprised smile tugging at her lips. "We're fine with that," she assured for the both of them.

Bast turned to his brother, his blue eyes cold and merciless. "Are you done bothering our guest, Corvus?"

The prick watched Belinda for a moment, his yellow irises glinting with something Mera couldn't name. Licking his lips, he raised one finger at her friend. "Oh, little starfish. What a wonderful beginning we've had."

"I wouldn't call it wonderful."

"Are you certain, Officer Tiderider?" Beta Three cocked his head toward her. "Your heartbeat is elevated, and your serotonin levels—"

"No one asked you, Beta Three!" Belinda's face turned a deep shade of crimson. "Gods!"

"Don't worry, *Belinda Tiderider*." Her name rolled easily off Corvus' tongue as he stepped closer. "I tend to have that effect on women. Increase their heartbeat, you see. It's a talent of mine."

"I'm sure it is." She scoffed before clearing her throat and stepping away, her hands joining behind her back. "Do all faeries enjoy shenanigans like this?"

Corvus turned to Bast, and both brothers shrugged before offering a resounding, "Yes."

"All in good fun, mind you," Corvus added, clapping his hands.

The sound startled Belinda since she'd probably had never heard it. The Night King grinned wickedly at that.

"My lord!" A Sidhe wearing a navy shirt and pants ran from inside the palace, heading toward them. When he reached Corvus, he whispered in his ear for a moment, then bowed and left.

Bast frowned. "What was that about?"

"Fabulous news. The council has decided the assembly will take place tomorrow in Lunor Insul. Things are looking good for the detective."

Mera gasped, but before she knew it, Bast was already trapping her in a hug so tight that she could barely breathe.

"Colin came through, *min hart*. He came through," he repeated, as if he couldn't believe his own words.

She hugged him back, fingers digging into his clothes, relief washing over her.

"I say we welcome them in proper Night Court fashion." Corvus' lips curled back like a beast eager to feast. "Wouldn't you agree it's only fair, Detective? Especially after what they put you through?"

For a moment, she considered taking his offer. Shaking her head, however, Mera opted for the wiser choice. It was what Ruth would have done. Her uncle and the professor too.

"We do this the right way. We need the council on our side, so no tricks and no nonsense, understood?"

"Must we?" Corvus waved his hand as if swatting away a bug. "Doing things the right way is terribly tedious."

"Following rules *bores* you?" Belinda scoffed, though a certain amusement beamed from her eyes. "What kind of king are you?"

Shrugging, Corvus gave her a charming grin. "Why, the fun kind, of course."

CHAPTER 24

By now, Mera had spent a great deal of time in the Night Court's throne room, but today, it felt different.

A round table had been set up in the middle of the space, and the councilors sat around it, their voices loud and angry as they argued with one another. Corvus stood next to Councilor Adams, his fangs sharp while he barked at the witch councilor. Adams had always been the voice of reason, but even he engaged in a heated argument with Harry Trotter.

On and on they went, clapping back at each other so viciously that they barely noticed when Mera and Beta Three stepped into the space.

The moment they did, however, a group of five supernaturals wearing black uniforms walled them in a circle—a bulky warlock with a thick beard, a thin-as-a-stick Summer fae, a werewolf in human form but with his canines on display, and a vampire as old as time—since she seemed to withstand sunlight. Plus, a bitter-looking human carrying an M-15.

"Is this our welcoming party?" Beta Three asked her, his metallic tone hinting at genuine curiosity.

"I suppose so."

Their escorts glared at Mera and the automaton as if they were a bomb about to explode. To be fair, they weren't entirely wrong in Beta Three's case, but if this was how the council handled the presence of one waterbreaker, she could only imagine what would happen if they knew about the thirteen sirens currently hidden in the palace's east wing.

Thankfully, Belinda knew how to hide their powers—using the same magic she'd harnessed to block Corvus' winnowing. Mera learned to do it too, since she felt what strings her friend pulled when she'd stopped the Night King's magic.

The power block was so effective, that it also hid the sirens' scents. After all, one had to be careful around shifters and vampires.

The councilors silenced when she and Beta Three moved forward. All guards followed along, standing between them and the exit at their backs.

A portal of night and stars suddenly opened ahead, and out came Bast. Crossing his arms, he arched one eyebrow at the soldiers. "Is this necessary? Mera is a guest, not a threat."

"This is preposterous!" The vampire councilor cried from the table. "Our warlocks blocked any winnowing around this room!"

"They did." Bast winked at Mera discretely, both hands behind his back as he strutted toward Corvus.

His message was clear. She might not be a threat, but that didn't mean Bast wasn't. Also, she was pretty certain that if the council decided she had to stand trial, her *hart* would winnow her out of there before the squad had a chance to arrest her.

Councilor Adams nodded a silent greeting at her. "Welcome, Detective Maurea. I trust you've been well?"

"Thanks to my people, I have." Taking his cue, she addressed the other councilors. "You have seen what Beta Three can do. Forgive me for my candor, but this meeting is a waste of time. You know the danger circling us, and it's past time to act on it."

"Aligning with Atlantea two millennia after the Great War is not a small feat, or an easy decision, Ms. Maurea," Harry Trotter spat, his hand fisted over the table. "Especially considering your antics."

Mera let that slide. She had to if they were to move forward.

"I betrayed your trust, and I am sorry for that. But you should see for yourselves that we're not the monsters history says we are. Tagradians and Atlantians are both trying to lead peaceful lives."

With that, Beta Three stepped forward. The plates in his chest opened to reveal a small, blue holo-screen. The engines inside him whirred, and the screen blinked, only to pop up again against a wall. When the projection grew ten times its original size, discrete gasps escaped the councilors' lips.

Uncle Barrimond soon appeared on the display, then bowed at the council with respect. "Greetings, esteemed rulers of Tagrad. I am Barrimond Wavestorm, king of Atlantea."

The councilors shifted awkwardly in their seats. None said a word, except for Councilor Adams, who smiled at him. "Greetings, King Wavestorm. I hear we have an enemy in common."

The human councilor might not have the power to strong-arm his peers, but he would certainly try. For that alone, Mera couldn't thank him enough.

"Indeed," her uncle confirmed. "For years, he who calls himself Poseidon has been wreaking havoc in our society. It seems recently, he's taken to doing the same to yours."

"Quite right," Councilor Adams said in an encouraging manner. "Hopefully, we'll be able to solve this situation together."

"Not so fast," the witch councilor leaned forward on the table, her curly blond hair grazing the left side of her face. "We've seen what your technology can do. If you decide to turn it against us—"

"We never have." Uncle Barrimond shrugged. "We could, of

course. It wouldn't be terribly difficult." The members of the council gawked in offense, but the king promptly raised his hands. "I do not mean to insult you. However, I must highlight the value of an alliance with us."

The werewolf councilor scoffed. "If your kingdom is so well developed, why can't you handle Poseidon yourselves?"

"His danger lies not only in his power, but in his words. His ideology. He targets those with weak minds, our angry and ignorant, and they follow him blindly."

Mia Hammond, the witch councilor, puckered her lips. "It seems to me that's *your* problem."

Uncle Barrimond watched her for a moment. "I fear I'm not being completely honest, Councilor. They follow Poseidon because I have refused to attack Tagrad for years. They see me as weak for never trying to conquer the mainland."

A deep, uncomfortable silence filled the space.

"Atlantea's defense system is weakened," Uncle Barrimond continued. "With a third of my city adhering to his ideals, it's not a matter of *if* civil war will break out, but of *when*. And if Poseidon conquers us, our technology will be at his disposal. Trust me, he will not be as kind to your peoples as I have been."

"What he means is that Azinor will have access not only to phasers, but to an army of automatons that, although not as advanced as Beta Three here, can cause a great deal of damage," Mera added. "This is not the time to fight amongst ourselves. It's time to unite."

The councilors exchanged a wary glance, except for Councilor Adams. He knew where he stood, what he was willing to do for the greater good. No wonder Ruth had liked him so much.

Trotter leaned back in his chair and crossed his arms. "As far as we know, Poseidon attacked Tir Na Nog to get his hands on Ms. Maurea. Why he did it remains a mystery to me."

Councilor Adams exchanged a fearful glance with Mera.

"If she's to avoid a trial on land, then I say we at least send her to him," Mia Hammond added. "That should keep him out of our territory until we can raise a new barrier."

"That might take weeks, if not months," Adams countered. "Also, we shouldn't be giving him exactly what he wants on a platter! Mera is a powerful agent in this fight, and has proven herself to this nation over and over again. I am getting tired of this." He slammed a hand on the table. "Focus on what matters, Councilors!"

The werewolf cleared his throat. "If that's off the table, *for now*, then there's another solution. If Atlantea is evacuated, we will send bombs that should obliterate everything in there, including your technology. It's the only way to ensure Poseidon won't get his hands on it."

"You have bombs?" Mera turned to Councilor Adams, waiting for an explanation, but he stared at his own hands instead.

No surprise, really. She hadn't known the human borough had jets, either. Still, the idea was so ridiculous, that she saw right through Trotter's game. "You want to destroy decades of hard work; an entire city filled with technology that could actually benefit Tagrad, only to secure a stronger political position?"

The werewolf shrugged. "Everything has a price."

Uncle Barrimond expelled water through his gills, but he seemed to consider it. "Bombing the city would be the best way to ensure Poseidon doesn't get our technology, albeit a painful one. It might work, especially if we shut down the dome. But what about my people?"

"I'm sure you can find another place to live." Mia Hammond tucked a blond curl behind her ear. "The ocean is vast, is it not?"

"You're asking them to start from scratch without any support?" Mera snarled. "Bombing Atlantea will slow down Azinor, but it won't stop him. If he goes after them, they'll be completely defenseless!"

"Not our problem," the witch countered.

Uncle Barrimond stared at someone off-screen, despair clear in his eyes. "Harold, they're out of their minds."

"How dare you insult us?" she barked.

"How dare *you*, Mia?!" Councilor Adams pushed his chair back and stood. "You just told them we'll bomb their home, and that they'll be left to fend for themselves. Your lack of compassion is astounding!"

"Cowardly *shigs*," Bast growled, and soon enough, the room exploded in argument.

Colin and the vampire councilor, however, watched the brawl unfold in silence. Mera wondered when they would step in, if at all.

In any case, she'd had enough. Opening her mouth, she let out a quick siren's shriek that was uncomfortable to hear, but not painful. The councilors winced, so did Bast, Corvus, and the black-ops soldiers near the exit.

"Enough! You're so blinded by your fear and hate, that you're missing the point. Azinor started the Great War, and—"

"He *allegedly* started the Great War," the werewolf councilor corrected.

How Mera wished she could punch the asshole right in the middle of his face. "Azinor started the Great War, *period*. Sirens had their own borough back in the day. We were Tagradians until he ruined it, and he's about to do it again. Do not let him!"

"A piece of Tagrad has been missing ever since the Great War," Bast stepped in, addressing the council. "A piece we must welcome back home if we're to survive what's coming."

The councilors seemed unconvinced, and Mera was tired. So fucking tired. What came next left her throat more out of instinct than anything else; a flurry of sentences she couldn't bring herself to halt.

"I am Mera Maurea, first of my name, citizen of Tagrad, and heir to the Atlantean throne. I am the Princess of Atlantea." She swallowed dry, watching the shock in the councilors' faces. "I abandoned my people once. I will not abandon them again."

Corvus stepped forward, standing tall with his chin raised proudly like the king he was. "If we're to obliterate their home to stop Poseidon, the minimum we can do is offer refuge. Any Atlantean seeking shelter in Lunor Insul shall have it, as long as they agree to be mind-screened to ensure they're not on the *suket*'s side."

"You can't do that!" Trotter snapped, his canines sharp. "You don't have the authority, and you're not a part of the council. The topic hasn't even been up to a vote!"

"I've heard enough." Colin Asherath stood from his chair, and Mera braced for disaster. "I can support many things, but destroying an entire city and leaving innocents at a madman's mercy isn't one of them. Therefore, the southern part of Tir Na Nog, which used to be a piece of the *akritana* borough, will be restored to its original owners."

"Colin?" Bast muttered, shock clear on his face.

The fae councilor smirked at him, then pointed at Corvus. "I can't let this *baku* take all the glory, can I?"

Mera expected a great many deal of things, but not that, and certainly not from Colin.

Councilor Adams was quick to follow. "The human borough would like to make the same offer as the Night King, and I also propose an exchange program to learn about Atlantean technology." He turned to Uncle Barrimond. "We'll give you the infrastructure to rebuild Atlantea once Poseidon is defeated. Do you accept?"

Her uncle blinked, still surprised by what was happening. "Yes."

"This is outrageous!" The werewolf slammed a hand on the table. "Have you forgotten what these people did to our nation? This is a council! We must put our decisions to a vote!"

"*These people* have always been a part of our nation, even

after we banished them," Councilor Adams stated harshly. "It's time to put an end to this. All in favor of aligning with Atlantea to fight Poseidon, and to offer asylum to its people, say 'aye'!"

"Aye," he declared it himself, almost at the same time as Colin. Corvus followed, even if his vote didn't count.

The witch and werewolf councilors didn't react, which meant it was up to the vampire.

"So, we'll shelter Atlanteans, then bomb their city to oblivion. I have a bad feeling about this, but..." Her palm lifted. "Aye."

Three against two.

The room erupted in cheers, when a loud boom suddenly reverberated through the screen, followed by a piercing shriek in the distance. A howl that seemed to come from a hungry beast, and it sounded eerily like...

A waterdragon?

Mera's pulse raced in her veins as she stepped closer to the screen. "Uncle?"

"Azinor broke through the barrier," the king muttered with horror, then faced someone else. "Guide groups A to D out, Harold, as we planned. The Guard and I will hold him off."

"I cannot leave you!" Professor Currenter countered offscreen.

"You must." Uncle Barrimond lifted the golden bracelet around his wrist to his mouth. "Automatons, engage. Now, Harold! Save as many people as you can!"

A second blast roared across the room, and the screen blinked out of existence.

Fear gnawed at Mera's stomach, her heart beating in her ears. "Uncle!"

Only static answered her.

CHAPTER 25

THE MARAUDER RUSHED FORWARD, propelled by Captain Flint's and Mr. Snipes' wind magic. Three officers from Belinda's team stood at the quarterdeck, moving their hands in frantic circles, breaking the water to boost the ship.

The vessel suddenly veered sharply to avoid a big wave, and Mera grabbed Beta Three's arm to balance herself. Belinda wasn't so quick, but the automaton latched on to her hand before she went overboard.

Once they found their footing, the two of them kept trying to contact Atlantea or the professor through Beta Three's screen, but only a deep, gut-wrenching silence welcomed them on the other side.

Their ship had set sail shortly after they lost contact with Uncle Barrimond, and while the council didn't stop them, they refused to add Tagradian resources to the rescue. It made sense, as much as Mera hated admitting it. The government had to focus on defending the mainland, and couldn't risk warriors and ships on a mission with little chances of success.

"Blasted krakens, this is pointless," Belinda grumbled after another failed attempt. Turning on her heels, she pointed at the

Night King, who stood a few steps away, next to Bast. "Do that thing where you disappear and reappear!"

He shot her a glance filled with pity and sorrow, but still raised his chin in contempt. "I don't *have* to do anything, *akritana.*"

"It's not that he doesn't want to..." Mera stepped closer to Bast, intertwining her fingers with his. "We're not in range yet. Once we are," she nodded to two oval-shaped cars strapped to the ship's deck, "they can give it a try."

"And pray that it works," Bast added.

Her hold tightened on his hand while the wind blew fiercely around them, making her low braid flail in the same rhythm as her *hart's* silver threads.

Mera's attention then shifted to Corvus. She still didn't understand why he had come. As king, he should have stayed within the safety of Lunor Insul, but he'd refused to sit back and watch.

"Bast will need me to make your plan work, so..." He'd shrugged. *"If it puts your mind at ease, I'll leave my most trusted advisor in charge, with express orders to contact our brother, Ben, if we don't make it."*

He'd said it so carelessly, that Mera wondered if he truly understood what he was preparing for...

Their death.

Captain Flint called it a suicide mission because any ship out there would be a sitting duck, especially if Azinor had taken over Atlantea already.

"But he'll have a hard time catching this particular duck, lass," he assured her with a wink.

The panels in Beta Three's torso closed. "We are nearly within range."

The professor had prepared for this scenario, so he gave the automaton certain coordinates where they could meet. The Marauder was fast, but not fast enough, which meant they would have to winnow at some point, and yet, Bast and Corvus couldn't transport the entire ship, plus the rest of Belinda's convoy—the cars followed behind the Marauder, keeping up to speed. So, two little vehicles would have to do.

If they got to the professor's coordinates in time, they would either be met with no enemies, or the bulk of Azinor's forces. Flint and the convoy wouldn't be able to help them—they would be too far away—but it was a risk Mera was willing to take.

Beta Three turned to Bast and the Night King. "Are you positive you'll be able to winnow the cars to the location? They're quite heavy."

"Of course!" Corvus snapped, but Bast didn't seem so certain.

Mera gave him a peck on his cheek. "Are you sure you're up for this?"

"Always, *min hart.*"

"Aye, ladies and gents!" Flint belted from the bridge as he steered the ship. "Get ready."

Down below, the rest of Belinda's convoy kept driving in their cars, following the Marauder like dolphins. Slowly, they submerged, boosting faster underwater. Beta Three jumped over the wooden railings to accompany them, splashing the surface harshly.

If everything worked, they would meet Mera and the others at the outer rims in a couple of hours.

She entered the first car on the deck with Bast in the backseat, and one of Belinda's officers as the driver. Belinda got in the second car with Corvus and another officer.

"Brace yourselves," Bast warned while pressing his palms against the vehicle's glass walls, "and pray to Danu."

Magic thrummed around them as he grit his teeth, his eyes closed. His entire body shook before he suddenly screamed in pain.

Mera felt his strain through their bond, watching as veins popped on his forehead. "Bast, stop! We'll find another way."

Suddenly, they weren't aboard the Marauder anymore. The car drifted among night and stars, their bodies becoming weightless. A gripping cold began taking over Mera's fingertips, and veins of ice spread over the windows. From one moment to the next, however, the stars vanished, and they reappeared underwater.

"It never ceases to amaze," the driver muttered. He didn't throw up, since he'd already winnowed once—when Bast took their convoy into Lunor Insul.

A weak moan escaped her *hart* before his chin dropped to his chest, and his entire body went limp. His seatbelt was the only thing holding him in place.

Mera grabbed his hand and pushed her magic into him, sending her energy through their bond, hoping it would work. After all, if she'd drained him at the beach, surely she could refuel him.

It wasn't healing per se, more like recharging—something she wasn't entirely sure she could do, and yet...

It worked.

As the siren on the driver's seat accelerated the car, Mera felt Bast coming back to himself, her magic pulling him back to consciousness.

"Wake up," she whispered, worry squeezing her chest.

Groaning, he blinked awake. Seeing the concern in her stare, he gave her a weak grin. "I'm fine, kitten."

Still, she pushed more of her power into him. If things went south and water breached the car, he would have to be strong enough to winnow himself out of there.

"It feels so strange," the driver muttered, watching the deep blue surrounding them, "being underwater while keeping a human shape, that is."

Mera narrowed her eyes at the vast emptiness around them. "Do you see anything?"

He motioned to the car's panel, which scanned the seabed, then shook his head. His curly brown hair bobbed like tiny springs. "No life signs so far."

Her skin felt suddenly warm and tingly, the sensation telling her the runes were twirling under her skin, and the voices—*her* voices—began chanting a strange word. *"Sejun."*

"Mer, do you copy?" Belinda's voice came through a round speaker on Mera's side of the car.

She pressed a blue button next to it. "Copy. Did you make it all right?"

"Yes. King Dickweed passed out for a moment, but he's awake now."

Maybe Mera was losing her mind, but she caught a whiff of worry in her friend's tone.

"The *Night King* is fine," Corvus grumbled drowsily from the other side.

"All right," Mera said. "Stay sharp."

They kept driving for what had to be half an hour. She assessed the car's panel and the deep blue ahead, but everything around them was empty. Silent. That was until the panel beeped, and an enormous convoy came into view.

It moved like a giant sphere, rolling slowly through the ocean. *"Sejun..."*

As they got closer, Mera realized that hundreds of automatons formed a protective globe around the convoy. They sheltered a second layer made by officers in black uniforms, who carried phaser guns and blasters. The officers seemed tired and weary; some of them were hurt and bleeding. Professor Currenter swam amongst them; the only waterbreaker wearing a tattered, white bodysuit.

The sphere had a third layer formed by hundreds of cars;

along with waterbreakers riding orcas, narwhals, and dolphins. They too carried phaser guns and blasters, plus an awful lot of crates, but they didn't wear black bodysuits, which meant they were civilians. Forming the core of the sphere was a legion of women and children.

"They made it out," Belinda breathed in relief through the speaker.

Either Uncle Barrimond had put on one hell of a fight—which might still be going on even after a day since they'd lost contact—or Azinor had deemed the convoy not worthy of his pursuit.

At least the refugees were safe. They weren't most of her people, not by a mile, but a good number of her kin who were now free from the prick's clutches.

Smiling, Mera hit the speaker in the car. "People of Atlantea, welcome. You are now under the protection of Tagrad."

This wasn't the middle, nor the end, but it was a start. And suddenly, as if a lightning bulb had blinked to life atop her head, Mera understood what *sejun* meant.

Prepare.

～

"Rogue patrols attacked us near the outer rims, but Poseidon didn't bother following us." Professor Currenter stood next to Mera on the harbor, his arms crossed as he watched nightlings mind-scan their people. "You know what that means?"

She nodded. "He has bigger fish to catch."

The refugees who had gone through the mind-scan were given blankets and cans of food, before being directed toward a squared building in the distance, where they would be sheltered for the time being. It was a slow process, but the waterbreakers seemed happy to comply.

The Atlantean officers, however, did not rest. After being

cleared by Corvus' people, they hauled the big crates up to the Night Palace; crates filled with phaser weapons and technology the professor had gathered before escaping.

Ahead, Bast welcomed and directed sirens, while Corvus helped Belinda carry a crate on the left.

"I've talked to Peter Adams, the human councilor." Mera didn't turn to the professor, her gaze locked on Bast and her friends. "He'll be arriving in Lunor Insul soon to go over our technology. Hopefully, they'll be able to adapt a few things."

He nodded.

"Also, you'll be glad to hear that the council voted against bombing Atlantea, now that Azinor is holding half of the city hostage."

"That's the merciful thing to do," he replied. "Are they patting themselves on their backs because they made a decent choice?"

"It's how politicians work."

"Well, even if they bombed us, it wouldn't make a difference. Poseidon has the shield up and in full force now," the professor went on, his gaze mournful, lost. "Their bombs wouldn't make a scratch."

"How do you know he has the shield back up?"

"I have a few prying fishes in town, though their numbers are dwindling."

She took that in for a moment. "Do you know if my uncle—"

"Last I heard, he was being held at the castle. No word on whether he's alive or not." With a burdened sigh, his gaze fell away from hers. "Poseidon's thugs are roaming the streets, and people are afraid. He started reprogramming the automatons, too. All twenty thousand of them."

Mera rubbed the bridge of her nose. "We knew this would happen."

"There's more. He has a waterdragon. A giant, *dead* water-dragon that obeys his every command. I never thought I'd see…" His voice cracked. "He calls it Icefire. Your uncle put up a good fight, but when that creature belched waterblaze over the western quarter of the city, all was lost. We're lucky it didn't follow us here."

Mera's throat knotted, and she fought the tears that pricked her eyes. She couldn't tell why she was certain Icefire was *her* waterdragon; she simply knew.

Professor Currenter patted her shoulder softly. "What I'm about to do next will not be easy, little fry, and for that, I'm sorry."

Her forehead crinkled. "What is it?"

"You have noticed I do not age like a normal waterbreaker."

"Yeah. I figured you used an anti-aging spell. It's not uncommon on land. Ruth looked sixty, but she was almost two hundred years old."

"Quite right, in a way. It was a spell at first, but after such a long time, I suppose it's become a part of me." Sighing deeply, he set both hands behind his back. "I was a child at the time of the Great War. This makes me the oldest living creature in this world, after Poseidon—if 'living' even applies to him."

"Almost two thousand years?" Pursing her mouth, she whistled. "That's a fine anti-aging spell."

His lips formed a sad smile. "My house on land was attacked during the war. Most of my family died, and I was severely injured, until someone healed me. Someone with black runes tattooed everywhere on his body. To this day, I don't know what he did to me. I don't think he knows it, either. Fact is, as long as he lives, I cannot die."

Still processing what he'd just confessed, she gawked at him. "But you've aged."

"I have, so very slowly. I still have decades ahead of me, but what might happen after that…" He shrugged. "Maybe I'll regenerate. Maybe I'll walk this earth as a pile of bones."

"I'm so sorry. We'll figure it out, I promise."

"That's not why I'm telling you this, little fry. You see, due to my condition, I have crowned every Wavestorm who sat on the throne after the Great War." Taking her hand gently, he bit his lower lip. "I'm terribly sorry, but there is no other way."

"Oh, no! You are the crown prince. You're next—"

"I'm not, and you know it." Never letting go of her hand, he dropped to one knee.

"Get up!" she begged, but he didn't move. "Please don't do this."

All waterbreakers around the port followed his cue. Even Belinda stopped what she was doing, and knelt with a proud smile stamped on her face.

No, no, no...

Bast and Corvus exchanged one amused glance before they too got to one knee. The nightlings in the port followed after them.

"What are you doing?" Mera whispered to the professor, her lips quivering, fear and dread spreading in her chest. "I'm not ready. I don't want to turn into *her*."

"Don't fear, little fry," the professor offered kindly. "You're not Ariella's daughter. You're Mera Maurea, first of your name, citizen of Tagrad and heir to Barrimond Wavestorm. And I hereby declare you Queen of Atlantea."

CHAPTER 26

BAST HANDED a kit of canned goods to a family of four, while Mera gave them the essentials for their hygiene. An officer next to her provided them with a fresh batch of clothes, and then the family went on their way. The line moved slowly, but Bast expected most Atlantean refugees would be supplied and settled before nightfall.

His *hart* might be a queen without a crown, but her people still bowed their heads whenever they saw her, even when she told them it wasn't necessary. As the line moved along, she began ignoring it. Either that, or she'd gotten used to it.

"Your uncle was a good king," the officer next to Mera offered while handing a batch of clothes to the next family in line. A slender male with a kind smile, the siren had a deep scar on the left side of his face that went from his forehead down to his jaw, passing over one blind eye. "I fought for King Wavestorm, and I will fight for you," he vowed.

Bast eyed Mera's reaction. She didn't look the siren in the eye, she simply kept handing kits to the refugees. "I don't deserve your devotion. I abandoned you."

"You came back." The officer turned to Bast, silently asking him to intervene.

Bast simply gave him a tiny shrug. He knew it was pointless. His *hart* carried the weight of the world on her shoulders, and all he could do was be by her side when she needed him.

"You were a merling without any options left," the siren continued. "You did what you had to do to survive, my queen."

"My uncle might still be alive. Let's not lose hope, shall we?"

Bast's heart squeezed. "Kitten…"

"If the king is alive, then he has my pity." The officer's one good eye glistened. "Being at Poseidon's mercy is a punishment worse than death."

A frown marred Bast's forehead. "You speak from experience?"

The siren pointed to the scar that created a valley over his skin. "This was only the beginning."

A cold, gut-wrenching fear spiraled inside Mera—Bast could sense it through their bond—but she didn't let it show.

"We'll bring him to justice," she promised, then winked at Bast. "Detective Dhay and I are famous for that, aren't we?"

A silly grin cut through his lips as he admired her. His *hart*. His queen. "We certainly are."

The officer didn't seem convinced. "Many have tried to defeat him, and all have failed. But if I must die one day, then let it be fighting him. For you, my queen. For Atlantea."

Another family stepped in front of them, but Bast pulled Mera aside. "If you'll excuse us for a moment."

Two officers promptly replaced them as he led her to an empty spot near some bushes.

"I like where this is going," Mera whispered with a naughty grin.

A smile hooked on the left side of his cheek. "Ah, do you?" Wrapping both hands around her waist, he kissed her forehead. "Your wish is my command, my queen."

"Don't call me that."

"You know you're not her, yes? That you couldn't be her, even in your worst nightmares."

"It's just so strange. I've run from Ariella, from this title, for so long. I don't know how to act now that I'm, you know." She motioned to herself from top to bottom.

"You're already a million times the ruler she was, kitten." Taking the back of her hand, he kissed it softly. "Besides, it has a nice ring to it. Queen Maurea, first of her name, ruler of Atlantea and *hart* of Sebastian Dhay, detective extraordinaire."

She shook her head, but couldn't hold the smile that sprouted on her lips. "You're impossible."

"Can't argue with that." A despondent sigh escaped his lips. "As much as I would love doing certain things with you behind those bushes, we happen to be late."

"We do?"

Without warning, he swept her in his arms and winnowed them to the throne room. Officer Tiderider, Corvus, Harold, and the *thing* waited for them.

Beta Three, Bast chided himself. The *thing* had a name, and given how helpful it—*he*—had been thus far, the least Bast could do was show *him* some consideration.

"Another meeting?" Mera grumbled, climbing off his arms. "Great. This gig isn't as fun as most people would think."

Corvus stamped the back of his hand against his brow. "You finally understand my penance, Detective."

"Penance?" Officer Tiderider chortled. "Being king, with servants tending to your every whim surely compensates for the stresses of your position, doesn't it?"

Shrugging nonchalantly, he leaned closer to her. "Not as much as the endless nights of fucking with women who demand more *results* from their ruler."

"You're all talk and no catch, Night King," Mera's friend fired back, but she couldn't hide the blush that rose to her cheeks.

Corvus raised his brow. "Want to see for yourself?"

"*Broer!*" Bast snapped. The *shig* was anything but subtle.

"Officer, the effect the nightling has on you is fascinating," the thing—*Beta Three*—noted innocently, his metallic tone carrying a hint of a child's innocence. "Despite his vulgar comment, your heart rate spiked considerably when—"

She shot the machine a narrowed glare that spoke of murder, and surprisingly, Beta Three seemed to catch it.

He was learning, as was his design. Bast couldn't tell if that was a good thing, though. Technology tended to go wayward, but then again, so did living beings. Maybe that was why Harold had shared Beta Three's override codes with him and Mera only a few hours ago.

"In case of an emergency," he'd admitted.

Bast didn't know what an override code was, but according to Mera, it could limit the machine's free will. It didn't seem entirely fair, yet perhaps necessary.

When he stepped onto the circle with his *hart* by his side, Officer Tiderider bowed her head slightly at Mera. "My queen."

"Oh, no." She shook her head. "Don't you start with that, too."

"You must acclimate yourself with the title, little fry." Before she could react, Harold clapped his hands. "On to the meeting, then. Beta Three, if you will."

The machine nodded. "I have linked my data core to the automatons that arrived with the convoy. They will now follow my every command." He paused for a moment. "I'm also trying to regain contact with Darwhal, the commissioner's informant, but he's gone silent. I'm afraid we must assume he's been caught."

"Keep trying." Harold straightened his stance, trying to mask his worry, yet Bast saw right through his façade. Reading people was a must for a detective.

"I can report that the human borough is learning fast. They

should start their mass production of phasers soon, which is great news. A certain Detective Smith in particular has been of great help to Councilor Adams." Harold faced Mera. "He asked me to tell you that the human and vampire boroughs are ready. He also said he's 'got this' and to 'tell Mera to go kick ass.' Whatever that means."

His *hart's* lips opened into a warm smile. "That's Julian, all right."

Bast's blood boiled, as it always did when Julian entered the picture, even if his jealousy was foolish.

Halle, he had bigger things to worry about now.

"I hate to follow up with bad news, but…" Harold exchanged a sorrowful glance with the Night King. "The government declared that every shore city must be evacuated to the mainland."

"Which means we must leave Lunor Insul." Corvus fixed his collar, as if the words suffocated him. Truth be told, they suffocated Bast too. "We have no advantage points here, and my barrier will lose strength soon. I can only hope Poseidon will pass by without doing much damage. I'll put a protective spell around the castle and set up a self-destruct in case he tries to enter the library. Thousands of years of records and spells should not fall upon his hands."

"Just in case, Brother." Bast patted his back, his lips pressed into a line. He shared Corvus' pain, his fear. After all, this was their home.

"Your island should be fine," Harold assured. "He will focus his attack on Tir Na Nog. It's the closest spot to Atlantea, and the most stable sea bed. Also, Mera will be there, and Poseidon isn't known for letting go of a grudge."

She nodded. "We have another problem. Ariella told me that chopping him into a thousand pieces won't destroy him, and I believe her. So, how do we stop the prick once and for all?"

Officer Tiderider scoffed. "Of course chopping him up will work. It's logical. She's just playing games with you."

Harold rubbed the bridge of his nose, seeming to consider it. "Actually, dismembering Poseidon could backfire stupendously, considering he can regrow himself. Who knows? We might end up with several copies of the bastard."

Officer Tiderider slammed both hands on her waist. "Well, then this entire thing is pointless, isn't it?"

"We might be able to find something in the library of night," Corvus suggested, curling a lock of her blond hair around his finger. "Up for a read, *Bel?*"

By the look on her face, she was either about to slap him or kiss him—could go either way. Instead, she rolled her eyes and let him show her the way. "Don't suppose I have much of a choice, do I?"

Corvus winked at her before taking her hand. Within a blink, he winnowed them out of the room, leaving Mera, Bast, and Harold alone with Beta Three.

"On to further matters," the professor started, when Beta Three's engines whirred loudly. His stance locked as if he'd turned into a metallic statue.

"Are you okay?" Mera asked.

A moment passed before he gathered himself. "I have received a transmission from Atlantea."

"Darwhal came through!" Harold's smile beamed with optimism. "Show it to us, Beta Three."

"I would rather not."

"Kitten," Bast warned, dread spreading in his chest. "You might not want to see what's on the other side."

A flash of cold anguish crossed her green eyes, and Mera swallowed dry. Taking a deep breath, she turned to the automaton. "Show it to us."

With a curt nod, his plates opened, revealing a blue screen.

Azinor floated in front of the camera, his face fully formed.

King Wavestorm hovered in the background with his ankles tied together. Dark clouds of blood puffed from the stumps where his arms used to be, and his head was lowered. Bast couldn't tell if he was alive or dead.

Harold stepped back, a cry simmering in his throat while Mera inhaled deeply, seeming to center herself—even if her entire body shook.

Bast gripped her hand. "Kitten..."

"I'm fine," she lied.

Floating next to the king was a dead *akritana* with nothing above his neck. His severed head hovered on the opposite side of his bobbing corpse, and the siren's long hair drifted around his face. His eyes had rolled back, his mouth hanging open as if he'd died midscream.

"Darwhal," Harold croaked.

Azinor grinned at the screen with a mouthful of perfectly white teeth, and although that was a recorded message, Bast could swear the *shig* was glaring directly at Mera.

"I have conquered Atlantea, child, and now, I shall lay waste to your precious land. I'll slaughter everyone and everything you care about. But you, Daughter, I will spare. You will become my new favorite toy." He turned back to the armless king, and a low chuckle reverberated in his chest. "Regneerik is coming."

The screen blinked out.

CHAPTER 27

MERA WATCHED Lunor Insul from the shore of Tir Na Nog, the mighty Night Island now only a blip in the distance. Black, metallic ships that seemed to be made of night sat scattered around the sea, along with the Marauder, which stood guard on the far left.

A few Atlanteans walked atop the ocean's surface, using their waterbreaking to keep themselves afloat, but they stood far from the nightbringers, not daring to approach.

Mera understood why, of course. Those onyx beasts were built to rip her people apart; death machines carrying iron harpoons, spiked hulls, and booming cannons.

Back when Mera was a merling, Atlantean technology wasn't quite as developed. So whenever a nightbringer cut through the surface, she and Belinda always hid in fear, watching the monsters' long, iron bellies cast a shadow upon the ocean floor.

Now, those same beasts guarded the shore against Azinor.

Behind her, beyond a massive stone breakwater that lined the back shore, thousands readied for battle where the promenade used to be.

Automatons helped carry heavy machinery, guided by humans and sirens. On the right, Belinda taught a group of witches how to fire a phaser, while Corvus and Bast talked to a squad of werewolves dressed in black ops wear. At the far back, the professor discussed plans with Adams and the vampire councilor—one of the few of her kind who could withstand being under the sun.

Everywhere along the shore, waterbreakers and landriders prepared for battle together, the differences between them forgotten. The Great War didn't matter anymore; all that remained was Tagrad, united, against Azinor and his army of sirens and automatons. His waterdragon, too.

Icefire.

Mera's stomach dropped at the thought of facing the creature.

"You seem to be in distress," Beta Three noted from beside her as she watched the promenade. "Is that what you call fear?"

"I'm fine."

He cocked his head with curiosity. "Is that what you call a lie?"

Mera chuckled, facing the ocean. "Maybe."

Her feet felt heavy in the sand as the waves washed lazily atop them. Closing her eyes, she tried to listen to the runes that danced inside her, their whispers ringing faintly in her ears. Like several versions of herself whispered to her from a great distance.

Over the past days, however, the voices had started sounding closer. As if they knew something big was coming, and yet, Mera still had a hard time deciphering them.

Some words she understood. *Ahatana*—Fear. *Menitute*—Courage. *Sejun*—Prepare. Yet, most remained an enigma.

Ariella told her the voices were her soul trying to speak to her. A shiver ran down her spine when Mera remembered the waterbreakers she'd killed. She avoided thinking about them, ignored what happened, because deep down she knew.

She'd sucked their lives dry as if they'd meant nothing.

Mera certainly wasn't a waterbreaker anymore. She wasn't a witch or a human, either. She was something else.

Soulbreaker.

"Why do they wear iron shields, Detective?" Beta Three's metallic tone jarred her from her thoughts.

When she frowned at him, he nodded toward the crew of a nightbringer close to shore. Some of the ship's members wore thin iron plates over their chest and backs.

"Ah. The shields help block the macabre, or at least slow it down depending on the siren's power. Human and weaker supernaturals wear them just in case."

"But if they go overboard, they will sink faster."

"They can remove the shields, but sometimes there isn't enough time. They think it's a worthy gamble. Better to drown than to explode into a million pieces, I suppose."

"Is it?" The wind blew gently around them. "Tell me, what is it to be afraid, Detective?"

She pondered what to say. How to explain fear to a creature with the emotional intelligence of a child?

"When you thought Corvus was attacking Belinda, you immediately went on defense mode. Fear is what made you do that. What makes someone wear an iron shield in the middle of the ocean. Point is, you feared losing Belinda and you acted on it." Her mouth curved with a grin. "Most people freeze, but you went into action. You just might be the best of us, Beta Three."

"Thank you. I appreciate that." The automaton focused on the ocean ahead, then nodded to himself. "After what happened to the king, I *fear* you will be hurt if I tell you the truth."

"What truth?"

"Someone in Atlantea has been trying to contact you. It is not a recorded message."

Mera frowned. "Do you know who it is?"

"They're using the automaton that accompanied Darwhal to connect, so I suppose it's Poseidon." A deep silence filled the air, lingering for a while. "I can feel what he's done to him, and I do not like it."

Him. Darwhal's automaton. One of Beta Three's people, in a way.

Mera set a hand on his shoulder, even if he couldn't feel her touch. "I'm sorry."

"It is not your fault." A whirring sound came from inside his metallic plates when he turned to her. "I do not want you to be hurt."

"I know, but it's *my* choice."

The voices inside of her whispered louder now, faster, but Mera couldn't understand what they tried to say; millions of different words she'd never heard, all interspersed with one another. Her skin thrummed slightly.

Shaking her head, she focused on the automaton. "Besides, if I keep him on the line long enough, we might catch something that could give us an advantage. We need all the help we can get."

With a nod, Beta Three opened up his chest.

To her surprise, it was Ariella's face that popped up on the blue screen. The bitch wore the Crown of Land and Sea, her hair woven into a low braid like Mera's.

Her jaw clenched so hard that she could barely bring herself to speak. "Why are you contacting me, *Mother*?"

Ariella looked to the sides, her voice low. "He wants your power, but by defying him, you've earned his anger. Now he'd rather torture you than simply use you. Nevertheless, if you bend the knee, he might reconsider. Join him, and he'll compensate you beyond your wildest dreams."

Mera nodded to the gap on Ariella's left cheek, then her

rotting skin. "Sure, Mother. I'll join him. After all, he has compensated you so well, hasn't he?"

The bitch's mouth contorted in a bitter curve. "I..." She couldn't finish; couldn't deny the truth.

Mera was tired of their never-ending dance; the ongoing cycle of pain and misery. "What's the point of this call?"

Ariella didn't reply for a while. Maybe she didn't know it herself. Then, finally... "I met *her* in the world beyond, after you killed me again. You know who I'm talking about, yes?"

Mera swallowed, remembering the times Mother had blabbed about someone in the afterlife. Someone that sounded awfully like... Tears pricked her eyes, and her heart shrank. "It was Ruth, wasn't it?"

The dead queen nodded.

A devastating longing stung Mera's heart, but she didn't show it; wouldn't give Mother the satisfaction. The voices kept whispering in the background of her thoughts, and though she couldn't understand them, she felt their sorrow, their pain, because it was Mera's own.

"What did she say?"

Ariella stared at nowhere in particular, a frown creasing her forehead. The blue holo-screen wavered slightly.

"When you die, there are no words. Only images, memories, sensations, everything at once. A second that lasts forever. You see thousands of pasts, presents, and futures, never knowing which one will be yours, which one will be real. You feel everything, you are everything." She stared at Mera, an ache burning in her eyes. "Some things are not meant to be shared."

Seeing a thousand futures. Maybe that was why she'd returned completely broken.

"You don't get to choose." Mera's tone quivered with unshed tears. "You took her from me. If Ruth told you something, I deserve to know. She was my mom—"

"She was."

Mera's voice left her. Had Ariella really admitted it?

Still, the monster didn't share what Ruth had told her.

Sniffing, Mera wiped the corners of her eyes. "I'm the product of Azinor's violence on you. You love and worship him, but you hate me. Why? I was a child. I had done nothing to you."

"Could you escape your nightling, even if you wanted to?" She looked away. "There's no running from your soulmate."

"Don't compare what Bast and I have to what you share with that prick. Bast loves me. He respects me. What you two have isn't love." She chortled, shaking her head. The voices growled in outrage; *her* outrage. "It can't be a mating bond either, and even if it is, you should have walked away. But no, you chose to be your abuser's little lap dog." Heat flushed Mera's head, blood rushing through her veins. "You're pathetic."

"If you won't help him, he will kill everyone, but he will leave the nightling for last. He won't stop until you beg him to kill your soulmate." She shrugged. "You saw what he did to Barrimond. Do not provoke him, Daughter."

Mera's hands fisted, her nostrils flaring. "I'll end Azinor before he gets to do that again."

The question was, how?

As if on cue, the voices rose louder, whispering a word that made no sense. *"Ethama, Ethama!"*

Shaking her head, Mera forced herself to focus.

Ariella stared at her with a hint of curiosity. "I used to think Regneerik was the end of times, but I see now that it's the end we face when our time comes. Endless Regneeriks, happening every second of every day." She swam closer to the screen, a new resolution in her eyes. "If you remove Poseidon's runes, you remove his immortality."

And if Mera removed his immortality, she could kill him.

"How can I do that?" she pushed.

The dead queen nodded to Mera's skin, more precisely, to

the tattoos that swirled under her flesh, unseen but always there. The origin of her voices.

"Ethama. Ethama!"

"You have some of his power. Use it, but beware, child. His force is greater than yours, and if you take it, your combined magic will consume you, body and soul. You wish to kill your father? Then take what's his, let it engulf you until there's nothing left. Accept your *Regneerik*."

Why would she tell Mera how to beat Azinor? This was yet another of her schemes, it had to be, but at the same time… Mera couldn't explain how she knew that Mother was telling the truth; she simply did.

Like a wall crumbling down, she suddenly understood what the voices had been whispering all along.

Ethama…

Sacrifice.

A freezing jolt coursed down her spine, and she stepped back. Her body trembled, and her throat felt drier than sand. Mera had felt this way once, when she was thirteen and about to fight Ariella above a ring of molten fire.

"Do not fear death," the dead queen offered quietly. "It is only the beginning. At least, you will be free of him."

"Detective, you can't possibly be considering this," Beta Three interjected. "You would be killing yourself. I cannot allow that."

Mera swallowed the knot forming in her throat. The automaton was supposed to keep her safe. Letting her do what she had to do went against his primary directives.

Ariella gave her a mournful smile. "Watch the sky the day after tomorrow. Land and sea will burn green."

She went offline, and Beta Three's metallic plates closed.

"We must go to the councilors with this information at once," he insisted.

"We'll tell them about the incoming attack, but not about the rest."

"I cannot comply with that." The automaton turned to leave. "I'm sure you understand. Your safety comes first."

"I know." Taking a deep breath, Mera nodded to herself, hating what she was about to do. "Beta Three, delete log for the past fifteen minutes. Override code seven, three, four, two."

The automaton stopped in his tracks, frozen in place.

"No…" His engines slowly went silent. The light in his eyes dimmed and his chin dropped to his chest. The rest of his body remained mid-action, as if he'd turned into a statue.

Mera stepped closer, facing him. "I'm really sorry."

His eyes had gone blank, but soon enough, Beta Three's engines started again. Within seconds, he blinked back into awareness and lifted his chin.

Cocking his head to the side, he observed Mera with his typical child-like curiosity.

"Tell me, what is it to be afraid, Detective?"

CHAPTER 28

THE FATEFUL DAY started like any other day, except for the thick fog that enveloped the shore of Tir Na Nog. Chilled droplets hung in the air, heavy and nearly suffocating, swallowing any sound.

Mera stood aboard one of the nightbringers out of the many peppering the frontline. Once Azinor came, if he came—the possibility that Mother had lied wasn't too farfetched—she would be one of the first to face him.

Mera glanced down at her special boots, which neutralized the iron on the ship's deck. Black and bulky, they felt surprisingly comfortable. She needed them because pure iron weakened the fae's powers—one of the reasons why Bast's people abhorred metal. Mera never felt that effect, but sirens were once called the sea fae, so her *hart* insisted on it. There was always a chance they weren't so different after all.

Her gaze drifted to the nightbringer's iron boards, and then to the four giant harpoons on deck; two near the quarterdeck and two near the bow.

Unlike her, Belinda refused to board the beasts that had

haunted their childhood. Instead, she led a squadron of Atlantean cars, joined by Beta Three's automatons. They gathered ahead, past the nightbringer armada, where they waited for any signs of their enemy.

Her friend's front, along with the nightbringer fleet, should be enough to stop Azinor before he reached the mainland. Once her friends were safe, Mera would ensure that he never hurt another soul.

Tears pricked her eyes, not because she would die today, but because the thought of never seeing Bast again left a hole in her chest. Nevertheless, she had to control her emotions; she couldn't let her feelings slip through their bond.

Clearing her throat, Mera crossed her arms, listening to the silence; the stillness before the storm.

"Something doesn't feel right," she told Bast, who stood next to her. He was clad in an onyx bodysuit, his silver hair up in a tight bun, and he wore boots just like hers. The leather belt around his waist carried two holsters, each with a phaser. Remarkable, considering Bast hated guns.

Desperate times, she supposed.

His clothing matched Mera's own—she wore an officer's black bodysuit with a silver belt around her waist. Like Bast's, the holsters in her belt held two phasers.

"Something is definitely off, kitten." His wings flashed to life with a loud flap, spreading behind him.

Corvus had stayed on land, leading an air battalion comprised of winged Sidhe and the occasional witch or warlock who could fly. Mera hated admitting it, but she missed the prick's presence. The Night King could be a dick, but at least he knew how to lighten the mood.

Her attention lowered to the silver bracelet looping around her wrist. Tapping it twice, she brought it closer to her lips. "Bel, anything out of the ordinary?"

A moment of quiet followed before her friend's voice came

from the other side. "Nothing yet. Can't see a thing with this fog. The cars underwater are registering zero movement in their sonars. Not even a little fish. It's like we're surveying a graveyard."

"That's not normal."

"Agreed." Her friend blew air through her lips. "I'll let you know if we catch anything."

Mera tapped the bracelet, shutting down the connection just as loud clangs came from the right side of the nightbringer's hull, making the ship wobble slightly.

Something was climbing aboard.

She glanced at Bast, her worry reflected in his eyes. They faced the quarterdeck together, dropping into battle stances.

Near that part of the deck, Professor Currenter led a squad made of warlocks and sirens. He stared back at her, his lips pressed into a line as he and his team prepared to fight. Instead of his usual white bodysuit, he wore a black uniform like Mera's. Today, he wasn't the commissioner, and she wasn't a queen.

They were Atlantean soldiers.

The clanging suddenly stopped, and then Beta Three jumped over the railing. The deck shuddered under Mera's feet when he landed.

The professor's shoulders slumped in relief, and he turned back to his squad. He addressed two newcomers—a werewolf and a human who wore iron chest plates. They looked nervous, especially compared to the stoic waterbreakers in the squad, soldiers who had already faced Azinor's wrath when escaping Atlantea.

The automaton paced toward Mera and Bast, his steps clanging against the iron deck while water washed down his metallic frame. "The sensors are in place," he informed them calmly.

Beta Three and his automatons had placed floating sensor

orbs beyond the thick wall of fog. They spread the orbs in a line that followed most of the shore, guarding both air and water. Thanks to them, Azinor couldn't possibly approach Tagrad without being seen.

"Well done," Bast said, then turned to the professor, watching him through narrowed eyes. "Are you sure bringing him along was wise? Harold isn't a spring chicken anymore. He should have stayed on land."

Mera smiled, warmth spreading in her chest. Professor Currenter was important to her, and so he was important to Bast. "I told him the same, but he wouldn't take no for an answer, especially after what Azinor did to my uncle."

Cocking his head left, Bast raised his brow. "I can certainly respect one's desire for revenge. In any case, I'll try to keep an eye on him."

She hugged her torso, staring at the gray fog that clouded the air. "I don't like the silence. The stillness."

Beta Three's metallic spine suddenly snapped straight, his neon-blue eyes blinking brightly in the mist. "Detective, the sensors have caught an alteration."

The plates in his torso opened, revealing a blue hologram screen that displayed a combined view of every single orb. The screen showed calm waters and the sunny sky beyond the fog.

Narrowing her eyes, Mera tried to spot anything unusual, yet found nothing. "Are you sure? Switch to underwater view."

He did. The deep blue was empty, devoid of life, but other than that, everything seemed normal. The sonars also didn't alert them to any changes.

"Are you sure, Beta Three?"

"I cannot confirm," he countered. "There was a reverberation."

"Isn't that normal?" Bast pointed to the lazy waves that made the ship wobble slightly. "Could it be a malfunction?"

The cogs under Beta Three's neck whirred loudly when he turned to Bast. Even though his expression showed nothing and he couldn't feel any emotions, Mera could swear he seemed offended.

"I do *not* malfunction."

Her *hart* raised his hands in surrender. "I apologize, but Azinor has a waterdragon, and an army of automatons. Any *reverberation* he caused would be caught easily, no?"

Beta Three's index finger rose, but he couldn't argue with that.

Ignoring them, Mera closed her eyes, trying to listen to the whispers inside of her. Perhaps, they could catch something or warn her of... the droplets in the air. They thrummed against her essence in an unnatural way. *Buzzing, restless.*

"It's a diversion," she muttered, just as a beastly belch cut the air.

Mera's blood chilled, not because the sound belonged to a waterdragon, but because it didn't come from the horizon and the sea before them.

It came from the mainland.

The unseen beast shrieked again, followed by a distant, loud gush that could only be a plasma burst.

"Menitute," the voices whispered.

Courage.

Bast stared in horror toward the mainland they couldn't see, his jaw clenched and his nostrils flared. *"Kura!"*

"Turn the ship!" the captain yelled from the bridge, and the engines ran at full speed, veering the nightbringer. "Prepare for battle!"

The crew hurried toward the four iron harpoons on deck.

"You can't aim at something we can't see!" the professor shouted at them.

Not to mention, they were too far away.

Closing her eyes, Mera centered herself. Her skin warmed as her siren's power stretched into in an endless web. It connected her to the droplets drifting in the air for miles and miles.

Her entire body shook by the giant effort, but in those seconds, Mera was the fog and the fog was Mera. Yet, she struggled to keep control.

"*Ternat,*" her voices whispered.

Free.

With one loud cry, she pushed the droplets away. Her magic exploded in a pulse that coursed through the web, swallowing Azinor's spell. The gray mist dissipated in an eyeblink to reveal the shore, and then a figure flying from the mainland toward the sea. When it vomited green plasma at the ground, an emerald hellfire consumed the suburbs of Tir Na Nog.

"*Fuchst ach,*" Bast muttered, watching the waterdragon approach the promenade.

Phasers shot at the creature from the ground, but it dodged the attacks, almost as if it was being guided by someone. Turning to a stunned human next to her, Mera grabbed a pair of binoculars he had hanging around his neck.

She adjusted the device to see a gray-skinned male with neon-green runes tattooed over his naked chest. He rode the waterdragon's thick neck with a wicked grin, bloodthirst and madness clear in his cruel face.

Some parts of the waterdragon's rotting body showed its insides, like the open gash on the beast's torso that revealed two poking ribs, but most of the creature was covered in smooth metallic plates similar to Beta Three's. One of its eyes had an emerald hue, while the other shone a neon-blue like an automaton. Lime-green tattoos had been engraved on the metal atop the beast's flesh, shining while they spread along its entire body.

They matched Azinor's.

A mix of magic and technology.

That waterdragon couldn't be Icefire; she was so certain, but her memory had to be playing tricks on her.

Bast's attention focused on the cloud of fae rising in the distance. They jumped in the air to face the creature—a sky battalion led by Corvus.

"Kitten, I have to go."

She nodded. "Be careful."

Bast was torn, she felt it in their bond. He didn't want to leave her, but when she assured him she would be fine—*a lie*—he shot toward the mainland.

Mera watched the beast in the distance. Something wasn't right, she could feel it in her bones.

Azinor's resources were at sea, so an attack from the mainland made no sense, and still, most nightbringers had already begun turning, heading toward the shore before understanding what the bigger picture might be.

"Detective," Beta three's monochromatic voice called out from the bow. He pointed at the horizon as she approached, and Mera lost a breath.

"Mer, are you seeing this?" Belinda's voice came from the bracelet around her wrist.

An army of screaming sirens in moss-green bodysuits ran on the ocean's surface. Hundreds of cars accompanied them, breaking through the water before plunging under the surface to strike.

A big explosion boomed from Mera's left, and heat slammed against her skin as the sound of torn metal shrieked loudly. A red plasma stream had swallowed half of the ship next to hers, quickly revealing a gash on its hull. The nightbringer split in two, sinking almost immediately while what remained of its crew jumped in the water.

"He must have cloaked the automatons with his magic," Beta Three muttered while his plates opened.

The blue screen showed thousands of machines walking on

the seabed or zinging forward, propelled by their engines. Their soulless eyes shone bright red, and when their mouths opened, red beams shot out, aiming at the surface—and at Belinda's convoy, as well as its accompanying automatons.

"For Atlantea!" Professor Currenter bellowed a war cry from the quarterdeck. Raising his phaser, he jumped ship, landing with a loud splash on the water's surface. Lunging forward, he drew from the sea, forming sharp icicles that swirled around him. All waterbreakers on deck followed suit, dodging the red bursts that broke through the surface.

"Let's show him what we're made of!" Belinda's shout came through Mera's wristband.

She was about to join her friends when another draconic shriek pierced the air, only this time, it didn't come from the mainland. Mera stilled, jaw dropping when her stare followed the line of water.

A second waterdragon zinged in the horizon; bigger, bulkier than the first, but equally dead. It had long spines atop its back, the skin on its wings tattered. Thin metallic patches covered the bigger holes that peppered its rotting corpse, and its emerald runes shone brightly. The creature grinned with sharp teeth, both eyes glinting a burning, neon-blue.

Icefire.

"Turn ship!" the captain ordered from behind, fear drenching his tone.

Too late.

Mera had to get to that beast, preferably before it belched waterblaze all over her friends. Pulling out her phaser, she turned to Beta Three. "Clear my path!"

"But—"

"Now!"

With a nod, he jumped overboard, and began shooting at approaching sirens from underwater.

As Icefire flew closer, Mera spotted a figure riding it. A female with russet hair and a ruby-red bodysuit.

Mother.

Jumping from the ship, Mera landed on the ocean's surface. "With pride," she muttered before rushing toward them.

CHAPTER 29

Bast didn't have time to wonder how Azinor had entered the mainland with a fucking waterdragon without being noticed, because he had to dodge a scorching plasma burst. The green substance—a mix of molten lava and gas—missed Bast, yet bulls-eyed a Summer Sidhe who'd been flying next to him.

The poor bastard didn't even scream. His flesh had already melted, and when the green storm faded, only his charred bones remained. They clanked against one another as they dropped to the ground.

Explosions boomed from the distance, coming from the waterline. One by one, the nightbringers guarding the shore blew up in red clouds. When Bast narrowed his eyes, he spotted a second beast zinging above the sea. It spewed green blaze at the remaining ships, enveloping the *akritanas* on the surface in a deadly stream.

"Mera!" he bellowed, ready to get back to her.

"*Broer*, wait! I need you here." Corvus shouted from above, then addressed a group of Sidhe behind him. "Divide!"

Half of the sky battalion rushed toward the sea, flying past

Bast. He thought he spotted Fallon leading them, but he couldn't be sure.

The waterdragon began to go after them, but Bast shot a gush of night and stars at the beast, calling its attention, and Azinor's. The *suket* glowered at him as his pet turned.

Halle, Bast's magic hadn't even made a dent on his shield. The creature zinged toward him, its wings flapping loudly.

Corvus was right. Bast had to stay. If he wanted to help Mera, he needed to defeat Azinor and his waterdragon there, on land.

His darkness rose around him, his hands fisting. He was ready.

A group of Autumn Sidhe on the left suddenly shot their magic at the beast, halting its advance before it got to Bast. Their orange and golden power slammed against the invisible shield, but failed to pierce it.

When a loud boom came from the distance, one of the things called *jets* zinged closer, firing mercilessly at the *suket* and his beast, giving the sky battalion a good advantage.

"Shield wall!" Someone yelled down below, a witch clad in black ops clothing, who led a battalion of twenty Evanorians near the stony breakwater.

The runes tattooed on their hands, arms, and faces glowed all colors of the rainbow, and then a magic shield that looked like a soap bubble enveloped most of the promenade.

Bast wondered why they'd done it, when he spotted automatons emerging from the water. They ventured through the beach slowly, each step heavy against the sand. Their eyes shone bright red, a stark contrast to the blue irises from the machines programmed by Beta Three.

The few automatons guarding the shore jumped down from the breakwater to battle their enemies. Beta Three's machines fought bravely, but Azinor had ten times as many, and some of them walked right past the metallic bodies that grappled with one another. They climbed up the stones to discharge red plasma at the shield.

The witches' magic took the blasts, protecting the soldiers inside it. It wouldn't hold forever, but it would buy them time.

The troops inside it fired at the automatons' heads, but new machines still bloomed from the water non-stop. At some point, the shield would crumble.

The jet kept firing phaser blasts at the waterdragon, along with the attacks from the sky battalion. Since they had things under control, Bast plummeted toward the beach, shooting spheres of darkness at the automatons. Yet as he neared the ground, his heart skipped a beat.

"Stella!" he roared.

His sister didn't hear him. From inside the shield, she prepared her healer's bag, then shoved a phaser in her belt's holster.

Fuchst ach!

Was she going into battle? Had she lost her *sarking* mind?

Bald sirens with gray skin began rising from the waves. They stepped onto the beach, watching the breakwater and the shield. Marching between the automaton army, they pulled out their phasers and began to shoot.

War cries erupted from below as wolves, humans, fae, and witches jumped through the safety of the shield, charging at their enemies without fear or hesitation.

Some were met with red beams, others with phaser blasts, and some with the macabre—witches and fae didn't need iron shields, but if a siren's magic was greater than theirs, they were in trouble.

Stella followed after them, brave fool that she was.

"No!" Bast bellowed.

Again and again, he shot blasts of darkness at the enemies who stood in her way. Yet, his sister kept running toward a wounded human, never looking back, never losing focus, and completely missing a large group of sirens with two automatons that rushed closer to her.

Halle!

Bast's darkness gushed from his palms, piling up into a raging cloud of night that burned the group beyond recognition. When his power retreated to his core, it revealed a crater on the sand filled with charred bones and metal.

The Tagradian soldiers down below cheered, and so did Stella, who smiled sweetly at him from the sand.

Some automatons whirred their heads toward Bast. Well, he'd certainly called their attention.

The machines' maws opened, ready to burn him to oblivion, but Bast winnowed just as the red streams engulfed the spot he was occupying. He blinked back high above, next to Corvus, who shot his magic at the waterdragon along with the rest of the sky battalion.

"It's looking good, *broer!*" the Night King shouted with an eager grin. The jet's relentless phaser blasts, aligned with the rushing bursts of magic muffled his voice, filling Bast's ears.

Perhaps too good.

Among the chaos down below, a bunch of sirens glanced to the sky. They locked eyes with Bast, and the flying Sidhe and witches trying to stop the beast.

"Raise your defenses!" he bellowed, but a witch in the battalion had already popped into a red cloud, macabred to death. So did the fae next to her, and the one right after.

"Keep attacking the fucking waterdragon!" Corvus' magic burst harder from his palms, but it didn't stop the beast from discharging green blaze at the jet, swallowing it whole.

A loud boom engulfed Bast's hearing, and hot air blasted against his body. He tumbled downward with Corvus, spiraling out of control. As he and his brother steadied themselves, they stared at the fiery, orange cloud that expanded through the air high above them.

The jet had been blown out of existence.

Sidhe and warlocks kept shooting their magic at the beast, but with one swipe of Azinor's arm, the waterdragon gushed a green cloud that ate through their magic shields as if they'd been made of air.

"Fuck!" Corvus shouted.

Explosions boomed from offshore, and Bast turned to the sea, anguish eating at his insides. He needed to make sure his *hart* was okay, but Mera was resilient, resourceful, and she didn't give up easily.

"We have to keep the *shig* distracted." Corvus tapped his shoulder, then pointed toward the ocean. "Poseidon can't join that fight. They won't stand a chance against two waterdragons."

He was right.

Bast's magic concentrated in his hands. He glared at the beast that now turned toward the promenade, uncaring about what remained of the sky battalion, which to its own credit, wasn't much.

When it vomited waterblaze at the far side of the beach, it engulfed not only Tagradian soldiers, but the *suket's* people as well. Azinor didn't care about his own; he only wanted the world to burn.

The witches' shields wavered, the magic shrieking like a dying animal. It wouldn't withstand another attack. Not only that, but the waterdragon now approached the section of the beach where Stella healed wounded soldiers.

Summoning all of his power, Bast shot a scorching storm of night and stars at the monster. It had to be enough to break Azinor's shield; the bastard simply couldn't be *that* powerful.

Gritting his teeth, he kept pushing his magic forward, engulfing the beast and Azinor in pure, raging darkness. Red beams shot from the ground, but Corvus blocked the attacks with a large magic shield, covering Bast's flank.

"Keep at it!" his brother bellowed, flinging magic blasts at the sirens who tried to macabre them from the ground, and at the automatons firing red streams in their direction.

Bast tried, but when his energy started to fade, he had to pull back. Panting, he watched as his cloud of night retreated to his core, revealing an unscathed Azinor and his pet.

"Fuck!" Bast mumbled to himself, breathing heavily. His wings flapped lazily behind him, and he could barely keep himself adrift.

The creature boosted toward them with its jaw wide open, and Corvus pulled at his arm, trying to drag him out of its path. "We have to go!"

Bast pulled at all the magic he had left. Raw power thrummed in his core, and a new storm of night and stars brewed inside him, eager to be set free.

He'd had enough. Let the *malachai* come.

"Go, Corvus!" He jerked his arm free, pushing his brother away. "Now!"

"You can't take on that thing alone!"

Maybe, but he had to try.

Azinor was so close that Bast could see the evil smirk cutting across his cruel face. Instead of staying on track, however, the *shig* turned slightly to the left, toward... Corvus glared at Bast before a green, scorching waterfall engulfed him. The burning stream sent Bast spinning, the heat singing his skin.

The waterdragon pierced through the emerald cloud as if to check if his brother was really gone, then swept up in a loop to gain momentum.

Nothing remained of Corvus.

"Brother?" Bast mumbled, a void eating him from the inside out.

The creature shrieked again, calling his attention. From high above, it plunged toward him, ready to rip Bast in two.

Nightblood bubbled in his veins, taking over his thoughts.

Anger and sorrow filled him with a maddening, bloodthirsty rage. Bast couldn't think, couldn't speak. There was no war anymore, no one and nothing else but him, Azinor, and the need to rip the *shig*'s head off his body.

His power thrummed under his skin, his breaths ringing loudly in his ears, and he clenched his teeth so hard that a jolt of pain went up his skull.

He would avenge Corvus today or he would die trying. Bast's magic wrapped around him in a midnight-black blaze. With a howl filled with anguish and wrath, he boosted toward the beast.

Suddenly, a portal of night and stars opened next to him, and out zinged Corvus, flying side by side with Bast. His brother winked playfully at him as darkness concentrated on his hands. He didn't have a single scratch on him.

"Miss me?"

Relief washed over Bast, and tears stung his eyes, but he didn't have the luxury of shedding them.

Azinor watched them coming, a hint of something like fear in his eyes, before lightning birthed everywhere around him, making his green eyes turn a bright blue. The magic crackled loudly around the waterdragon; a storm of thunder ready to ram into them.

"It's an honor to die by your side, *broer*," Corvus vowed.

"We'll get through this." Bast increased the pace, though deep down, he knew his brother might be right.

They had almost reached the *shig*, when a red blast came from the beach and slammed against Corvus.

The Night King toppled over, plummeting toward the ground like a dead bird.

Bast plunged in a curve to catch him, forgetting all about the waterdragon. "Brother!"

Azinor followed them. His pet's mouth opened wide and too

close to Bast's feet, but he had to grab Corvus before his body hit the ground.

A green glow shone from behind, and the heat of plasma licked Bast's legs.

Almost there...

The second he grabbed Corvus, he turned around to stare at a blinding green light. It washed over him, mingling with the beast's rotting breath. Sharp teeth loomed above and below him, the heat of its breath vaporizing the sweat on Bast's skin.

If the creature snapped its jaw, he and his brother would be history.

Too late to winnow. Too late to run.

Forgive me, kitten.

CHAPTER 30

MERA RUSHED through the chaos on the ocean's surface. Water splashed everywhere as she dodged battling bodies and phaser blasts. When a roar came from above, green plasma rained upon her and the nightbringer right next to her.

Just as the plasma hit the surface, she dove underwater, waterbreaking to a safe depth. A loud boom came overhead, and the ship's upper deck exploded in a fiery storm. The blast pulsed through the water, pushing her back, but Mera kept her stance. The vessel's metallic shriek howled across the sea, rumbling deep in her bones.

What remained of the nightbringer plunged toward the battle taking place on the ocean bed. The crew's charred bodies plummeted along—wolf, witch, human, it didn't matter. The iron plates around their torsos made their corpses sink faster.

Below, Atlantean cars and automatons fired at their enemies. Sirens wearing black bodysuits clashed violently against Azinor's forces, waterbreaking for their lives. For Atlantea.

For Mera.

Taken by a need to join the battle, she began swimming down, but she couldn't lose sight of her goal, couldn't join her people. Not yet. With a displeased grunt, she boosted back to the surface and kept running. When she looked at the sky, she found Icefire dodging a blue blast that had come from an automaton on her far left. Beta Three's head peeked above water, and he waved at her.

The beast shrieked as it made a loop in the air, quickly plunging toward him. Facing Icefire, Beta Three spewed blue streams once again, but thanks to Ariella's steering, the waterdragon dodged every blast.

Swerving, Mera rushed toward Beta Three, but she wouldn't reach him in time. "Dive!" she yelled.

He couldn't hear her.

Crap!

The Marauder's dark wooden frame suddenly cut through her path. Captain Flint winked at her from the upper deck, then turned to his crew. "Harpoons, fire!"

The bulky wooden weapons fired at the waterdragon, piercing its side. The beast shrieked and swiveled, missing Beta Three by an inch as it plunged into the ocean with a mighty splash.

Her metallic wristband chimed, and Belinda's voice came from the other side. "Mer..." Her tone was weakened.

Injured.

"Where are you, Bel?"

"South from the Marauder."

Heart breaking, Mera gave Flint one last glance, then rushed forward, trying to find her friend before it was too late.

She searched through the battling bodies on the surface, carving a path that snaked between the scattered ships that still remained. Soon, her frantic gaze found Belinda near a sinking nightbringer, cornered by a group of sirens wearing moss-green bodysuits.

Her friend had a bruise on the left side of her face and one purple eye, her hair a scrambled mess. A deep cut extended over her right thigh, bleeding a vivid crimson. Belinda had lost her weapons, but still stared defiantly at the group closing in on her, even if she couldn't take them all.

Mera gripped her phaser tighter, her feet skating on the ocean's surface. Aiming at one lackey's head, she pulled the trigger and quickly vaporized his skull. She then summoned an ice spear that pierced the chest of another siren, leaving only two.

Taking advantage of their shock, Belinda launched herself at the closest enemy and snapped his neck. Just as the remaining siren was about to shoot her, Mera nailed a phaser blast to his head.

"Just in time." Belinda smiled through the specks of enemy blood that peppered her face, but winced in pain when she tried to step forward. Nodding to the battle raging everywhere around them, she clicked her tongue. "We'll die today, won't we?"

She couldn't tell her friend that she would give her life to stop Azinor. That while Mera wouldn't live to see another day, she would ensure Belinda and her friends did. "You'll be fine, Bel."

The water beneath their feet warmed up, sizzling, and Mera yanked Belinda out of the way just as a red beam broke through the surface, coming from an automaton under them.

The beam suddenly stopped with a loud boom that reverberated against the soles of Mera's feet. A moment passed, until Beta Three's head popped up from the water again, and he saluted them both.

Mera searched for the Marauder, but just as she found it, Icefire broke through the sea's surface. The beast flew so high and fast that it dragged the ship along, nearly lifting it from the water.

"Jump," Mera gasped, willing the crew to save themselves.

Flint's golden lightning whipped and crackled against the

shield Ariella had around the beast, but failed to pierce it. Icefire's chest puffed, and within a second, it spit a plasma stream that engulfed the Marauder in an emerald hell.

"No!" Mera yelled, hoping Flint and Mr. Snipes had enough power to survive the attack.

She watched the ship burn and begin to sink, a knot tying in her stomach. As the battle raged on the surface and under the sea, Mera realized Azinor had won, and worst of all, he wasn't there; hadn't even given her the chance to face him.

Battle cries suddenly rang from the sky, and a cloud of Sidhe and witches plummeted toward the surface, snatching bald sirens with moss-green bodysuits like seagulls ready to feast.

Some killed their enemies with clouds of deadly magic, others gave in to the advancements of technology and shot them instead—not a small feat when it came to faeries. The lackeys' bodies splashed violently on the surface.

The sky battalion also snatched survivors from the ship-wrecks—witches, wingless fae, wolves, and humans—and took them to land.

Handing Belinda one of her phaser guns, Mera quickly pulled out the second. "Stay low."

"Can't do much while that thing is still flying." She nodded to Icefire. It had just spit a green cloud at a couple of flying warlocks, burning them to a crisp.

Swimming closer, Beta Three propelled himself up to his waist. "Poseidon's automatons will reach land soon. I'm afraid I must leave you."

With Mera's nod, he sank back into the endless blue.

Above them, Icefire shrieked, then enveloped yet another nightbringer in green blaze. As it did, Ariella macabred a Sidhe on her right, leaving a red nimbus in the fae's place.

Fuming, Mera bit her own teeth. "I have to get on that waterdragon."

"You will." Belinda waved to a group of soldiers nearby. "Blizzard, cover the queen. Make me proud, Officer!"

Nodding, the male held his phaser high. His companions did the same, belting a war cry in unison, "For Atlantea!"

"Take cover, Bel," Mera ordered more than said. "You're in no condition to fight."

With a wink, she smiled.

Exchanging one last glance with her friend, Mera ran toward the waterdragon, her feet splashing on the ocean's surface. Blizzard and his officers followed.

A line of water rose to her hands while she looked up, her focus locked on Icefire. The line began solidifying into malleable ice—meltwater, at the tip of her fingers.

When she turned back to Blizzard, the officer caught her cue.

"Fire!" he ordered, and blue comets rushed up, aimed at the beast. Most of them missed the creature, but two slammed against its side.

Icefire dove toward them with a shriek, waterblaze burning at the back of its throat.

"Dive!" Mera ordered.

They plummeted just as the plasma heat blasted along the surface, but the waterdragon plunged right behind them. It sunk its teeth into Blizzard, chewing him in half.

Cursing under her breath, Mera turned in a circle and gained momentum, waterbreaking after the beast, who now followed another officer. The creature prepared to vomit melting plasma on him, but Mera whipped her meltwater rope, tying it around Icefire's ankle.

Glaring at her, the beast seemed to forget all about the officer. So did Ariella. The bitch pushed Icefire forward, cutting into the deep so fast, Mera had to waterbreak a shield to avoid falling behind.

The waterdragon swiveled, looping around as it tried to

break free, but she wouldn't let go. Gathering her magic, she pulled at the whip until she landed on Icefire's back. Water rushed past the shield that helped keep her in place.

"Let go, Mother!" Mera aimed her phaser at the bitch's head.

Ariella glanced back at her from Icefire's neck. "The water-dragon obeys my magic only. If you shoot me, it will attack everything and everyone in its path."

"Then we have a problem, don't we?"

"Not really." Standing, Ariella walked atop the beast's spine, approaching Mera. The strong currents that slammed against them passed right around their shields.

Mera gripped her weapon harder. "Stop where you are!"

"I won't fight you, child." Lifting her hands as if in surrender, Ariella whispered things Mera couldn't understand; ancient words that matched the whispers in her head.

"What—?"

Ariella tapped her own temple. "The language of souls, Daughter. Understanding them has always been within your grasp, but first, you must learn to listen." She thumped her feet twice on the waterdragon's hide, and the creature slowed down, gliding seamlessly through the sea.

"What did you do?" Mera asked, maintaining her aim.

"I gave you the reins."

"And how am I supposed to ride this thing?"

"Listen."

Before she could ask what the hell that meant, Ariella jumped off the beast, diving toward the ocean's depths.

"Damn it!" Mera didn't have time to go after her. She had much bigger fish to fry.

Carefully, she pulled herself toward Icefire's neck. The last time she'd mounted it, the waterdragon had been alive.

"I'm sorry it came to this," she mumbled, patting its moon-silver skin.

She closed her legs around the beast's neck and grasped two

spikes at the base of its head. Leaning her body to the left, she tugged the spikes in the same direction, but Icefire didn't obey.

"Come on!"

Technically, that should have worked. Then again, Mera didn't have a lot of experience riding a freaking waterdragon.

As if on cue, whispers echoed in her ears, and when she glanced at her own hands, those strange, black runes had already rose to the surface, dancing on her skin.

"Hertenah," the voices urged.

Control.

Yeah, no shit.

Mera tightened her grasp on the waterdragon's spikes, finding a certain stillness inside herself. Energy sizzled in her veins, jolting to her palms before swimming down the creature's skin and reaching its core.

The whispers kept repeating, *control, control,* and her tattoos glowed a bright blue. So did Icefire's runes. Their neon-green shifted to the same sapphire hue of her power, connecting them.

Suddenly, Mera saw the ocean through Icefire's eyes. When she opened her mouth, so did the beast. She thought about turning right, and to her surprise, the waterdragon did it.

Becoming one with the beast was a hollow sensation, like being trapped inside a giant, empty cavern. Maybe it was because the creature was dead; maybe because its body didn't belong to Mera. It didn't really matter.

Waterblaze tickled her ribcage, and currents drifted past her spine, gushing through the open spots in her ribs.

Well, Icefire's ribs.

A wicked grin cut through her lips when she ordered it to turn around and fire waterblaze upon the lackeys fighting her people near the sea bed. The pricks glared at her with a mix of shock and hatred before the scorching blaze engulfed them. And then, they were gone.

Atlanteans cheered as she zinged across the currents,

charging at their enemies without mercy. One, two, three gushes, and her soldiers already had an advantage. But if she were to end this war, there was only one enemy she had to face.

Turning the waterdragon in an upwards loop, she stared at the surface. Icefire broke through it with a mighty splash, zinging high into the sky.

As they approached the mainland, Mera spotted Bast, Corvus, and what remained of the sky battalion attacking Azinor and his beast.

"Hold!" A Sidhe with red hair yelled from her right, stopping a group that was scouting Mera's flank, ready to attack.

The Sidhe was none other than Fallon Asherath, Bast's captain, who gaped at her in shock when he realized she wasn't Ariella. Nodding, he ordered his soldiers to stand down.

Icefire charged faster toward the mainland. Wind gusted furiously around her while the beast flapped its wings non-stop, cutting through the air itself.

As they flew closer, Mera watched a gruesome battle below. She spotted Beta Three spewing blue blaze out of his mouth, taking out three automatons at once with his attack. His form mingled into the flurry of grappling bodies and machines fighting at the promenade.

When she opened her mouth, waterblaze burst from Icefire's maw, annihilating hundreds of evil automatons, and giving the witches, fae, and wolves below the upper hand.

Ahead, Corvus and Bast flew head on toward Azinor's waterdragon.

Had they lost their minds?

A red stream from the ground suddenly hit Corvus, and Bast dove through the air to catch him. Despair pooled in Mera's core as she watched the creature chase after them. It opened its mouth, ready to chew her *hart* apart.

With a scream, she willed Icefire to go faster. It rammed into

Azinor's pet just in time, pushing it away before it could snap its jaws closed.

They fell down in a deadly spiral, but the look of shock in the prick's eyes had been worth it.

"Mera!" Bast screamed from above, but she couldn't look back; couldn't hesitate.

Icefire clawed at its kin without mercy, locking their bodies in a free-fall. She willed the beast to push its enemy away from the shore; away from everyone she loved.

Their wings flapped furiously, both waterdragons locked together as they rushed past the battles at the beach and the ocean. They jerked from side to side violently, and Mera nearly lost her grip.

Almost out of range...

With a loud shriek, Azinor's pet bit Icefire's neck, and Mera dodged a sharp tooth that nearly pierced her calf. As clotted blood gushed from her waterdragon's neck, she wondered if that was it for Icefire, but her beast didn't falter. It grabbed the other creature's chest plate and ripped it off its flesh, revealing rotting organs underneath it.

Looking down to the ocean's surface, she tried to keep the waterdragons on a parallel trajectory. If they hit the water at that speed, she would break every bone in her body.

"Hash, fash," the voices whispered.

Claw, bite.

Icefire followed the commands before Mera realized what they'd meant. Her waterdragon sunk its jaw into the other's neck, ripping out a huge chunk of flesh. Gurgling blood, Azinor's beast let out a horrid shriek while they spiraled farther over the ocean.

"Let go!" he bellowed.

"Fimna," the voices urged.

End it.

Clawing at one of the waterdragon's wings, Icefire ripped it to shreds. Mera held on to her beast as they plunged harder, faster, fighting the centrifugal force that pulled her away.

Azinor glared at his maimed beast, his eyes filled with fury. "You forget one thing, Daughter!"

Raising his hand, he snapped his fingers, and the tattoos on both creatures stopped glowing, as did the runes on Mera's skin. The waterdragons' eyes went blank and their bodies limp.

Staring at the approaching sea, Mera uttered a curse under her breath. She jumped from Icefire just in time, moving her hands frantically to break water, trying to ease her fall.

The beasts crashed violently against the surface, shattering bones and splattering old, clotting blood everywhere. Their bodies, or what remained of them, began sinking all too quickly.

Thankfully, the thick column of water she'd summoned swallowed her, slowing her descent. Plunging into the cylinder, she quickly came out on the top of the ocean.

Mera stabilized herself on the shock waves of the crash, while the cylinder melted behind her. Salty wind blew gently everywhere, and for a moment, the sea became so very quiet.

Azinor stood ahead with a bloodthirsty grin, his fists closed. The magic enhancer hung from a chain around his neck.

Her hand went to the holster attached to her belt, but she'd lost her phaser during the battle. She only had her fists and her magic.

So be it.

"It ends here," she shouted.

"For you, it just might." A siren's shriek burst from his throat, breaking the air toward Mera.

A shriek of her own tore through her vocal cords, and their voices clashed in a loud boom that tossed both of them in opposite directions.

Hitting the water like a skipping stone, Mera quickly forced herself to come to a halt. She watched the asshole far ahead, who also recovered from the blast.

No time to waste.

Rushing toward him, she bellowed a war cry while summoning hundreds of ice spears that followed her. Mera flung them at the dickface, but Azinor turned each and every one into powdery snow.

She'd almost reached him when an icy blade grew from his hand. *A sword.*

Two could play that game.

An ice blade bloomed from her palm too, just as she jumped toward him, and their weapons clashed violently. With each strike, the ice swords shattered then regenerated. Seeing an opening in his defense, Mera snatched the enhancer and ripped it off his neck.

Power rushed inside her for a moment too quick to count, until the asshole sucker-punched her so hard that she rolled away. As she crashed over the water, the enhancer escaped her grasp.

"No!"

It plopped downward, and though she tried to waterbreak it back, Azinor blocked her magic, replacing it with his own. The enhancer began rising toward the surface—toward *him.*

Heat coursed under her skin, the air around her crackling. Mera's power slammed against his, obstructing his magic. She couldn't keep the enhancer safe from Azinor, not during their fight. Teeth gritting, she pushed it to the bottom of the sea.

Azinor cursed under his breath. "You're quite a nuisance."

The enhancer soon plunged into the depths of the ocean, escaping both her radar and the prick's. Sweat bloomed on her forehead, but she kept a fierce grip on her power, blocking his.

"Now that you're out of advantages..." Boosting toward him, Mera nailed a perfect punch to his face.

He tumbled back. Wiping the black blood that trickled down the edge of his mouth, he grinned like a tiger about to feast.

"Oh, child. You thought I needed the enhancer to defeat you?"

Before she could react, he punched Mera in the ribs, then grabbed her wrist and twisted it behind her spine, trapping her back to his chest.

Fuck, he was fast.

"Enough playing." His free hand wrapped around her neck and squeezed. As she grappled for air, the asshole leaned into her ear. "Welcome to your end, Daughter. Rejoice."

CHAPTER 31

AZINOR'S PALM squeezed Mera's neck, depriving her of air. "Give me your magic, child. Give it willingly, and I will ease your suffering. Fight me, and you'll regret it."

She held down a yelp from the pain stabbing her twisted arm, but it came out as an indignant whimper.

"Fuck... you," she croaked, trying to breathe as much as she could through a squeezed windpipe.

Mera pushed her magic, and it burned through her veins, splitting into thin rivulets that cracked the air. They spread around them like billions of shiny blue veins, a flower of power blooming to life.

Laughter reverberated in Azinor's chest. Her attempt at fighting back clearly amused him. "Wrong choice."

Sapphire lightning bloomed from the bastard's frame. His bolts crackled, then plunged into her, burning and hissing through her flesh. Mera bit back cries when the lightning dashed into her essence, soon connecting to the power in her core.

Azinor's magic began swallowing hers, growing stronger. "You defy me, again and again, like a puny bug who won't give up." His stinking breath fanned against her cheek, and his palm closed tighter around her throat. "I am eternal. I am invincible. Your fickle attempts bore me, Daughter."

His magic crackled louder, expanding into a thunderstorm ready to swallow her. Millions of shiny bolts split the air, and their heat prickled her skin before they plunged deeper into her core.

Mera's entire body clenched, her flesh and muscles feeling as heavy as iron. Exhaustion pressed down on her, and her legs wobbled, but she forced herself to stay standing. She wouldn't give the dickface the pleasure of seeing her fall.

"*Er et tu sa! Er et tu sa!*" her whispers urged, but Mera couldn't understand what they said.

A sharp pain coursed through her bones as she tried to change the flow of magic. Energy, raw and pure, filled every pore in her body, charging Mera to the brim, expanding beyond herself and into his lightning.

"Foolish girl!" he barked, squeezing her neck harder.

His magic blocked hers too easily, but Mera wouldn't give up, even when her vision began to tunnel and the little air she had left escaped her lungs. With her last strength, she summoned ice daggers that burst from the water behind them, aiming at the asshole's back.

He didn't turn, but right before the daggers reached him, they popped into oblivion thanks to his waterbreaking. One by one they disintegrated, but the attack had been enough to distract him. As his grip on her arm and neck loosened, Mera elbowed his stomach, prying herself free.

She dashed atop the ocean's surface, then made a U-turn to face the asshole. Panting, she steadied her thoughts, ignoring the despair that curled up inside her.

Defeating him would be impossible.

Nevertheless, she would try.

When the last of her daggers snowed upon him, Azinor

cocked his head left, watching her. "Get back here, child. You will regret it if you don't."

"You can't subdue me like you did Ariella, *Father*."

Opening her mouth, Mera shrieked from the top of her lungs. Soundwaves broke through the air, rolling toward him. The creep barely had time to shriek back. His voice clashed against hers at the last minute, two unseen, deafening forces grappling with each other.

Mera kept shrieking as she pushed herself forward, her steps making ripples atop the ocean's surface. Yet, she couldn't scream for much longer; already she was running out of breath.

The moment her lungs gave in, she sank underwater, escaping the blast of Azinor's shriek. Mera couldn't falter, couldn't hesitate, so she sent a rush of frozen water toward him, trapping him in a giant icicle that broke through the surface like an iceberg.

She propelled herself back up, jumping from the water like a flying fish. Taking deep breaths, she steadied her footing atop the lazy waves.

Azinor glared at her from the glazed ice as if she was a fly he couldn't swat away, not a real threat.

Never a threat.

"*Er et tu sa! Er et tu sa!*" the voices insisted, louder this time.

"*You wish to kill your father?*" Ariella's voice echoed in her memory. "*Accept your Regneerik.*"

And just like that, she understood what the voices were saying.

Let go.

Let go of herself, of everything, and everyone.

Cracks spread atop Azinor's frigid prison until he broke through with an explosive bang. A million pieces of ice rained down on him, plopping on the water.

Breathing heavily, he pointed at her, hate beaming from his

clear blue irises, which matched the color of the lightning that whipped around him. "This is the end, child!"

A certain calm washed over her. "It is."

Lightning spread from Mera's back, growing around her in a sapphire flower of magic. It was as if a door inside her had opened, a door she could never close.

The runes on her skin glowed again, her magic tuning into Azinor's. His power sung in her ears, and it followed Mera's voices until their energy reverberated in unison.

"What?" he barked, stepping back, but it was in vain.

He couldn't run.

Her bolts shot at him, plunging into his thorax. The prick shrieked, and his back arched as her magic lifted him from the water.

Clenching her jaw, Mera strained to keep control. His power flooded her, mingling with her own. Her blood boiled, her flesh roasting from the inside out, but she didn't stop.

With a cry, her lightning pierced deeper into his essence, and though his magic thrashed and snapped at hers, Mera engulfed it as easily as a thought.

His screams intensified the more she syphoned his energy, taking from Azinor all that made him what he was. The tattoos on his body began ripping from his skin, flowing through the lightning, and leaving behind scarred patches. They rushed into Mera's core, becoming one with her.

"Kitten!" Bast's voice rang from above, his figure a speck in the distance as he zinged toward them. "Stop!"

Not yet.

Gritting her teeth, she let go a little more. Power, raw and unending, flowed through her; a force larger than life, larger than herself. Whether it belonged to Azinor or not, she couldn't tell—the lines between their magic blurred with each passing second.

A rivulet of all that power dove into the ocean beneath her

feet, and a giant dome of water swelled around them, turning to ice in a flash. The water under her feet solidified, too.

Thumps came from the thick ice ceiling seconds after, and Mera spotted Bast's shadow on the other side. His fists and shoulder slammed against the dome. Her power blocked his winnowing, preventing him from coming inside.

"Mera!" His shouts sounded muffled. "Let me in!"

Suddenly, a storm of night and stars swallowed the structure, drenching the dome in rumbling darkness. If not for the sizzling blue glow of Mera's lightning, she wouldn't have been able to see a thing.

Bast could try as much as he wanted. She wasn't using only her power; she was using Azinor's too, and he couldn't fight against them both.

"*Kitten!*" his voice echoed in her mind, the cold sting of his desperation piercing his tone. "*Take from me!*"

If she did, who could say when she would stop? How much would be enough? The faces of the lackeys she'd killed by accident flashed in her mind. After what had happened at the isles, Mera wouldn't let Bast fuel her; couldn't risk it.

Especially now.

Closing her eyes, she smiled. In her mind, she stamped a ghost kiss on his lips. "*Thanks for everything, partner.*"

"*No!*" he bellowed, his attacks growing stronger. "*Mera! Don't!*"

She closed her side of the link.

Azinor's screams died in his throat while he thrashed against her lightning. His once bulky and strong body deflated, as if she wasn't taking only his magic, but every ounce of strength he had.

She was almost done—there were only a few glowing runes left on his skin. Dark circles spread under the asshole's eyes, onyx veins crawling up his neck.

Their power scorched her from the inside out, eating her up

bit by bit. Mera's time neared, she could feel it the way one felt coming rain on a cold autumn morning.

"Take everything from me, if you wish." Azinor hissed in pain as her lightning lowered him to the icy floor. His legs shook, struggling to keep him standing while Mera swallowed what little was left of his power. "When you're done, I'll still be here. I shall remain, and you will be dead."

Mera gave him a fierce grin as patches of her skin burned. Their combined power sizzled in her veins, its weight crushing her. Her flesh and bones slowly began turning into dust.

"You'll be mortal when I'm done." Trembling, she glanced at the roaring storm of night and stars that tried to break through the dome. "You will survive, but you won't survive *him.*"

The asshole glared at Bast's darkness rumbling outside the dome. Loud thunders of night lashed against the ice, thunders that echoed Bast's screams. His magic channeled his pain, his fury, and turned them into sound, building a gut-wrenching melody to her final moments.

A painful yelp escaped Mera's lips as she fell to one knee, hitting the cold, harsh floor. Her body was giving up.

"More," her whispers demanded, so more she would take, until every bit of her turned into dust.

Snarling, she fueled up on the creep's energy. Soon, she would reach the peak of her doom, her own Regneerik. As long as those she loved were safe...

Mera smiled through the pain.

The icy floor ahead suddenly cracked. She lost a breath, panic rising inside her as the crack opened into a hole. She stared in disbelief as Mother pulled herself into the dome, the magic enhancer in the palm of her hand.

"No," Mera croaked, despair taking over.

She couldn't syphon Azinor's power, stop Bast, and fight Ariella at the same time, especially since the bitch had the enhancer. If Mother helped the asshole, then all would have been for nothing.

Kneeling on the icy floor, Mera begged, her voice weak and barely there. "Please... don't."

Up ahead, Azinor laughed loudly, his joy overcoming the pain her magic was inflicting, because he knew. He knew he'd won. "A pointless end to your pointless life, child!"

Paying him no mind, Ariella stepped between them, facing Mera. Her expression had always been full of hate and anger, but this time, Mera swore Mother looked at her with... kindness?

"Don't stop," Ariella whispered with a smile, then lifted her closed fist, the enhancer tucked safely in her palm.

A green aura of magic flowed around her, like a flame igniting around a torch, but the color quickly changed to sapphire. Her eyes began to glow bright blue as she took the power flowing between Mera and Azinor, acting as a buffer.

Shock coursed through Mera. She couldn't believe or particularly understand what was happening.

The former queen's scrawny figure thrashed as Mera continued syphoning Azinor's magic, yet it was Ariella's body that took most of the blow. The heat threatening to eat Mera from inside out slowly vanished—Mother was taking it away.

Ariella winced in pain, her lips pressed in a line, but she never screamed.

"What are you doing?" Mera mumbled.

"Wench!" Azinor barked from the distance, unable to move. He couldn't get to her because Mera's lightning kept plunging into him, sucking the last of his runes. "Free me! Now!"

Ariella kept her back turned to him as her rotting skin started puffing into ashes that went up in the air. It was too much power for her. Too much for anyone, even with an enhancer.

"Be happy, child." A smile cut through her lips while chunks of her thighs and arms turned into dust, flowing with the energy that gushed around her. "I am free of him... I am proud of you. And I am sorry."

When the last rune left Azinor's flesh, Ariella's strong demeanor crumbled, and she screamed in pain. Lumps of her quickly disintegrated into dust, their rivulets curling in the air. Her screams died midway, in a throat that didn't exist anymore, and just like that, she was gone.

The magic enhancer fell on the ice with a thick clank, spinning towards Mera. The emerald encrusted in its middle had cracked.

She glared at the ashes that danced in the air, ashes that had once been the queen. The pile-up of magic which took over Mera started to dwindle.

Azinor watched in shock from the opposite side, crumbling to his knees on the icy floor. Once muscular and strong, his flesh now stuck to his bones. The mighty Poseidon resembled a living skeleton.

He stared at the spot Mother had occupied not a moment ago, his eyes glistening. "You stupid wench..."

Bast's night and stars retreated from above, letting in sunlight. With one loud kaboom, he broke through the dome's ceiling, landing right next to Mera. No surprise really, since the magic was ebbing away, dispersing in the air.

Free.

Kneeling at her side, her *hart* cradled Mera in his arms, his fingers digging into her skin. "Kitten!"

She held him back, feeling his body shake against her own.

Ahead, Azinor pushed himself up on trembling legs, then summoned an ice sword from the floor with what remained of his magic. "You will pay."

Mera blinked, drowsy, exhausted. She couldn't fight, couldn't even stand.

Cupping her cheeks, Bast kissed her forehead. "Rest, min *hart.*"

He turned to the prick, and his eyes became pitch-black. With a snarl, his fangs sharpened, and when he glanced back at Mera, she understood the silent plea in his stare.

Let him finish it...

Rushing toward them, Azinor raised his ice sword, an angry howl filled with sorrow bursting from his throat. Before Bast could fight him, Mera summoned the little magic she had left and slammed both hands on the frigid floor.

Her waterbreaking zinged through the ice, until a giant stalagmite broke through the surface, crashing right into Azinor's chest. Its slanted, ragged point impaled his skeletal frame as it grew, lifting him into the air. His feet dangled above the ground, and his ice sword crashed onto the frozen floor, shattering into a million pieces.

Azinor's cold blue eyes filled with shock and rage while he spat black blood. "You pitiful... damned..." he croaked, unable to finish the sentence.

Life vanished from his eyes, and his body fell limp. Just like Ariella, he was gone from one moment to the next.

A storm of night and stars immediately burst from Bast's palm, engulfing the prick. In an eye blink, her *hart's* power retreated into his core, leaving only a pile of wet ashes in Azinor's place. They floated atop the puddle of meltwater that had been a stalagmite only a moment ago.

Mera turned to the spot Ariella had occupied. She couldn't understand why the former queen had sacrificed herself for her. Ariella didn't know love; wasn't particularly fond of it.

Bast hugged Mera closer, pressing his face against the curve of her neck. "It's over. You're safe."

A sob threatened to push through her lips as she kept staring at Ariella's final stand. Her fingers clawed at Bast's back, her breathing rushed.

She fought against the sorrow creeping up her chest, against the irrational pain chewing at her soul, but Mera was weak and tired, and she couldn't fight any longer.

A heart wrenching sob escaped her, and she finally let go, doing the impossible.

Mera mourned her tormenter. Her villain. Her savior...

Her mother.

CHAPTER 32

5 YEARS LATER...

MERA WATCHED her uncle through the screen in Beta Three's chest. Once blue, the display now supported every color, building a crisp image of the palace, and the king.

Behind him, waterbreakers rushed around as they prepared the main hall for the festivities.

Every year, Atlantea celebrated the coming of the new tide, when warmer currents from the gulf graced the city for a whole cycle. Something akin to Evanora's solstice festivities, and just like the witch's celebration, it tended to last weeks on end.

From the other side, Uncle Barrimond shook a metallic finger at her. "You're working too much, Councilor."

"I'm fine." She smiled. "The crown never rests."

"Yes, but—"

"I'm your representative in Tagrad, am I not? That means you trust me, so believe me when I say I can fulfill my duties perfectly well. If that wasn't the case, you would be the first to know."

"Stubborn child," he grumbled. "I simply don't want you to exert yourself. Harold and I *will* take the express train to Aquatia to ensure you're getting proper rest, understand?"

"Oh, don't tell that to Captain Flint or Mr. Snipes."

"What is it they say? *'There is no flair or elegance in taking a train'.*" He shrugged. "Still, it *is* faster than the Marauder 2.0."

"The Professor loves Flint's moonshine, though."

"I know." A weary sigh escaped him. "It's a lost battle more often than not."

"How is he, by the way?"

When Azinor died, Professor Currenter began aging normally, as he should have centuries ago. Thankfully, his body didn't catch up at once, which meant he still had decades ahead of him, yet eventually, he would be gone, like every other living being in the world.

"Harold is busy, but fine. He can't wait to see you, Bast, and Leon for the festivities next week." He clapped his metallic palms, the clang coming clearly through Beta Three's speakers —wherever they were placed.

After the war, Mera returned to Atlantea to discover that Ariella had saved her own brother, which was yet another act so unlike her. Uncle Barrimond never shared what he discussed with his sister at that time. All he told Mera was that in the end, Ariella understood, though he didn't bother to explain any further.

Not long after they reunited with the king, Beta Three found a solution to Uncle Barrimond's missing arms. He snatched the limbs from an inactive automaton left from the war, and with the help of Stella, they performed the first robotic implant in Tagradian history. The king even came to prefer his metallic limbs, saying they gave him a fierce aura, which to his own credit, wasn't entirely wrong. His arms looked pretty badass.

"Well, we'll certainly be attending, but we might not be able to stay for the full week." Mera clicked her tongue. "Things have been busy in Aquatia, and with the due date coming up..."

"Of course! That's not an issue, my dear. We don't want you straining yourself."

"All right, then. I'll keep you updated." With a wave she hung up, and the plates on Beta Three's chest closed.

Once the war ended, Mera was happy to return the title of ruler of Atlantea to her uncle, but that didn't mean her duties as princess vanished. The king insisted she become councilor of Aquatia, the new siren's borough in Tagrad. Mera had snuck out of ruling duty, but she couldn't escape it twice. Besides, she couldn't oppose, not when her uncle needed her.

"Consider it your training," he'd suggested. *"For the future."*

Thanks to her *training*, she hadn't worn a badge in over two years. She missed detective work every now and then—being a politician could be frustrating at times, especially when she had to argue with Mia Hammond, that thick-headed witch—but Mera had a duty to her people, and she wouldn't let them down, nor her uncle.

Besides, acting as a link between land and sea had its perks. During the rebuild, she guided the waterbreaker integration process in Tagrad. It was on-going work, but it had been a smooth transition so far. Just the other week, she'd sent a couple of new siren recruits to work with Julian back in Clifftown.

"Detective Tiderider won't be happy about her new mission," Beta Three said in his metallic monotone as they followed a dirt path to the Night Palace.

His movements now flowed easily and remarkably human-like. His new engines barely made a sound, the metallic plates on his body showing no gaps. Sometimes, Mera forgot she was even talking to a machine.

"Belinda will be fine," she replied. "Her duty is to Tagrad and Aquatia, and I decide what's best for both, don't I?"

"You do, but if I recall correctly, she and the Night King are not on good terms."

"Were they ever?" Mera shrugged. "They'll be fine. You'll see."

"I trust your judgement, as always." His eyes wandered to her swollen belly, which was covered by a flowy emerald dress. "My sensors detect your blood pressure is slightly elevated."

"Yeah, that's what walking does to a 'carbon-based life form'." Patting his metallic shoulder, she offered him an assuring smile. "I'm fine. Stella said the baby isn't due for a few more weeks." Her hand drifted down, rubbing her round stomach. "Then again, we know how impatient nightlings can be."

"Certain waterbreakers, too."

"Wiseass."

"You're seriously still working?" Belinda's voice came from behind, just as they reached the arched entrance to the palace's vast gardens.

Her friend's long, blond hair was tied in a low braid, and she wore the Aquatian detective's uniform—navy jeans, white shirt, and a dark-blue leather jacket.

Rolling her eyes, Mera let out an annoyed gruff. "What is it with everyone today? I'm fine!"

"And also as round as a puffer-fish." Belinda pointed at her. "I doubt Bast is okay with you working so close to your due date."

"He is… as long as Beta Three accompanies me at all times."

The automaton bowed his head.

"That's because he knows how stubborn you are." Waving carelessly, Belinda nodded toward the palace. "Anyway. Let's get this over with, shall we?"

They ventured through the gardens, passing by faeries who bowed at them politely. They soon reached one of the many arched entrances that led to the inside of the castle.

Halting, Belinda stared up at the white construction that

wrapped around the mountain like a chalky waterdragon protecting its nest. Her throat bobbed. "Why on the seven seas do you want me to work a case here in Lunor Insul? It's not even my jurisdiction."

"You're my most trusted officer. Also, it seems the case might tie to one of our people, but I'm sure Corvus will tell us more once we see him." Her attention shifted to the top of the castle, and she pointed to the throne room on the last floor. "The Night King wasn't very forthcoming with information, I'm afraid."

"Is he ever?" Belinda grumbled.

They went inside, their steps clanking against the vast marbled halls. When they reached a set of stairs, Beta Three lifted Mera into his arms without asking for permission.

"Hey!"

"Your husband was very clear, Councilor. No exertions." With that, he began climbing the stairs.

Huffing, Mera crossed her arms at the indignity of it, but her belly was heavy and her feet swollen, so she didn't oppose.

"Bel, Corvus asked for you *specifically*, by the way." A knowing grin tugged at her lips.

"I don't see why," she countered casually as they went up, but a blush still rose to her cheeks.

Her friend was the smartest, most loyal detective she knew, but when it came to Corvus, Belinda was clueless.

They soon reached the throne room, where the Night King ran around with a two-year-old latched onto his back. The child —a boy with silver-white hair, chubby cheeks, and green eyes— giggled while Corvus trotted like a horse.

"Leon Maurea Dhay!" Mera called out in the most severe tone she could muster, which wasn't much considering she couldn't hide her amused smile. "I thought I told you to behave."

"Don't blame Leon, Councilor. This is all on me." Corvus winked back at her boy. "Besides, a king does what a king wants, and if said king wishes to be a pony, then he shall be a pony."

Leon giggled from Corvus' back. "Unclie pony!"

"You have a good life, King Dhay," Belinda remarked nonchalantly, while Beta Three set Mera down on her own feet. "From what I've seen, you let your councilor do most of the work."

With a sigh, Mera scratched her forehead. "You're provoking him."

"Of course I am." Belinda frowned at her, as if she couldn't understand why that might be wrong.

"I'll have you know that my councilor is quite happy with his assignments, *Belinda*." Corvus' yellow eyes shone with a certain wildness. "Unloading some of my responsibilities onto the Night Prince gives me time to deal with other matters."

Mera could only wonder what said matters might be, but by the blush in Belinda's cheeks, her friend knew exactly what he was talking about.

Kneeling on the ground, Corvus let Leon climb off his back. He ruffled the boy's long, white hair, then motioned to Mera. "Off you go to your *amma*, nightling. Uncle has business to attend."

Leon hugged Corvus' legs before rushing to Mera with his chubby little arms wide open, his steps heavy and unsteady.

"Mommy! Unclie and me did magic today!"

"Did you?" Arching an eyebrow, she pressed her lips into a line. "Only the good kind, I hope?"

Corvus' palm raised in a silent promise. "Rainbows and night puppies, I assure you."

The moment Leon reached her, Mera pulled him up into her arms, kissing his forehead. "My cheeky sea monkey."

Belinda tapped his little shoulder. "Hey, Auntie Bel deserves some love too, no?"

Giggling, Leon threw himself into Belinda's chest. He

wrapped his arms around his auntie's neck, but accidentally kicked Mera's stomach in the process.

"Be careful with your sister, baby," Belinda warned as she held him.

Leon blinked, his big eyes glistening. It was uncanny how much he resembled his father. If Leon hadn't inherited Mera's green eyes, she doubted anyone would guess he'd come out of her.

"Sorry, Mommy! I didn't mean to." He bent down, almost throwing himself off Belinda's arms to kiss Mera's belly. "Sorry, Ruth!"

Pushing himself away from his auntie's embrace, he reached for his mother. Mera took him, quickly kiss-attacking her boy.

His giggles filled the room, when the popping sound of winnowing suddenly came from behind them. Leon's eyes immediately widened, and the largest smile bloomed on his lips. Practically throwing himself over her shoulder, he shouted, "Pappa!"

A despondent sigh escaped Mera. Leon worshipped his father. In fact, whenever he was around, their boy barely paid her any attention.

The charms of Sebastian Dhay, she supposed.

"There's my nightling!" Taking him in his arms, Bast spun him around twice before blowing on his belly. Leon laughed loudly.

Still holding him, Bast leaned closer and stamped a soft kiss on Mera's lips. "Did she behave, Beta Three?" he asked without turning to the automaton, who watched them from the left.

"Other than a slight spike in blood pressure, her levels are perfect, Councilor Dhay."

"Good." He turned to Corvus. "I struck a deal with Harry today. He wants to import Ben's wine, and since Lunor Insul distributes it to Tagrad, we agreed on a nice little margin."

"Splendid! That's why you're my councilor, *broer*. Without

you, I would never be able to go on my little adventure with Detective Tiderider."

"You mean a case," Mera chided. "You need Belinda to help you solve *a case*. By the way, you still need to explain what's going on."

"Surely." He clicked his tongue. "See, someone stole the Crown of Land and Sea from its vault in the Library of Night."

Mera's blood chilled, and she exchanged one worried glance with Bast. "That's not good."

"You think a siren did it?" Belinda asked, stepping closer.

"Quite right. I believe we're dealing with one of Poseidon's remaining loons." Straightening his spine, he cleared his throat. "I trust you and your work, Belinda. You know your people like the back of your hand, and since Councilor Maurea Dhay has retired from the force, you're my best chance at catching the culprit."

Staring at him, Belinda seemed surprised at the sudden compliment. "Thanks, I guess."

"It looks like you two have a lot of work ahead." Bast held Leon against the left side of his body and wrapped his free arm around Mera's waist. "If you'll excuse us, we've had a long day. Good luck."

With that, he winnowed them out of the castle and back to their home in Aquatia. They landed in their large balcony, which offered a magnificent view of the ocean. Far ahead, Mera could spot Lunor Insul.

"I wish you wouldn't have done that." A slight pout puckered her lips. "I wanted to know more about the case."

"No, you wanted to see what would happen between Belinda and my brother."

"Stupid soulmate bond," she grumbled under her breath.

"You have to let them find their own path. In any case, you and Ruth had a long day. It's time to rest. Also, I'm sure Belinda will fill you in later." Bast lifted their boy and smelled under his armpits. Quickly turning his face, he stuck out his tongue. "You stink, nightling."

A loud, carefree laugh burst from their son. "Stinky kitty!"

"Time for a shower, then." He pecked Mera's cheek, the tip of his tongue lingering for a second longer, hinting at what might be waiting for them once Leon went to sleep. With a wink, he smiled. "See you inside, kitten."

"Wait, Pappa!" Leaning over, Leon followed his father's example, giving her a peck on her cheek. "See you later, Mommy!"

With that, they went inside. Her precious boys.

Inhaling the salty tang of the ocean, Mera watched the sun lower on the horizon, drenching the sea in a warm glow.

Once she finally defeated Azinor, her whispers vanished, and so did the hidden runes in her skin. Maybe the magic rush that had killed Mother used all of Mera's newfound power; maybe the whispers had fulfilled their purpose. The fact remained, she wasn't a soulbreaker anymore, and it was blissfully, wonderfully quiet now.

Caressing her belly, she appreciated the silence broken only by the rolling waves in the distance, and the soft breeze that caressed her russet locks.

Ariella's voice echoed in her memory.

"Be happy, child."

With a smile, Mera went inside to fix supper.

∾

THE END

∾

Looking for your next great read? How about BLESSED FURY, the first book in the Angels of Fate Series?

BLESSED FURY

Once you face the devils, there's no going back.

Guardian angel Ava Lightway has spent a century watching over her charges, whispering the words of the gods in their ears. But her peaceful existence ends when she's assigned to Liam Striker, a supernatural detective with no memory of his past.

Liam might be Ava's biggest challenge yet. Stubborn and dangerously captivating, he'll stop at nothing to find the demon who murdered his father. Even if it costs him his life.

Keeping death away from her new partner is an impossible task. Ava has never failed a charge, and she doesn't plan on starting now. But even if their investigation doesn't destroy her, succumbing to Liam's smoldering touch just may.

Read the sizzling, breath-taking tale of angels gone bad!

Note to readers: This is a forbidden romance featuring a sinning rogue and the angel who'll stop at nothing to help him. Perfect for fans of dark supernatural romance.

Available on Amazon

ACKNOWLEDGMENTS

Thank you so much for making these characters I adore something more than just words scribbled on a page. Thank you, for making them real. I hope you've enjoyed Mera and Bast's journey.

Oh, and if you enjoyed this book, do consider leaving a review. They make an author's day!

$\sim$

Join the Wildlings (*subscribepage.com/kateam*) to be the first to know when new books are coming out. You will also get a FREE copy of BLESSED LIGHT, an urban fantasy romance novella!

ALSO BY C.S. WILDE

Urban Fantasy Romance:
  Hollowcliff Detectives:
  TO KILL A FAE
  TO KILL A KING
  TO KILL THE DEAD
  TO KILL A GOD

Angels of Fate Series:
  BLESSED LIGHT
  BLESSED FURY
  CURSED DARKNESS
  SACRED WAR

SWORD WITCH *(Standalone short story)*

Paranormal Thriller Adventure:
  A COURTROOM OF ASHES

Science Fiction Romance:

The Dimensions Series:

FROM THE STARS

BEYOND THE STARS

ACROSS THE STARS

THE DIMENSIONS SERIES BOXSET

ABOUT THE AUTHOR

C. S. Wilde wrote her first Fantasy novel when she was eight. That book was absolutely terrible, but her mother told her it was awesome, so she kept writing.

Now a grown up (though many will beg to differ), C. S. Wilde writes about fantastic worlds, love stories larger than life and epic battles.

She also, quite obviously, sucks at writing an author bio. She finds it awkward that she must write this in the third person and hopes you won't notice.

For up to date promotions and release dates of upcoming books, sign up for the latest news at www.cswilde.com. You can also join the Wildlings, C.S. Wilde's exclusive Facebook group.

Printed in Great Britain
by Amazon

41216292R00158